"Engaging." —*Publishers Weekly*

Dirty Little Secret

a novel

Jennifer Echols

Award-winning author of *Such a Rush*

The critics love
JENNIFER ECHOLS
Dirty Little Secret

"A perfect mix of Nashville, emotion, and protagonist."

—*Chick Loves Lit*

"Stand-out characters."

—*RT Reviews*

"The characters were authentic, and their dialogue felt real. I found myself wrapped up in the story and burning through the pages."

—*Super Librarian*

"Another winner. . . . The story came alive through the words on each page . . . [and] the book ended just the way I wanted it to."

—*Book Binge*

"Lots of drama, music, and heart. . . . *Dirty Little Secret* put a smile on my face."

—*The Reading Date*

"Engaging. . . . [Echols peppers] energetic music scenes with girly jealousy, self-doubt, and revelations from a likable, relatable protagonist."

—*Publishers Weekly*

Such a Rush

"A twisted love triangle that had us scratching our heads and biting our nails. . . . An emotional story—complete with funny, sarcastic characters and mean-girl confrontations—that you're sure to enjoy."

—*Seventeen*

"I've come to expect certain things from Jennifer Echols' writing: candid characters, passionate chemistry, and equally poignant and hilarious moments. *Such a Rush* has all of this and much more."

—*Lost in the Stacks*

"Perfectly flawed but relatable characters. . . . Knee-weakening, steamy scenes."

—*The Reader's Den*

"A brilliant lead, hot twin boys, and airplanes! What's not to love?"

—*The Overflowing Library*

"Fantastic. . . . A must-read for contemporary romance fans."

—*Book and Latte Reviews*

"[A] blend of romance, interesting characters, witty dialogue, and dramatic intrigue. . . ."

—*The Reading Date*

Love Story

"Comical and sexy, *Love Story* is intriguing and will most definitely live up to expectations for a lusty read. With two central characters who hold a thick tension between them, and a well-developed supporting cast, this one easily sees sparks fly in more ways than one. . . . A fun and engaging tale."

—*A Good Addiction*

"Excellent. . . . Another must-read for fans of Jennifer Echols."

—*Chick Loves Lit*

Forget You

"Sexy and full of surprises.... An enchanting tale of searching and finding.... Addictive and special, and oh-my-God, so searingly sexy...."
—*Girls Without a Bookshelf*

"The romance in this book is outstanding, the story is superb, and it's a story you can't put down. *Forget You* is a must-read!"
—*Chick Loves Lit*

Going Too Far

"Brave and powerful.... Searingly romantic and daring, yet also full of hilarious moments."
—R. A. Nelson, author of *Throat*

"The perfect blend of romance, wit, and rebelliousness."
—Niki Burnham, author of *Shot Through the Heart*

"A thoroughly engrossing look into two people's personal stories of loss and strength, this atypical romance is a powerful one."
—*Parkersburg News and Sentinel*

"Edgy, tense, and seductive.... Humor and sarcastic wit alternating with terribly tender and sneakily seductive scenes."
—*Smart Bitches, Trashy Books*

"A big roller-coaster ride.... A torrent of different emotions...."
—*YA Book Realm*

"*Going Too Far* has everything a teen love story should have."
—*Book Loons*

Other Romantic Dramas by Jennifer Echols

Available from MTV Books

Dirty Little Secret

Jennifer Echols

GALLERY BOOKS MTV BOOKS

New York London Toronto Sydney New Delhi

Gallery Books
A Division of Simon & Schuster, Inc.
1230 Avenue of the Americas
New York, NY 10020

Copyright © 2013 by Jennifer Echols

MTV Music Television and all related titles, logos, and characters are trademarks of MTV Networks, a division of Viacom International, Inc.

First MTV Books/Gallery Books trade paperback edition April 2014

GALLERY BOOKS and colophon are registered trademarks of Simon & Schuster, Inc.

For information about special discounts for bulk purchases, please contact Simon & Schuster Special Sales at 1-866-506-1949 or business@simonandschuster.com.

The Simon & Schuster Speakers Bureau can bring authors to your live event. For more information or to book an event, contact the Simon & Schuster Speakers Bureau at 1-866-248-3049 or visit our website at www.simonspeakers.com.

Designed by Aline C. Pace

Manufactured in the United States of America

10 9 8 7 6 5 4 3 2 1

The Library of Congress has cataloged the hardcover edition as follows:

Echols, Jennifer.
  Dirty little secret / Jennifer Echols.—First Gallery Books hardcover edition.
    pages cm
  1. Sisters—Fiction. 2. Country musicians—Fiction. 3. Fame—Psychological aspects—Fiction. I. Title.
  PS3605.C48D57 2013
  813'.6—dc23
                          2012050507

ISBN 978-1-4516-5803-3
ISBN 978-1-4516-5804-0 (paper)
ISBN 978-1-4516-5806-4 (ebook)

For my dad,
who plays banjo

Acknowledgments

Heartfelt thanks to my editors, Lauren McKenna and Emilia Pisani; my agent, Laura Bradford; and my critique partners, Catherine Chant and Victoria Dahl.

On Tuesday I was in a band with Elvis. Lucky for me, he wasn't the overweight Elvis from the 1970s, eating a peanut-butter-and-banana sandwich and wearing a sequined jumpsuit, the version most impersonators go for. In that case, Ms. Lottie, the wardrobe lady, would have decked me out in a Las Vegas costume with a huge headpiece, a sheer body stocking, and sequined pasties over my nipples. Everybody in the band was supposed to match, more or less. So if the lead singer had been drugged-out Elvis on death's door in Vegas, his fiddle player would have been a bare-breasted showgirl.

And to think: my sweet granddad had gotten me this afternoon job. If I'd had to wear an outfit like that, it would have served the rest of my family right.

Fortunately, I'd been hired as a fiddle player to fill out tribute bands in Nashville, not Vegas. The bandleader for my first gig was the young rockabilly Elvis from a 1950s movie, wearing a broad-shouldered suit with a skinny tie and wing-tip shoes. Ms. Lottie had an honest-to-God circle skirt for me. Considering what I'd imagined when she'd first said "Elvis," I was relieved. The skirt was way too big, though. She had to fold darts into the waistband and sew me into it.

Then she eyed my hair, lifting short black sections with her carefully manicured pinkie nail, squinting at my locks through the rhinestone-framed reading glasses on the end of her nose. "I know you're going to feel warm in a wig, hon, but that's what you need. With some of the girls, I can pile up their hair and pull off an Audrey Hepburn, but yours isn't long enough." She pinned a red-headed ponytail wig onto my head.

Ms. Lottie also made me wash off my makeup so she could start over. I asked her if she was doing this because the casting company in charge of the band wanted me to look tasteful. She was way too polite to be baited into admitting my look was the stuff of her nightmares, though. She said the company wanted me to look "period," with my makeup redone in soft tones that played up my natural beauty (according to her gracious bullshit). With a chiffon scarf knotted around my neck above the starched white collar of my fitted blouse, I eased out of Ms. Lottie's chair, my thigh still sore from the wreck last Saturday night. I went out to meet Elvis.

His singing voice and guitar picking were tolerable. He imitated the King pretty well, too, but he was ten years too old to be Elvis in his twenties. I wondered what he was doing here in the middle of the day on a Tuesday. Shouldn't he be working at his real job? This gig sure wasn't paying his rent. Usually people figured that out by his age.

The other guitar player rounding out our trio was an elderly man I'd already met, Mr. Crabtree. I would never know all the professional musicians in Nashville because there was a constant influx of new ones trying to make it big. But I'd played the bluegrass circuit long enough that I'd encountered Mr. Crabtree over and over. He was also my granddad's friend. My granddad must have used his connections in the music industry to get a job for his poker buddy *and* his screwed-up granddaughter.

I hadn't played in a wandering band of minstrels like this before, but I wasn't nervous. I was well trained in jumping into a group and blending in with no rehearsal. My parents had dragged my sister, Julie, and me to every bluegrass festival in the country for as long as I could remember. They'd taught innocent, impressionable young me to say yes anytime some crazy lady asked me to get onstage with her. I didn't always know who the adult musicians were at the festivals, but my parents did, and the crazy lady *might* turn out to be Reba McEntire about to discover Julie and me and propel us to the fame and fortune that had been so elusive our whole young lives. Yes yes yes!

Besides being an old hand (or hack) onstage, I knew just about every song there was. The ones I didn't . . . well, there were basically three chords in all of popular music—major one, major four, and major five—with an occasional minor six or (gasp!) crazy-ass minor three thrown in to get everybody titillated. The solo break came at the same place in every song. The fiddle took a solo first, guitar second. I always knew what key we were in. I could predict where the music was going. Anyway, the audience didn't notice mistakes. They noticed hesitation.

Or would they? I'd been told that some days in this job, I would be traveling with a band to a local shop's grand opening or car dealership's sale extravaganza. Today we were staying right here in the vast shopping mall, playing country standards as a gimmick to attract customers. I doubted anybody on a mission to buy a new bathing suit for the summer would give the Elvis-impersonator band a second glance.

But a gig was a gig, and I would do my best. I played a few chords with Elvis and Mr. Crabtree outside Foot Locker to make

sure we were in tune. From there we jumped right into one rockabilly song after another. As I'd predicted, it was a lot like being onstage with Some Lady Who Might Be Reba McEntire but Wasn't.
I took the melody in the intro, then backed out and played easy
staccato chords on the upbeat while Elvis sang and swayed his pelvis and hopped around on the industrial tile floor. In the chorus,
Mr. Crabtree sang the lower harmony and I took the higher one.
During the second verse, I went back to staccato chords, and I
added a lilting string line in the third verse for variety. We sounded
like we'd been playing together for years. Musicians and their instruments and vocals were interchangeable building blocks in a
song, with no soul at all.

I hadn't allowed myself to think too hard about it, but I realized
now that I'd hoped playing with other people again would lift me
out of the funk where I'd spent the past year. Instead, I was going
in the opposite direction, backing farther into my cave. I was finally
playing in a band again. But without Julie, the magic was gone.

If she were here, I would glance over at her when she missed
a note, see the shocked look on her face, and cringe to keep from
cracking up at her. We would roll our eyes at the questionable
fashion choices of the customers strolling by. We would tease each
other about any cute guy who seemed to notice us. Our mom
would scold us later for acting unprofessional. After she stormed off
angry, our dad would buy us an ice cream as a consolation prize.
Between bites we would tell him what had been so funny, and he
would laugh with us and recount something that had happened to
him while playing in a Knoxville biker bar in the early 1990s.

I had thought I missed performing, but it was my family I
missed. And since they'd left me behind, music was nothing for
me now.

Of course, I had no ties to the real world anymore, so nobody noticed I was having a tragic epiphany. Elvis and Mr. Crabtree rocked on blissfully, oblivious to the fact that, during their fun rockabilly beat, my heart was breaking for the umpteenth time. The salesmen dressed like referees came out of Foot Locker to stare at us.

A couple of girls I'd seen at school slipped out of the salon next door, showing each other their freshly painted nails. I did my best to duck my head while keeping my chin in place on my fiddle. We weren't friends, but I was that girl everyone vaguely knew—didn't she have a younger sister who was about to become famous?—and nobody was friends with. I was afraid they would text everybody in their contact lists that they'd seen me. It would get back to my ex, Toby. He would bring his friends here to sneer at me. But the girls never stopped for our music or looked up at us. I might as well have been a mannequin in the window at Abercrombie.

It was two thirty on a Tuesday, a dead time at the mall, and no other customers passed us. Thinking we might have better luck if we moseyed into the next wing, we set up camp between Victoria's Secret and Sephora and played a couple more tunes. This time a few shoppers actually paused to listen. They gave us a smattering of applause. They heard happiness in our music where I didn't.

Then, as we moved toward the food court, Elvis leaned over and asked me what I had on under my circle skirt—if it was like a Scotsman and his kilt.

I was not going commando. I was wearing black lace panties. They'd become my habit in the last year, mostly to scare the hell out of my mother on the rare occasion when she was home to do the laundry, but partly so I'd look sexy and tough when I stumbled into a party and ended up behind the garage with a boy. It wasn't much of a goal, but it was all I had just then. Very little got me off anymore. Being alone with a hot guy at least made me feel something.

If Elvis had been a cute boy at school in years gone by and he'd asked me a lewd question like this, I would have giggled in embarrassment. If he'd been a cute boy at school in the past year, I would have come on to him and called his bluff. But the closer Elvis got to me, the older he seemed. I could tell from the uneven texture under the layer of makeup Ms. Lottie had applied that his tan skin was weathered. His black hair was thinning on top, with not quite enough to fill out his pompadour.

My feet ached from standing in high heels, my bruised thigh throbbed, and I was in no mood to be toyed with. I told Elvis that under my circle skirt, there was a Glock. (There wasn't. I was just a skinny girl with a punky screw-you haircut and no balls at all.)

Elvis was not dissuaded. As we chose our place with our backs to a blank wall between Baskin-Robbins and McDonald's, he murmured, "Pull up your skirt and let me see it."

My first thought was for Mr. Crabtree, who stood close enough to us that he should have overheard what Elvis said. He would think it was *my* fault that Elvis wanted to see the imaginary gun in my undies. He would report this to my granddad at the next poker game. My granddad would tell my parents, who would basically disown me by refusing to pay my tuition to Vanderbilt. That was their deal with me for the rest of the summer. If I wanted them to fork over tuition and room and board as they'd always promised, I had to stay out of trouble and avoid doing anything that would embarrass Julie.

I wasn't supposed to draw attention to myself in any way, and that specifically included playing fiddle with a group. But I hoped I was safe from my parents' wrath when they found out about this gig. It had been my granddad's idea, not mine. He'd promised to take the blame if my parents got angry and swore to withhold my tuition, and to help me convince them to let me keep the job for the whole summer. I'd been pretty mopey yesterday—Memorial Day. Toby and his friends had spent the holiday at the lake while I moved my shit from my parents' house to my granddad's. I figured my granddad had gotten me the gig because, after one day with me, he wanted his guitar shop and his privacy back in the afternoons.

I guess he didn't buy my parents' reasoning behind keeping me away from gigs, and neither did I. Julie's record company was afraid of a public relations disaster if the tabloids found out she'd been signed to the label while the older sister she'd always played with had been locked out. That wasn't the shining success story girls wanted to read about in *Seventeen*. Personally, I didn't think the press would care what Julie's loser sister did with her afternoons. For Julie's future fans, I would never rise to the level of importance of Julie's boyfriends or Julie's clothes or Julie's hairdo.

But as Elvis sneered at me, I realized *this* was a situation ripe for a tabloid sensation and a major embarrassment to Julie's baby career. If Mr. Crabtree told my granddad what was happening here, my granddad would pull the plug on me and maybe even confess to my parents about this gig. The potential story of Julie Mayfield's older sister dressing up like a mental patient and threatening Elvis with a Glock . . . that might upset my parents enough to cut me off. They were dead serious about Julie's success. Mine was expendable.

As I turned around to sneak a peek at Mr. Crabtree, though, I realized I'd panicked for nothing. Judging from his facial expression, he hadn't heard a word that had passed between Elvis and me. In his tacky trousers and shirt and tie—which could have been his original clothes from the fifties for all I knew—he gazed out at the crowd, half smiling, like a golden retriever waiting for his master to throw a ball.

Reading my mind, Elvis informed me, "He's deaf. I can say anything I want to you."

I felt my face flush with anger at Elvis's challenge. The food court wasn't crowded, but the few patrons close by would overhear if I laid into him like he deserved. I squared my shoulders, glared at him, and said quietly but firmly, "No, you *can't* say anything you want to me. I'm a professional musician, and I won't put up with it."

Elvis straightened to his full height, reminding me how much bigger than me he was. His nostrils flared as he spat, "Oh, *you're* the talent now? Let me tell you something, toots. *I'm* the talent here. You're in a band with *Elvis*. *I'm* not in a band with . . . I don't even know who the fuck you're supposed to be. Can't help falling in love."

I was used to boys who seemed willing enough to put their hands all over me, then told me off when I didn't play submissive girlfriend with them like they wanted. It had happened all year. It had happened with Toby.

I was *not* used to a middle-aged man who asked what was under my skirt, then told me off when I didn't play submissive girlfriend, then declared his love for me.

Soon enough, I was glad I'd stood there with my hands on my hips, bow in one hand and fiddle in the other, rather than responding to him in a way that would have embarrassed us both. He wasn't declaring his love for me, duh. He was naming our next tune. He repeated very loudly to Mr. Crabtree, "'Can't Help Falling in Love' in D." Mr. Crabtree obediently strummed the D-major chord, setting the rhythm. Elvis joined in with his own guitar. As far as he was concerned, my opinion and my anger didn't matter. I was dismissed.

I joined in, too, doing my part for the intro, bowing the lush melody in the key of D-sharp instead of D. It took a *lot* of concentration for me to sound this bad, because I had a sensitive ear. I made sure my fiddle line was the loveliest tune the crowd had ever heard. My instrument had a mellow tone. My fingers on the strings created a wide vibrato that only seemed easy. It just so happened that every note I played was a half step up from the key Elvis and Mr. Crabtree were playing in.

And that made Elvis sound like a train wreck. The people at the table closest to us, teenagers munching soft pretzels, got up suddenly and took their trays to the other side of the food court.

Between verses, Elvis slid close to me with a tight smile and whispered in my ear, "We're in D."

In the middle of my solo line, I pulled my fiddle away from my chin to say, "And *I'm* in D-sharp." I tucked my fiddle under my chin again and resumed my soaring fiddle line, taking extra care to make it a Grand Ole Opry–worthy performance, only gratingly off-key. As Elvis and Mr. Crabtree continued their accompaniment on their guitars a half step too low, every nerve in my body vibrated with the need to tune down.

I tried to get my mind off it by gazing out at the audience, such as it was. A few customers remained at tables at the far edge of the food court, involved in their own conversations, not even glancing at us across the atrium. Maybe they were so tone-deaf that they hadn't noticed anything wrong. More likely they were just here to shop for new shades, man, and our performance meant nothing to them, our drama less than nothing.

My heartbeat slowed to normal. I'd returned to the mind-set that had helped me survive the past year, in which I acknowledged how little I mattered and how little anybody cared. When the tortuous song ended and Elvis stepped close to tower over me again, I faced him with a smug expression, batting my eyelashes sarcastically, ready for anything.

"You're going to get us both fired," he growled under his breath.

"Only if we keep accidentally getting our wires crossed," I said in an innocent tone to go with my chiffon scarf and my ponytail. "That won't happen, because you're going to apologize to me."

His lips parted. His eyebrows shot up. Suddenly, despite Ms. Lottie's makeup, he looked nothing like Elvis. He was an older man I'd just met. I knew zero about his real life, his motivations, or how far I'd pushed him.

He seethed, "I will report you."

"I don't fucking care," I lied. It was important that I said *fuck* because he'd used it first. I had to show him I wasn't scared of him. But I was beginning to be. I was such a wuss that I couldn't even hold his angry gaze. My eyes darted to Mr. Crabtree to make sure he hadn't heard me say the F-word in the middle of the mall.

Mr. Crabtree still smiled out at the food court. "How about 'Love Me Tender' next?" he asked, turning to Elvis. "Such a pretty tune."

Sure, a pretty tune, I supposed. The scales and arpeggios progressed from major one to major five like a thousand other rockabilly ballads. The song stood out solely because the rote major four in the middle had been replaced with the rogue madness of a major two. And Mr. Crabtree couldn't even hear it. After years of work as a musician, losing his hearing must have been a nightmare for him. He hardly seemed to notice. Maybe the change had been so gradual, the letdown so gentle, that he'd landed in a soft place, and his memory of one, two, five, and one was as good as the real thing. It was only when the rug was jerked out from under you that you fell on your ass.

After that, Elvis and I both stood down. I didn't screw up another song for him. He didn't say another word to me, but the tension between us was frightening. I felt more awake than I had for a whole year, and not in a good way. Before, my school day and an unhappy night at home had seemed like I was trapped in a losing battle. I was outnumbered and unarmed. Now I was still outnumbered—the whole world was against me—but I'd discovered I could use music as a weapon. I could at least have the satisfaction of giving one attacker a bloody nose before the pack of them cut me down.

♪ ♫ ♪

My shift ended at six. When I drove back to my granddad's house, he had dinner waiting for me, and we made small talk over the pot roast. At my parents' house I would have stayed sullenly silent, just in case they'd forgotten how I felt about them, but my granddad was only trying to help.

"How was work?" he asked. He'd stressed to me when he got me the mall job that I couldn't blow it off. A professional musician knew playing music was a job and viewed it seriously. In referring to my afternoon at the mall as "work," he was warning me against treating the job as I'd treated everything else in the past year: like shit.

"So much fun." I was lying like a dog. "Thanks again for getting me this gig, Granddad. And, oh—Ernest Crabtree was in my band today."

My granddad's eyes widened through folds of old skin. "How did he do? He's gotten deaf as a doornail."

"He did great!" We laughed about poor Mr. Crabtree, and then I steered the topic away from work. The thought of Elvis made bile rise in my throat.

I washed the dishes, then sat down with my granddad to watch *Antiques Roadshow* on PBS. This was the life of a girl doomed to spend the summer between high school and college living with her grandfather. After it was over, he got out his guitar, I opened my fiddle, and we played together for a few hours. Our music wasn't electric, like performing onstage with Julie, or such a part of me that I hardly noticed, like practicing by myself, but a relaxing way to pass the time, like lying on my back in a warm lake, staring up at the sky.

At ten, the phone interrupted us: an actual phone plugged into the wall in the kitchen, because my granddad didn't see the need for a cell. I could tell from his "Heeeeey, sugar pie, how's Minneapolis?" echoing around the old house that he was talking to my mom. My parents were with Julie on the final and most important leg of her pre-album tour before they came back to Nashville next week for the debut of her first single.

"What?" my granddad asked. "Trouble? No, she's been an angel."

I settled my fiddle under my chin and played softly enough that I wouldn't disturb my granddad but loudly enough that I couldn't hear what he said.

"Bailey," he called over my tune. "Come talk to your mom."

I could feel an ugly expression tighten my face as I packed up my violin and closed the case. In the kitchen I took the receiver my granddad held out to me and leaned against the 1960s wallpaper printed with dancing forks and spoons. "Hello."

"Hey, sweetie," my mom said. "Behaving yourself?"

"Yes, ma'am, I'm five years old and I'm behaving myself."

"If you feel you're being treated that way, maybe you should ask yourself why." My mother's voice thinned out, pitching into the same guilt trips and threats she'd laid on me for a year. I wasn't listening anymore. I didn't need to. I knew what she'd say because I'd heard it a million times, and because, nauseatingly, I was exactly like her.

I'd inherited her high-strung anxiety about success, along with my dad's easygoing willingness to practice his music dogmatically— the terrible combination that had made me a proficient has-been before I was old enough to vote. Julie was unlike either of them. She loved music, she wanted to be successful, and she'd enjoyed the bluegrass festivals that had made up our childhood. But privately to me, she often said she longed to quit it all so she could go to the movies with her friends on Friday night, or get a job at the Gap. In short, she was the only one in the family who was normal. That's probably what the record company saw in her when they tapped her (and not me) to become famous.

When my mom took a breath, I asked, "May I please speak with Julie?"

"Julie is not ready to speak with you."

"She doesn't want to talk to me, or you won't give her the phone?"

"She's sitting right here, shaking her head no."

I believed it. For the past year, every night that Julie had been out of town, I'd called her around ten. But she'd told me the night of my accident that she wasn't speaking to me anymore. Last night, for the first time, she hadn't answered when I called.

"Here's your father," my mom said. They murmured in the background. Then my dad said brightly, "I miss you, Bay."

My stomach twisted into a knot, my nose tickled, my eyes watered, and suddenly I was sobbing silently, turning my mouth away from the receiver so I didn't gasp in my dad's ear.

"Bay?" he prompted me.

I couldn't talk to him, but I didn't want to hang up on him, so I leaned through the doorway and stretched the spiral cord to hold out the receiver in the direction of my granddad.

He jumped up from his chair, surprisingly spry for an old guy, and took the phone from me. As I walked into the living room to grab my fiddle case and escape up the stairs, I heard him saying, "Mack, I think she's really tired right now. I worked her pretty hard around the shop today. . . ."

I closed myself in the bedroom I was using and dealt with my feelings the way I had for a year. I rummaged in my purse, pulled out my now-battered notebook printed inside with music staffs rather than blue lines—my fifth notebook since I'd started over without Julie—and wrote a song. This one was about crying suddenly, unable to speak on the phone, and afterward wondering why. As always, I wasn't so sure about the words, and I would continue to tinker with them, but I was dead sure about the melody and the crazy chords that held it up like pillars under a highway.

As I considered the song, playing it over in my mind, I decorated the edges of the pages in doodles of hearts and flowers, shading them with delicate strokes in colored pencil. I'd never had the urge to do that in the notebooks I'd filled with songs as a child. I'd played those tunes with Julie. I'd gotten her to sing them with me when they weren't even done so I could hear where I was going. But for these new notebooks, I had nobody to play with. I might spend a lifetime as an anonymous costumed fiddle player at the mall and never hear my own compositions—not in real life. The drawings of hearts and flowers were a strange compulsion. I felt better when I added them, as if they were a consolation prize, a sympathy card after a loss.

It wasn't until I rolled into bed that I realized my granddad had been half-right when he made an excuse for me over the phone to my dad, saying I was tired because I'd worked hard. I was so upset with my mom and Julie and myself that my dad's kindness had been too much of a shock. But I probably wouldn't have reacted that way if I hadn't had such a hard day at work with Elvis.

I was afraid Elvis would turn me in for ruining "Can't Help Falling in Love." I suspected he wouldn't dare. Musician jobs were too hard to come by in Nashville, which was chock-full of wanna-be's. Elvis would prefer to fly under the radar. He wouldn't want to cause a stir at the casting office by complaining about a coworker.

Even if he did, it would be his word against mine. My boss would believe him, though, because he'd worked in the tribute band longer. I would be fired. My granddad would be disgraced because he'd put in a good word for me and I'd let him down. He would report my failure to my parents. They would carry through on their threat to withhold my college tuition. For the rest of the summer I would spend not just the mornings but the afternoons, too, helping my granddad in his shop, sanding guitars and sweeping up wood shavings as if they were pieces of my own soul that had sloughed off my body and fallen onto the floor.

Or, if my parents were cutting me off anyway, I could buy a bus ticket to L.A. Wasn't that where runaways went? Out there, pass-ersby probably didn't even throw a dollar to rock guitarists on the street, but a bluegrass musician from Nashville might be a novelty. Playing my fiddle would keep me out of prostitution for a whole day before I had to pawn it.

Or I could be proactive and tell on Elvis before he told on me. He was the guilty one, after all. I had to keep reminding myself of this. He was the one who'd made lewd comments. I'd only played in the wrong key in response.

♪ ♫ ♪

The next afternoon, I parked in the mall's vast lot, walked around to one of the loading docks, and swung through the employee door of what used to be a Borders bookstore. My plan was to let

Ms. Lottie make me up like a demure 1950s teenager, then march
into the casting office and file my complaint against Elvis. I'd rehearsed my speech in my head so many times that I'd memorized
it. And I'd strategized that I should complain in the squeaky-clean
ponytail wig Ms. Lottie pinned on me rather than my normal bad-
ass hairdo, so my boss would more likely believe me.

The bookstore was too big to be this empty, books long gone.
Only a few comfy chairs and a couch remained where the café
used to be. Now it was a lounge area for musicians to tune their
instruments and wait for the rest of their group. But nobody had
their instruments out today. Willie Nelson watched and occasion-
ally interjected a comment while Elvis argued with Dolly Parton.
I couldn't hear what they were saying, but Elvis's tone and body
language were a lot like what he'd used on me the day before.
Good—at least I knew he wasn't really a king around here. I likely
wasn't the only fiddle player who'd ever pissed him off.

I slipped into the restroom to scrub off my makeup, plus the
fine sawdust that had stuck to it during my morning of helping my
granddad build guitars. Then I returned to the wardrobe area set up
at the front of the store, near the floor-to-ceiling windows onto the
mall, now covered in brown paper to protect us from the curious
stares of shoppers. I plopped into Ms. Lottie's chair.

"You know, hon," she said, peering at me over the tops of her
rhinestone reading glasses, "you could come in without makeup.
Then we wouldn't have to go through so many steps."

"I never leave the house without makeup," I told her. "I'd feel
naked." All of which had become true in the past year. I'd been
hiding behind inky black mascara and a scowl since I cut off my
long hair. Nobody messed with a tough-looking chick like me. I'd
felt like I was surrounded by a force field when I'd passed Elvis in
the lounge area just now. I got in trouble only when I washed my

makeup off and Ms. Lottie made me up nicely to look like the high school portrait of my now-dead grandma.

"Um," I said as Ms. Lottie fitted a wig of long, straight blond locks over my head. With my hair color back to natural and no makeup, in the mirror I looked more like myself than I had in a year, which made me uncomfortable. "Does this hair go with Elvis?"

"You're not with Elvis today, hon," she said, wrapping the wig with a bandanna printed like the American flag. "You're with Willie Nelson."

"Why?" I asked her reflection. Even without mascara, my blue eyes looked huge. I tried not to seem so obviously panicked. Elvis must have complained to the management about me already. I'd been transferred but not fired. Not yet.

"Elvis only works a few days a week," Ms. Lottie explained. "He bartends the rest. We couldn't put you with him all the time. Everybody's schedule is real irregular because nobody can make a living doing this. And then, of course, sometimes we have people out sick. Or they lay out of work, more likely." She placed her hands firmly on either side of the flag bandanna and gave the wig a hard jerk to straighten my fake scalp. "Even if you were all here every day of the week, we'd switch up the bands so you didn't kill each other. You musicians are impossible, and Elvis is the absolute worst. Didn't he come on to you?"

I was so surprised that another "Um" was all I could manage.

"Didn't he ask what was under your circle skirt?" Ms. Lottie insisted, leaning forward to find the foundation she used on me.

"Yes," I said.

"Sounds like Dolly is telling him off, though," Ms. Lottie pointed out as the noise of their argument rose over the empty bookshelves.

She came in close to work on my face and coaxed me to relax my jaw. I couldn't let go. My mind whirled with the speech I'd rehearsed for the last twenty hours. Now I didn't need it. I should have been relieved. Elvis wasn't going to tell on me. He'd insulted me and then had an argument with me because he did that to everybody. I could still tell on *him* if I wanted. Other employees and Ms. Lottie would probably back me up.

Instead of relief, though, I felt let down and exhausted. All my hours of scheming and plotting were a big departure from my usual routine of boredom and apathy. I was left with that buzz of adrenaline, and now I had nowhere to put it.

I was even a little disappointed to hear that Elvis came on to anything in a circle skirt, not just me. When I'd thought I was something special to him, at least I'd felt adult and sexy. Now I pined for this pervert to have eyes only for me. There was something seriously wrong with me.

"Hon, we can't have tears. I've already done your eyeliner." Ms. Lottie dabbed the corner of a tissue at my lash line, then stood back to look at me. "What's the matter? Boy trouble?"

"I wish." How delicious it would be to get this upset about a hot guy who cared about me instead of any of the hot guys I'd hung with that year, who would throw me to the piranhas rather than get their feet wet.

"I don't know about that," Ms. Lottie said, feathering mascara through my lashes to replace the thick mascara I'd just taken off. "Be careful what you wish for."

♪ ♫ ♪

After all the drama of Elvis Tuesday, Willie Nelson Wednesday was laid-back. Ms. Lottie costumed me in a tight tank top and a denim miniskirt with a frayed hem. I passed for a member of Willie's be-draggled 1970s entourage, I guessed. Either that or a girl from the boonies dressed in her finest for a tourist trip to Nashville.

Our quartet moseyed down the loading ramp to pile into a van, which drove us to the state capitol building. After the governor signed a tax bill into law on the marble steps, we entertained the lawmakers and lobbyists sipping punch with "Always on My Mind," "Help Me Make It Through the Night," and "Mammas, Don't Let Your Babies Grow Up to Be Cowboys," each song in the key of D. I'd never noticed that everything was in the same key.

Yeah, maybe Willie Wednesday was a little *too* laid-back. I should have loved this field trip because it got us away from the mall, outside in the sunshine. The huge capitol building was a fake Greek temple set on a grassy hill at the edge of downtown, with skyscrapers in front of us, and hints of country music wafting to us on the breeze from the tourist district on Broadway. But whenever I got close to Willie to confer about the next few tunes, he reeked of pot. So did the guitarist and the mandolin player in similar hippie garb. I thought about asking them for a toke, joking that it went with the outfit. But if I could smell it on them, my granddad would be able to smell it on me when I returned to his house that night. Which meant no toking up behind the bushes on the grounds of the state capitol.

♪ ♫ ♪

On Thursday, because God did not love me anymore, I played in a band with Hank Williams at a ribbon cutting for the city's new sewage treatment plant. At least it didn't smell yet. And to their credit, unlike Willie's band, these guys hadn't imbibed Hank's poison of choice. The bass guitarist was a talented musician who looked—and smelled—sober. Hank played guitar reasonably well and sounded fine when he sang in his normal range, but the yodeling. Oh, the yodeling. For a musician like me burdened with perfect pitch, being deposited in a band with a pitchy Hank Williams singing "Long Gone Lonesome Blues" was torture, pure and simple. I'd thought I needed to concentrate to play in D-sharp when Elvis was playing in D, but that was nothing compared with the Zen-like place I retreated to in my mind and the deep, measured breaths I took to keep the look of distaste off my face while Hank yodeled.

♪ ♫ ♪

Friday I thought I was prepared for anything, but Ms. Lottie threw me a curveball and announced I was playing at the tenth anniversary of a steak house out near the airport with Dolly Parton. Dolly was the version of Ms. Parton from her most popular, glitzy 1970s era. That meant cleavage, and not just for Dolly. For all four of us in her band.

I'd dressed up in costume from age seven to age seventeen, looking more like a pageant toddler than a bluegrass musician. Julie and I had worn matching "country" outfits that nobody out in the country could ever pick beans or herd cows in: custom-made dresses with knee-length skirts standing almost straight out like we were square dancers. When enough sequins sparkled around our necks and our blond curls were sprayed stiff underneath our cowgirl hats, people noticed only how alike we looked, not how different we were. They feigned astonishment that we weren't twins even though I was two years older. I found this fun at seven, nauseating at seventeen.

But no country costume could have prepared me for dressing up like Dolly Parton's right-hand girl a few weeks after I'd turned eighteen. I'd been wearing sexy clothes in the past year—*provocative* clothes, my mom had said with distaste—but to me that had meant choosing a body-hugging minidress for the homecoming dance, or slicing a deeper V in my threadbare White Stripes T-shirt. I'd never shown this much boob in public.

Ms. Lottie acted like it was nothing. Costumes were part of showbiz, after all, even the steak house version of showbiz. She pinned my bouffant brunette wig in place—only Dolly got to wear a platinum wig. Ms. Lottie had already taken in my spangled maxi-dress a few inches before I arrived. All she had to do was pull it, shift it, give up, and make me add some padding to my bra, then pull and shift the gown again and shove my precocious fake cleav-age into place. She stood back with her hands on her hips to survey her work, then reached out to coax one of my baby boobs a little higher. "Sorry, hon. That's the best I can do with what you've got. Just stay behind the others." She gave me an encouraging pat on my sequined ass as I staggered on high heels into the bombed-out Borders to find Dolly.

Ms. Parton was a tolerable musician. So were the other two ladies on guitar and mandolin. Best of all, Ms. Parton had the Dolly act down, with lots of self-deprecating humor about breasts and plastic surgery. She made some jokes so off-color that even *I* thought they might be inappropriate for the families from the sticks enjoying a long lunch before they visited Junior at the state prison. I almost enjoyed the afternoon.

But I couldn't shake the idea that my dress of the day had been designed as some sick parody of my life, a combination of the costume I used to wear with Julie and the costume I'd donned for my wild senior year of high school. I hadn't wanted to expose my boobs to this crowd going back for seconds and thirds at the chocolate fountain, but that's what I'd *acted* like I'd wanted all year.

I'd acted like my goal was to get drunk with Hank Williams, or get stoned with Willie Nelson, or have an older man like Elvis imply he wanted to screw me. This job was a catalog of everything my parents had screamed at me about over the past year. *Is that what you want? Because that's what you're acting like!* It was a mythical series of tasks I had to perform to prove myself before I claimed my prize—except there was no prize. Unlike Hercules, I was not worthy.

♪ ♫ ♪

And on Saturday, I was assigned to wander the mall again, this time in a band with Johnny Cash.

"Plus his son," Ms. Lottie said. "Such a cutie-pie."

I'd noticed Mr. Cash sitting on the couch on my way in. I hadn't noticed his son. Maybe at the time he'd been bent over, fishing something from his instrument case. Maybe he wasn't much to look at, or he was way older than me, so my brain hadn't even registered him, and Ms. Lottie was putting me on.

"You will liiiiiiiiike him," she insisted, looking at me pointedly in the mirror and raising one carefully penciled eyebrow above her reading glasses. "I hear he's a heartbreaker, though, so watch out."

I scowled at my reflection. As on the first day, she was making me up in the style of the 1950s, all traces erased of the blond, angelic version of me from a year ago, and the current evil version, too. I needed my usual heavy mascara and black hair and black T-shirt to make this heartbreaker take me seriously when I scowled at him and told him where to go. He sounded like a replay of Elvis.

"This is ridiculous," I told Ms. Lottie. "Johnny Cash's wife didn't even play fiddle. She played everything but. What kind of authentic Nashville experience *is* this?"

"You don't have to be June Carter Cash. You could be a session musician from Studio B. Trust me, you want to be with the Cashes today." Ms. Lottie nodded toward the lounge area, where Johnny Cash and his heartbreaker son were tuning their guitars. "A couple of mornings ago, weren't you wishing for boy trouble? You just found it."

2

"We'll see about that," I grumbled. With my circle skirt sweeping behind me, I spun in Ms. Lottie's chair and stepped out of her hair-and-makeup alcove. I opened my fiddle case on an abandoned bookcase with a "Romance" sign on top. Better that than "Addiction" or "Family Planning," which was where my parents thought I was parking my fiddle these days. I ran the bow across the strings, making minor adjustments with the tuning pegs. I didn't need a tuning fork. I could tune my instrument by ear and I was always right. Other people didn't believe me, though, and I often spent a whole set of songs gritting my teeth and playing A at a fourth of a step up or down from 440 hertz.

Determined not to let that happen this time, I marched across the bookstore with a smile on my face, which seemed a lot more natural while I was in costume. Mr. Cash and his son sat in chairs on opposite ends of the lounge area, playing their guitars. I would charm them into doing things the way I wanted.

I watched them as I walked closer. Johnny Cash was a man about my dad's age with his dark hair greased and combed into a pompadour. He wore a dark suit with a white shirt and a bolo tie, which worked fine for Mr. Cash but also wouldn't have turned heads anywhere in Nashville. People around here were a little eccentric about bolo ties.

Ms. Lottie had coaxed his son's hair into the same glossy pompadour, but his clothes could have passed for current, too, part of the Buddy Holly aesthetic so popular right now at Vanderbilt. He wore low-top black Chuck Taylors, black jeans folded up a few turns like greasers wore them in the 1950s, and a plaid shirt with the sleeves rolled up above the elbows. The material stretched tight across his chest and biceps. He was big enough to have played football.

As I approached, Mr. Cash never looked up. There was no reason for him to. The lounge area was always busy at this time of the afternoon with musicians milling back and forth between the couches and Ms. Lottie's area. A 1950s fiddle player coming closer shouldn't have been an unusual sight.

But his son looked up. I was watching them, listening to the cacophony as they played two different songs in two different keys. I saw the exact moment when Cash Jr. realized someone was making a beeline for him. His dark eyes widened at me, his stare so unabashed and his expression so intent, as if reading my face, that I felt myself blushing in response.

And then he grinned at me. His eyes sparkled. The corners of his mouth lifted through a day's worth of dark stubble, which didn't quite jibe with the pompadour. He definitely was only a few years older than me, and so handsome that I wished for the millionth time I'd never cut my blond hair off and dyed it black. Then I remembered I was wearing my red ponytail wig, which was even worse.

Now I knew what Ms. Lottie had meant when she said he was a heartbreaker. And he hadn't spoken one word to me yet.

I hadn't bothered to impress anyone in a full year, but I found myself doing it now. I stopped in front of the sofa and called above Mr. Cash's continuing guitar notes, "Hello, I'm June Carter Cash," in imitation of the way the real deal used to say, "Hello, I'm Johnny Cash," at the beginning of his television variety show in the early 1970s. My parents had the complete set of DVDs.

"She didn't play fiddle," the son said, never taking his eyes off me as he stood. "You're definitely not her." His words were innocent enough, but his knowing tone of voice told me he got the joke that I was married to his father, and he himself was my son. And he didn't like it.

By now his dad was standing, too. His dad said, "I'm Darren Hardiman and this is my son, Sam," at the same time Sam said, "I'm Sam Hardiman and this is my father, Darren." They both heard each other as they started talking, glared sideways at each other, and finished their sentences a little louder. I hadn't been around boys and their fathers that much, but these two were easy to read, their expressions open like cartoon parodies of themselves, as if they were thoroughly tired of each other and didn't care anymore if they stepped on each other's toes.

Their interaction was even more fascinating to watch because they looked so much alike. They were dressed differently, and Sam's face was softer and more youthful despite his five o'clock shadow. But their pointed looks at each other were the same. Their dark, piercing eyes were the same. They were both tall and fit, and they stood exactly the same way, with one hand balancing the body of their guitars, the other hand never leaving the neck.

They both held out a hand for me to shake. Whichever hand I chose first, I was bound to piss off one of them. I should have taken Mr. Hardiman's hand, since he was in charge, but I took Sam's and was rewarded with an even broader grin, his eyes crinkling with the pleasure of one-upping his dad.

"What's your real name?" he asked, squeezing my hand briefly in his warm palm.

I turned to his dad, shook his hand, and gave my fake name. "Bailey Wright." Bailey was my real name. Wright was my grand-dad's last name, my mom's maiden name, and my middle name. It was close enough to the truth. My granddad had gotten me this job on the condition that I introduce myself using his last name rather than mine, which ought to keep the curious from drawing links between the loser sister and Julie once her career started to heat up. I was still mortified and angry that my family wanted to keep me hidden, but after a year, I was getting used to it.

Besides, I'd thought my parents had turned on me a year ago, but their first betrayal was naming me Bailey Mayfield at birth. Who gave their child a ridiculous, singsong name? They'd never honestly wanted me to bloom into a country sensation with a name like that. I was glad to get rid of it.

"Pleasure," Mr. Hardiman said, not quite getting the whole word out of his mouth before he dropped my hand and bent his head to his guitar again.

But Sam still watched me. "Bailey Wright." He puzzled through it. "Are you related to Mr. Wright who makes guitars?"

"Yyyeah," I admitted, simultaneously thinking I shouldn't have. If he knew who my granddad was, maybe he would figure out who my sister was, too. But I doubted my granddad went around offering Julie's story to anyone who wandered into his shop. And it sounded like Sam knew of my granddad only in passing. "He's my grandfather," I said.

"No shit!" Sam exclaimed. "He made both of ours." He nod-ded to his father's guitar, then showed me his own, with "Wright" inlaid in a light wood on the head. It wasn't my granddad's top-of-the-line model, but it was definitely more expensive than a mass-produced instrument, lovingly constructed for someone who took music seriously. Sam added, "My mother doesn't understand."

"Mothers and wives usually don't." My granddad told stories about customers canceling their orders for pricey handmade instruments when their women found out and protested—sometimes violently.

"Bailey Wright." Sam ran his eyes down my outfit. "Well, that explains some things."

What it explained, I wasn't sure. The fact that I was a teenage fiddle player? Yeah, only someone who'd grown up in a bluegrass family would suffer this cruel fate. The fact that I was dressed like a cult member?

He prompted his dad, "Bailey is related to Mr. Wright, the guitar guy."

"Well, how about that," Mr. Hardiman said noncommittally. And he was right. In Denver or Honolulu, he might have been astonished if he'd met the musician granddaughter of the man who made his guitar, but not in Nashville.

So much for my attempt at impressing them. In a last-ditch effort, I said brightly, "I'm already tuned. Do you want to tune to me?"

Mr. Hardiman's brows went way up. He didn't try to disguise the fact that I was out of line. It was his band. I should have tuned to him, or waited for him to say otherwise. He took a breath to tell me so.

Sam broke in, "She has perfect pitch, Dad." He turned to me and asked, "Don't you?"

I was so surprised Sam had guessed something private about me that I just stood there with my mouth wide open. I pictured myself wearing this expression. At least Ms. Lottie had painted my lips impeccably in classic red like a model on a 1957 cover of *Vogue*.

"You were making a face on your way over," he explained. Turning back to his dad, he said, "We must be a little off. We're torturing her."

"Not as bad as Hank Williams on Thursday," I assured them. "Yodeling."

They both nodded sympathetically. "Oh," Sam said. His dad echoed, "The yodeling."

"Well, why don't you start us off?" Mr. Hardiman asked me, nodding to my fiddle. He was back in charge.

Obediently I played a long, low E and let them tune their guitars to it. I felt relieved and strangely giddy that I was getting what I wanted for once. It wouldn't last, though. Guitars slowly unwound and went flat. In two hours I'd be gathering up the gumption to face off with Mr. Hardiman again.

But for now, I was good. Mr. Hardiman headed through the glass door that had been fitted into the storefront of the ex-Borders. Following him, Sam held the door wide open for me while backing against it so I could squeeze by him and his guitar. This was no big deal. Men held doors open for women in Nashville. They were rude if they didn't. His dad would have done it if Sam hadn't.

What set my heart racing was the way his chocolate eyes followed me as I passed him in the doorway, my bare forearm brushing against his. He gave me the smallest smile, soft-looking lips contrasting with the older look he was trying to pull off. The term *handsome devil* came up in country songs a lot. Now I understood why.

He fell into step beside me as we trailed his dad up the wide corridor. He said quietly, as if he didn't want his dad to hear, "I would kill for perfect pitch." In his voice I heard admiration of me, and a mournful longing.

"No, you wouldn't," I assured him. "If you had it, you'd wish you didn't. It's more trouble than it's worth." Life in a tribute band would be so much easier if I didn't mind Hank Williams's yodeling—or if, like Mr. Crabtree, I couldn't hear when the song went south.

"That's exactly what all of you say," Sam told me as we parted ways and parked ourselves on either side of Mr. Hardiman, who'd stopped in front of Banana Republic.

"'Five Feet High and Rising,'" Mr. Hardiman said, which made me smile despite myself. That song had special meaning to Nashville musicians. A few years ago we got seventeen inches of rain in two days and the Cumberland River swelled to flood the Grand Ole Opry. I expected Mr. Hardiman to add that the song was in B-flat, the key in which Johnny Cash had recorded it. He didn't. He just started with a strum of major one on his guitar. Sam matched him on the first beat, and I jumped in with the melody. Mr. Hardiman must have taken me at my word—or, rather, taken Sam at his—that I had perfect pitch. Only a very experienced or very jaded musician would accept that fact without teasing or questioning. He'd been around the block a few more times than his son or even Dolly or Hank or Willie or Elvis.

The song was made up of ones, fours, and fives like so many others. But the key kept changing higher, B-flat to D-flat to E-flat to F, reflecting the water rising to flood the farm where Johnny Cash grew up. It also had the characteristic Cash boom-chucka rhythm like a train chugging down the tracks, lots of fun to play after so many sad country ballads this week. Best of all, Mr. Hardiman and Sam were good at this. Mr. Hardiman sang in a deep, strong voice that matched Cash's nicely, and he and his son both had their guitar licks down pat.

The song featured a slow beat, as if Mr. Hardiman was testing me with an easy pace first. I must have passed, because next he announced "Hey, Porter," and both guitars jumped right in with the speeding freight-train beat. I handled the fiddle harmony fine. The challenge came during the solo section in the middle. A fast song like this could easily wreck a fiddle solo.

I might have become a lot of things in the past year. A failure. A bitch. A bad sister. I was not, however, rusty. As I pulled off the solo, first Sam and then Mr. Hardiman looked up at me in surprise.

With the smallest nod, Mr. Hardiman indicated that Sam should take a solo next. In general, playing fiddle was harder than guitar. I didn't have frets as anchors to tell me where my fingers should go. But fiddle solos were easier than guitar solos. At least I had a bow. All Sam had was one pick to enunciate every note of a lightning-fast improvisation. As I played my staccato accompaniment quietly to stay out of his way, I watched his hands in awe. I'm sure my face mirrored the expressions of so many non-musicians I'd played in front of over the years. Their wide-eyed question: *How'd you get so good?* The answer: *You start when you're five.* In Sam I'd met my match.

He knew it, too. About halfway through, he looked up at me again and grinned.

Another small nod from Mr. Hardiman told us he didn't want his turn at a solo. We moved on to the next verse of the song. But I still focused on Sam. He reminded me of a boy I'd met a long time ago at a bluegrass festival. Those days were full of cocky children trying to one-up me. This particular boy had been kind and friendly. We'd gotten assigned to the same impromptu band. And when I'd garnered louder applause for my solo than he got for his, he didn't stick out his tongue at me. He smiled at me like he'd run into an old friend. I'd looked for him at every festival since, but I'd never seen him again.

My sigh at the end of the song was partly for that lost boy, partly from relief. Drops of sweat were forming on my scalp and running down to the edges of my wig.

"Why didn't you take a solo?" Sam asked his father quietly.

"You two were busy impressing each other," Mr. Hardiman grumbled.

Sam leaned around his father's back to see if I'd overheard. When he saw I had, his eyes widened in horror. Then, with a little shake of his head, he was back to normal, brushing it off. He crossed behind his father to talk softly to me. "Been at this long?" he asked with a knowing smile.

"A week," I said, pretending I thought he meant the job rather than the fiddle in general. "But we haven't been playing this fast."

"You like it fast?" He was flirting with me, but he blinked at me innocently. He never would have admitted to the double entendre if I'd called him on it. He was testing me, like his dad had, but deliciously.

"Yeah," I said, "I like it fast."

"Remember you asked for it," he whispered. He crossed behind his father again to resume his place. "Dad," he said. "'Cocaine Blues.'"

"Yep" was all his father said before launching the song. This time when we ended, my bowing arm was sore, something I hadn't felt since I was a young player with no stamina. Sweat crawled down my face and pooled in my subtle 1950s cleavage.

"Let's walk up to Macy's and grace those folks with our presence," Mr. Hardiman said. He took off in that direction without waiting for us.

I didn't want to look like a groupie, but when Sam didn't follow his father immediately, I waited with him. Grinning, he pulled a handkerchief from his pocket and held it out to me. He'd noticed my unattractive sheen.

"Hey, that's period," I joked. The only people I'd seen using handkerchiefs, other than actors in old movies, were elderly bluegrass musicians who smelled funny.

"Isn't it?" he agreed happily. "Here."

"I couldn't. I'll get Ms. Lottie's makeup all over it."

"That's what it's for," he insisted.

I held my bow and fiddle in one hand while I took the handkerchief in the other and carefully blotted the sweat from my face. Sam produced another handkerchief from his pocket and did the same to his brow and the back of his neck.

"Keep it," he said when I tried to give my handkerchief back to him. I hid it in my circle skirt and made a mental note to always carry my own tissues when playing with musicians who were better than me.

"Let's go," I said, inclining my head toward Mr. Hardiman, who'd turned around beside the Hallmark to watch us with an exasperated expression. When we started walking, he continued toward Macy's.

Quietly I asked Sam, "Has your hair always been that dark?"

He gave me a quizzical look, mouth drawing up into a quirk. "No, it was blond when I was a kid. My dad told me I glowed like a flashlight."

"Did you ever play at bluegrass festivals?"

"I've been to a few. Are you saying we've met?"

"Yes." I marveled at how sure I was and, despite how different he looked, how little he'd changed.

He walked backward in front of me, taking a closer look at me. "Are you blond?"

Definitely not now. "I used to be." I neglected to add that, unlike Sam's natural progression from blond child to tall, dark, and handsome man, I'd chopped my blond hair off last year and dyed it night black. If he never saw me without my redheaded ponytail wig, he'd never know.

He pointed at me. "You have a sister."

He remembered exactly what I'd been trying to forget.

"But you're the *older* sister," he added, weighting his words to let me know older sisters were the world's most desirable creatures.

I wanted to flirt back, but it was hard for me. I'd lost the ability to laugh without sounding sardonic. And past Sam's shoulder, Mr. Hardiman stood near the entrance to the department store with his guitar slung over his back and his arms folded, staring up at the ceiling with deliberate patience, as if he'd been waiting hours for us.

"Your dad doesn't like me very much," I murmured.

"No, he doesn't like *me* very much." Sam gave me one last bright grin before we parted ways on either side of his father.

Mr. Hardiman strummed his guitar. "A little old-time blue-grass?" He wasn't looking at me, but I figured he was talking to me rather than Sam. I couldn't picture him okaying anything with Sam before he did it.

"Yes," I said.

"Awesome," Sam murmured, lips curving into that adorable smile, pick at the ready over his guitar strings.

"What do you know?" Mr. Hardiman asked.

Again, I assumed he meant me. "Everything." Even to my own ears, I sounded weary as I said, "I know everything."

"'Soldier's Joy' then, in E." He had to name a key for me this time. The song was older than America and had probably been re-corded in all twelve keys.

I felt my adrenaline spike at the idea of playing one of the first tunes I ever learned on fiddle, a staple of late nights messing around at the edge of a bonfire after the main events at a bluegrass festival were over. The casual audience had gone home by then. Only us die-hard campers, my family and several other families of musicians we'd grown close to over the years, were left to close down the night with ones and fours and fives and ones. Somehow this happy tune woke up those tired chords for me and made their familiarity a good thing.

Or maybe it was Sam who'd turned my mood around. As was typical, we played a couple of verses, took turns with solos, and then sang one verse. Bluegrass singing was about harmony rather than anyone having a strong voice. I automatically took the higher line in a group. Hearing Mr. Hardiman on the bottom with Sam in the middle, I wanted rather desperately to know what Sam's singing voice really sounded like, but I couldn't pick it out with my own voice filling my head.

The singing was over almost before it began. We ended the tune with another instrumental verse, then jumped into "Cripple Creek" almost immediately. This day was so different from my other days on this job. The music was faster, the musicians were better, the backup guitarist was a hunk from heaven, and we gathered quite an audience of customers coming out of Macy's laden with shopping bags. Some got caught up in the infectious rhythm, tapping their toes. A gaggle of tween girls edged closer to Sam every time he looked up and flashed them that sweet grin. A toddler girl stood so close to me, staring way up at my flashing fiddle bow, that she made me uncomfortable. I looked around for her mother. If this little one caught the bluegrass bug, God help her. Better to spend her childhood watching TV and throwing rocks.

Though we amassed a big audience, we were supposed to be a traveling band. Mr. Hardiman was getting itchy, waiting for the proper time to end the set. It came when some teenage skater boys started their bad imitation of buck dancing at the edge of the crowd. Genuine buck dancing broke out at bluegrass festivals all the time, and admittedly, Julie and I had made fun of those backwoods people and their spontaneous jigs. But fake buck dancing to our real music was an insult. It reminded me of Toby raising a pierced eyebrow and sneering every time he caught a glimpse of my fiddle.

Sure enough, at the end of that song, Mr. Hardiman announced, "I'm Johnny Cash. Thank you very much," and started down the corridor without a word to Sam or me. Sam and I exchanged glances—mine startled, his resigned—and hurried after his father.

The rest of the afternoon passed that way. I did twice as much playing as I had with any other band. As we moved from our stop at Zales to our stop at Bath & Body Works to our stop at the Gap, Sam and I practically ran behind Mr. Hardiman. I was sorry Sam didn't get much of a chance to flirt with me and I didn't get much of a chance to respond with all the enthusiasm of a block of wood. I got the feeling Sam didn't want to talk to me anyway. Not in front of his father.

A few minutes before six o'clock, we made our last stop in the food court, which was crowded with weekend shoppers. "Dad," Sam said before his father could launch a song. "We've gone flat. Let's take a minute to tune to the human pitch pipe here." He flashed his brilliant grin at me.

People munching pizza and kung pao chicken from plastic trays snapped their heads up at us as I bowed an E for Sam and Mr. Hardiman to tune to. Over the note, Mr. Hardiman said, "I don't know about you two, but I'm plumb tuckered out."

He meant the three of us had tested each other that afternoon. He was attempting to be friendly.

"Wow, I don't blame you," Sam told his father. "Tired after four hours of work."

Mr. Hardiman stared Sam down, Sam stared back, and I wasn't sure what this animosity meant.

"'Old Joe Clark' in A," Mr. Hardiman barked. Turning to me, he added, "We dress it up a little with a major G."

I laughed at the idea of a seven chord turning this ancient song avant-garde. "Wow, a *major* G chord?" I exclaimed sarcastically before I thought.

Mr. Hardiman's eyes narrowed at me. Suddenly he looked more like Johnny Cash than he had yet, stern and gruff and not afraid to play concerts in maximum-security prisons.

"Um," I backtracked, feeling a blush creep up my neck. I'd meant all afternoon to make a chord joke to Sam. My attempt had come out at the wrong time. Sheepishly I asked Mr. Hardiman, "Where does the major G go?"

He nodded smugly. "You see? You've gotten too big for your britches. All that talent doesn't mean shit if you won't shut up long enough to listen to instructions so you can play with the group."

That stung. Everything bad that adults said about me stung, because all of it was true.

But the pain didn't have time to settle before Sam stepped in to draw the fire. "Dad!" he called, letting his guitar hang from his neck by the strap so his hands were free to wave between us. "Over here."

Mr. Hardiman glared at Sam, then at me, then down at his guitar, tuning his E string like I was dismissed.

Sam leaned toward me behind his father's back. "Sorry," he mouthed.

I tried to smile a little, to show him I appreciated him sticking up for me, but my lips couldn't make it.

I played "Old Joe Clark" perfunctorily. The fun was gone for me now, and Sam looked as grim as I felt. Despite our lack of enthusiasm, we gathered another crowd, because we were more interesting to listen to than the Muzak that the mall piped in over the loudspeakers. We played a few more Johnny Cash tunes, and then Mr. Hardiman said, "Last one. 'Folsom Prison Blues.'"

This was another song with a breakneck pace and Cash's signature freight-train beat. Whenever I stole a glance at Sam, his smile was creeping back, which made me try a little harder when my solo came around. He took his solo, Mr. Hardiman took his and sang the last few verses, and I thought the song would end.

As we were wrapping it up, Mr. Hardiman called over the music, "Not again. Don't do that, son. I'm warning you."

I watched them, puzzling through what they were talking about. I couldn't see that Sam was doing anything unusual, and then I heard it. Under Sam's pick, the freight-train beat on a major one chord morphed into a slightly different but equally driving rhythm. Confused, I followed along, retracing the one chord with my fiddle, until something developed. I finally recognized the song a measure before Sam started singing it: "Shake Your Body" by the Jacksons.

Mr. Hardiman's face was beet red by now, but he played along with Sam's funky beat. He had no choice. Professional musicians didn't stop in the middle of a song.

I was more intrigued by Sam. I was finally hearing his voice. And it was *good*. Strong. Soulful. White boy was singing the hell out of some Michael Jackson.

I wasn't sure what part I was supposed to be playing. For a while I just backed up the chords and doubled the bass line. Then I remembered this was a disco song with violins, so I played the soaring part from memory. That was the right answer, apparently. Sam had stopped singing, anticipating that I would know what to do in the bridge. He flashed me his biggest grin yet and melted my heart.

He picked up singing again in the next verse. His voice was deeper and fuller than Michael's, but he wasn't afraid to imitate the wails that made Jackson famous. The crowd loved him, and not just the tweens this time. Shoppers stood three deep around us, gazing at him with their mouths open. Mr. Hardiman could do a mean Johnny Cash, but there was no question who was the star of this show.

The song as I remembered it was drawing to a close, assuming it didn't morph again into something equally bizarre for a Johnny Cash tribute band like a Bach fugue or a Gregorian chant. Mr. Hardiman watched Sam, presumably for the cutoff. I did, too. As our last notes rang around the vast room and the crowd burst into applause, I finally smiled. My face and my whole body felt light for the first time in a long, dark year. I turned to Sam to tell him so.

But he was looking at his father. And his father lasered him with a glare that made the one they'd given each other when we first met look like a smiley face.

Mr. Hardiman said slowly, clearly, loud enough for the crowd to hear, "Don't you *ever* do that again."

Quite a few people in the audience deduced that if the band was arguing, the good times were over. They exchanged a few words with each other and moved off. But those who'd never seen the likes of a Johnny Cash impersonator get in an argument with his son at the mall sidled into the front spaces the departing crowd had vacated, eager for more.

Sam seemed to realize this was not the time or place for the discussion his father wanted to have. He glanced up at the crowd, then over at me, making my heart jump. He whispered to Mr. Hardiman, "I didn't co-opt your song. You went with me."

"I only went with you because *she* was going with you"— Mr. Hardiman shot me a mean look, then glared at Sam again—"and I wasn't going to fight two of you in the middle of a performance. You know it and I know it, so cut the shit."

Sam blushed. His eyes never left his dad's. He was embarrassed at the scene his dad was causing, but he wasn't going to give in.

"Quitting time," I sang with a glance at my watch, which of course neither of them saw because they still glared at each other, even now that I'd spoken up. "Maybe we'll have this much fun the next time we play together." As I whirled around to get out of there, my skirt spun in a wide circle. The material whacked Mr. Hardiman on the leg of his loose suit pants. I had to elbow my way out of the persistent crowd, protecting my fiddle and bow in front of me.

3

As I hurried out of the food court, toward the shell of a Borders, shoppers followed me with their eyes. I didn't blame the small children or the adults. My clothes were obviously a costume because of their anachronism as well as their thick durability. They had a peculiar odor, like Ms. Lottie had sent them back in time for authenticity and they'd returned with a scent of Brylcreem and tomato aspic. Seeing me roaming the mall alone was like running into Snow White buying a pack of crackers and a fountain drink in an Orlando gas station.

I did, however, blame the teenagers who snickered behind their hands and didn't bother to keep quiet. I had never fit in with them, not in this costume, not in my everyday one, not before I'd started wearing one. I was an anachronism no matter what I wore, an expert on a sixteenth-century instrument nobody wanted. I'd thought I could enjoy this job. Instead I'd been sexually harassed by one dead rockabilly, and I'd developed a hopeless crush on the son of another.

I wasn't supposed to have a crush at age eighteen. Crushes were for little girls without the maturity and confidence to ask for what they wanted, and without the strength to pursue it anyway if they were denied. Yet here I was, eleven all over again, quaking in my cowgirl boots when a fresh-faced, blond Sam smiled at me. For the rest of the summer I would be on edge every moment at the mall, hoping for another glimpse of him. If Ms. Lottie was right about the randomness of the schedule, I might never play with him again.

I could ask to be assigned to Johnny Cash permanently, unless he or his son objected to being saddled with a saucy fiddle player. But I didn't *want* to feel this way, did I? Staring at Sam with my mouth open because he was so handsome, hanging on his every word, shivering when I brushed past him? I'd be better off following Dolly Parton around from now on. Maybe I could make it to August without seeing Sam again.

Yeah, right, that's exactly what I wanted. I caught myself looking around the mostly empty Borders on the slim chance Sam had miraculously beaten me there.

Dolly Parton gave me a hard squeeze instead. I didn't recognize her at first without her blond wig and boobs. I actually had a split second of panic that I was being attacked by a mall groupie with a fetish for impersonators. Then she said in my ear, "Bye, hon! Have a great weekend!" and I figured out who she was. The outsize breasts might be a put-on, but the Appalachian accent wasn't.

I hadn't realized I'd earned such an emotional response from her after playing in her band once. I needed to get this outfit off as soon as possible and put my usual makeup back on to warn away good-hearted middle-aged country singers. And hunky teenage guitarists dressed like Buddy Holly. Feeling closed down over the past year had been awful, but it might actually have been more awful to think that music and this boy had opened me up. In a state of something like despair, I mumbled a good-bye to Dolly and slid into Ms. Lottie's chair.

"Uh-oh," Ms. Lottie said, seeing my pouty expression in the mirror and sticking out her bottom lip in sympathy. "Did Sam steal your heart already? That's got to be some kind of record, even for him."

I didn't want to talk about it. I explained instead, "He and his dad got into an argument in the middle of the food court."

"Yeah, I've heard that about those two. I've seen it in here." She nodded toward the empty lounge area, then lowered her voice. "Darren is a drinker when he doesn't have a gig. He's hard on Sam, and Sam is hard on him. I feel sorry for both of them. You run into that again and again in this town. So talented, and they're their own worst enemy." Shaking her head, she pulled out a few bobby pins and lifted my hair off.

After she disassembled me, I stepped into the changing room, a cubicle with no ceiling. Way up on the wall hung a decorative poster left over from Borders. James Joyce frowned down at me, which made me feel even more naked as I pulled off my heavy costume. I glanced up at his creepy gaze behind his glasses and fought the urge to hide my bruised thigh under my circle skirt again.

Then I paused, wearing only my black lace undies, and listened to the larger room on the other side of the partition. A banjo strummed. Ms. Lottie laughed. There was no guitar music, and there were none of Sam's quips under his breath. Yet my body thought it could feel him there.

Ms. Lottie's commentary had made me wonder again about his argument with Mr. Hardiman, and his snide laughter when Mr. Hardiman said he was tired after working four hours. I'd thought Sam was just a handsome guy. Now that I knew he had problems at home, he was complicated and, in a twisted way, more intriguing.

Which didn't change the fact that he was gone.

I'd almost forgotten his handkerchief in my circle skirt pocket.

I pulled it out and examined it for the first time. It wasn't stained with my makeup after all. It didn't have his initials embroidered on it, either. It was just a store-bought square—I marveled briefly that a shop still sold these—and any sweat on it was mine, not his. I didn't have to cling to it like he was a rock star.

Rolling my eyes at myself, I pulled on my tight jeans, stuffed Sam's handkerchief into my snug pocket, and ducked into a tighter T-shirt. Emerging into Ms. Lottie's area, I scrubbed my face clean and started over with my makeup for the third time that day. While Ms. Lottie deconstructed the fake boobs of a banjo player who'd followed Dolly around that day, she kept glancing over at me, carefully maintaining a neutral expression as I applied my black mascara, liquid eyeliner, and blood-red lipstick. The ponytail wig and four hours of sweat had matted my hair. I brushed it out and fluffed my curls until they hung correctly, longer on one side and jet-black all over. Then grabbed my purse and fiddle case and bailed out of Borders.

Out on the loading dock, the summer heat hit me like a rock, and the evening sunlight blinded me. I couldn't see, but I could hear a guitar to the left. Blinking and then opening one eye, I recognized Sam on the retaining wall. The pompadour was gone, his hair damp. Without all the gel or whatever Ms. Lottie had used to stick it together, his hair was surprisingly wavy and wild, which worked a lot better with the scruffy beginnings of his beard than the pompadour had. He'd traded the plaid button-down for a tight T-shirt, which he wore with the same skinny black jeans, rolled down now, and black sneakers. He was dressed a lot like me.

At first he didn't seem to notice I was looking at him. He didn't seem to concentrate on his music, either. His fingers moved automatically over the guitar strings, playing an old tune brought to the Appalachians from Scotland and written before the system of chords in Western music had been regularized, so it was full of progressions that sounded strange to the modern ear. The chords were minor, as if the song was meant to be sad, but the lyrics were ironically upbeat. Sam wasn't singing them, but I knew the words. He stared into space, in my vicinity but beyond me, through me, like he was thinking hard about something else. His dark brows were knitted, and he squinted a little. The hot breeze moved one dark curl across his forehead, which must have tickled, but he didn't brush it away.

I considered standing in front of him until he acknowledged me. What did I want out of that, though? He wasn't interested in me, and I shouldn't be interested in him. So I just kept walking and hoped he wouldn't notice me.

I was all the way past him, stepping from the concrete ramp to the asphalt road, when I heard him call behind me, "Bailey!"

I stopped automatically, then wished I hadn't. Now I couldn't pretend I hadn't heard him. He was making everything more difficult. The more I interacted with him, the harder I was going to fall, and the worse the rest of my summer without him or anybody else was going to be.

The damage was done, though. I turned to face him as he jogged the few steps between us, holding his guitar by the neck. "I've been waiting for you. I almost didn't recognize you." He stared at me, taking in my eyes, then my hair, but not with the appraising expression girls wore when they commented on my looks. A small smile played on his lips like he appreciated the way I was done up but also—a little disturbingly—found it amusing.

To break the silence, I finally said, "I don't wear the June Carter Cash wig home. Or the Dolly Parton Does Vegas outfit on my Dolly Parton days."

His brows shot up. "You have Dolly Parton days?"

"And Willie Nelson days, and that's just the first week." I confided, "Mr. Nelson was a bit fried."

"I'm sorry." Sam sounded genuinely sympathetic.

"The outfit was okay, though, in comparison. How did you get away with wearing your own jeans and shoes while Ms. Lottie sewed me into a circle skirt? Only your hair got caught in the time machine."

"Yeah." He laughed, putting one hand through his damp waves. "I've been doing this awhile. I know what Ms. Lottie will put up with and what she won't. The real question is, how did *you* snag so many days a week of work so soon after you started?" He lowered his guitar to rest on the toe of his shoe and spun it as he said, trying to sound casual, "Your granddad must have a lot of sway."

"Somebody at the casting company owed him a favor," I acknowledged. "But he doesn't have any real clout in Nashville. If he did, everybody in my family would have had a recording contract years ago." I shifted my fiddle case to my other hand and gazed impatiently at the parking lot like I had something to do tonight besides watch television with a seventy-year-old man and hate myself. "Why were you waiting for me?"

"Oh." He swallowed. "I just wanted to apologize for all the drama between my dad and me."

"Don't worry about it." I did worry about it, and I wanted to know more, but I waved the drama away with one hand. "I was playing at the very same place in the food court on Tuesday when I got into it myself with Elvis."

"Oh, man, they stuck you with Elvis, too? Who *didn't* they give you to? Was he a prick to you?"

"You could say that." I decided not to inform Sam about my night of intense anxiety or the fact that in my mind, Elvis had caused me to become a homeless prostitute. "Anyway, maybe there's something about standing between Baskin-Robbins and McDonald's that drives us all batty and makes us turn on each other. In high school I knew groups like this were playing around town. I might have passed Loretta Lynn once or twice on my way to shop for shoes, but I never pictured myself actually having this job. And I sure never knew the concert in the food court turns into a reality show. They should advertise it. People would come to the mall just for that."

"We musicians are impossible," he said in a dead-on imitation of Ms. Lottie.

I almost laughed. Almost. I opened my mouth, but all that came out was a short noise. I did want him to know how funny I thought he was, so I said dryly, "You sound just like her."

"Ms. Lottie is full of wisdom," he said. "She used to do makeup and costumes for the Grand Ole Opry, and once upon a time she was married to a record company executive."

"I guess she doesn't have the sway to get anybody a contract, either," I said. "Everybody in this town knows somebody who was Somebody with a capital S at some point." When he didn't say anything, I finished with a zinger that reflected what I'd suspected when he mentioned my granddad. "If she had any clout, you would have used her by now."

He lifted his chin and turned his head, as if he couldn't see me clearly, and looking at me with the other eye might help. "Why does that bother you?" he asked. "Wouldn't you do anything to get a recording contract?"

"No," I said too loudly. My voice echoed against the flat, blank concrete walls of the mall. "Absolutely not. I wouldn't use somebody."

His dark eyes widened in surprise—which surprised me in turn. Though I'd walked around the mall with him for hours, I hadn't had the chance to watch him much. He'd stood on the other side of his father most of the time. Only now was I noticing how expressive his eyes were, and how tall he was, and how young he seemed all of a sudden, like he hadn't been tall for long and he wasn't yet used to his own height.

But what he said next surprised me more than anything else he'd said or done. "I am so disappointed you feel that way, because I wanted to use you."

He uttered this with such confidence that I thought his innuendo was intentional. And despite the fact that I did not—*did not*—want to be used, chill bumps popped up on my arms in the hot sun.

His eyes grew even wider. "That's not what I meant." He closed his eyes and cringed. "God, what else can I say to embarrass the fuck out of myself?"

He'd teased me that afternoon, but this time I could tell his discomfort was sincere. And it was adorable. I wanted to hug him and help him out of it.

I couldn't, though. I stood paralyzed in front of him, letting him flail as if I enjoyed watching it.

With a final tortured look at me, he burst out, "When I first met you, I wasn't sure how old you were. It's hard to tell whether somebody is thirteen or thirty without seeing what they're wearing."

Perplexed, I asked, "How old am I?"

"Eighteen, like me. Please, God, say you're eighteen like me."

He sounded so desperate that I repeated automatically, "I'm eighteen like you."

"And I'm so glad," he rushed on, "because I didn't figure a thirty-year-old woman would be interested in my band." He looked around the empty loading dock and over both shoulders at the parking lot like somebody might be crouching behind the cars, listening in. "I couldn't say anything when my dad was around.

I mean . . ." He rolled his eyes at his own words, just as he'd done several times that day. I got the impression that his mouth moved faster than his brain. He seemed to blurt out a lot of things before his brain caught up. "My dad knows about my band. It's not a secret. But he doesn't want me to pursue music as a career because *he* wasn't successful and therefore there's no way *I* could be successful either, get it? My only musical activity that gets his approval is backing up his loser impersonation job."

"Got it." I didn't, exactly, but I wanted to hear the rest.

He talked fast. "So I have this parentally acknowledged and yet discouraged band that plays country and rockabilly. Some Cash, actually. Alan Jackson. Zac Brown."

"Michael Jackson?" I ventured.

He grinned and opened his hands, forgetting he was balancing his guitar on his foot. He snatched it up before it touched the concrete ramp. "See," he said, "I *knew* you would get it."

I flushed with pleasure, basking in the glow of his approval.

"Yes," he went on, "the Johnny Cash songs do have a tendency to morph into Michael Jackson's funky deep cuts, and the Zac Brown will sometimes give way to Prince. There might be some Chaka Khan thrown in. . . ." He slowed, less sure of himself as he saw my skeptical expression. "And some Justin Bieber for irony, and maybe a little Ke$ha. Look."

He stepped closer and stooped so that he looked straight into my eyes. I got the feeling he'd done this before. Maybe he'd never asked a punky fiddle player to come see his band, but he'd persuaded plenty of girls to follow along with his outlandish schemes. In his words I could hear the echo of every other time he'd done this to every other girl since he was a blond kid.

"A good song is a good song," he said. "You know that. The most important thing is the unrelenting beat. We're a dance band, a crazy party band, emo with a side of redneck. So far people seem to like us, but we've only played our friends' parties and a street festival and my mom's cousin's retirement party, and then it's a long story but there are a lot of immigrants from Laos living south of town and we were fortunate enough to get on the Lao wedding circuit. But tonight we have a *gig*." Remembering to secure his guitar this time, he opened only two fingers of that hand and all the fingers of his other hand as he said *gig*.

"A *gig*," I repeated, imitating him by opening my own hand, not the one holding my fiddle case.

"Yes," he exclaimed, delighted that I was mocking him, "and it's at a *bar*!"

"A *bar*!" I echoed, trying hard not to laugh at the ecstatic expression on his face. He was excited about this gig. He wanted me to come see him play. And I couldn't, because I was grounded—at least, as grounded as a legal adult could be. "Good luck!" I stepped past him.

"Wait, what? No." He jogged backward until he was in front of me again. When I didn't stop moving, he kept walking backward into the road. "This bar where we're playing may not be on Broadway," he said, "but it's close, in the District. I want to take the band to the next level. We're getting there, but slower than I want to go. We're not getting the attention we deserve. There are too many bands around town for anybody to give us our big chance. You know what we need?" He tripped backward over a curb around a tree.

"What?" I asked at the same time I instinctively caught his elbow to keep him from falling. Too late I realized he weighed a lot more than I did.

Using his guitar as leverage, he managed to balance himself again and keep me from falling in turn. We both held our instruments out to one side and gripped each other's free elbows. A shock ran through me—the pain of his strong fingers wrapping around my arm, and the tingle of awareness that went with it.

If he felt the tingle, too, he was oblivious to it. He released my elbow, then patted my arm as if to make sure he hadn't hurt me, that's all. "We need a fiddle player! I knew it as soon as I heard you play."

It had seemed to me yesterday that my trials with these bands were a test to prove I wasn't worthy—as if I didn't know this already. Now, here was the final task. I was being given the chance to do the one thing I wanted most in the world: play. The chance was presented to me by a guy so gorgeous, my skin turned to fire when he touched me. And joining a band was the thing I was most forbidden to do, the thing that would ruin my future.

Sam was still talking. "I thought so when you were dressed like 1956. But now that I've seen you for real . . ."

I walked past him, over the curb and around the tree to the parking lot on the other side, hoping he wouldn't see how my face had fallen. He *hadn't* seen me for real. He never would. That me was gone. Who was the real me anymore, anyway? Had I ever existed?

All of which was unbearably self-centered. I couldn't seem to stop focusing on myself these days, and frankly I made myself sick. "What are you saying I look like?" I shot back at him over my shoulder. It came out more bitter than I intended or he deserved.

"Like you belong with us. Some of the bars on Broadway are really friendly to new bands. At least, it seems that way at first. They have a reputation for hosting the hottest new acts in Nashville, and record company execs wander in and discover bands that way. These bars will let anybody upload an audition video. But I did that last month. They said our sound was there but we needed something extra to bring people in. You are that extra."

I turned to face him, leaning against my car and letting the sun-heated metal warm my back through my shirt. The car was a small secondhand Honda that I should have been grateful my parents had bought me. It didn't compare with the red Porsche Julie had earned, which was sitting in the garage at my parents' house, hardly ever driven, waiting for her to come home.

Out with it. It was a simple admission, but every word felt like a knife in my mouth as I said, "I can't join a band right now."

Stopping a few paces across the asphalt from me, he watched me for a moment and narrowed his eyes, as if he could read in my expression how loaded that statement was. How badly I wanted to join his band and play funky Michael Jackson covers on my fiddle, and how important it was to my future that I walk away.

Nodding, he said carefully, "Sure, you don't want to commit when you haven't played with us yet. Come try us out tonight, just this once."

I couldn't. But despite myself, I pictured it for a moment: a night out with this adorable guy, who had reined in his enthusiasm to avoid scaring me off, but whose intense, dark eyes still gave away how desperate he was for this. I winced as I repeated, "I can't."

"You can use our amp," he said. "Do you have an electric pickup? I can scrounge you up one if you don't."

"I have one." The equipment to amplify my fiddle had been coiled in my case for the past year, waiting for the son of a Johnny Cash impersonator to sweep me off my feet.

"Then what's the prob? Please, Bailey." He moved forward and put his hand on mine—this time on the hand holding my fiddle case. "I really want to play with you again."

If he heard his own double entendre, implying that he might play with me in more ways than one, he didn't acknowledge it. His hand rested lightly on mine, putting no pressure on me, holding back the pressure to come.

I felt myself relax, reluctantly, under his touch. I knew this gig was going to get me in trouble, and I was fully aware of the exact moment I started rationalizing that maybe it wouldn't. My parents didn't want me to play in public, yet my granddad had gotten me the mall job. He would let me play with Sam, too, just for fun, just this once.

Now that I'd decided to take this step, suddenly I realized I might not be able to after all. I let out a frustrated sigh. "What time is the gig? I have to make a phone call around ten."

I figured he would want to know more about the phone call. He would declare that he wasn't going to plan his gig around a phone call, and if that's the way I wanted it, he could find another Goth fiddler.

Briefly I considered giving in if he insisted. It *was* ridiculous for me to demand to make a phone call at a certain time in the middle of a gig. But no. The consequences were too steep. I was calling Julie to let her know I still cared about her, whether she cared about me or not.

I'd worried for nothing. Sam said, "The gig starts at nine and lasts until eleven. Ten would be a good time to take a break. I lose track of time, though, so you'll have to poke me in the ribs with your bow. What's your phone number? I'll text you the address of the bar." He looped his guitar strap over his head and settled the guitar behind him on his back. Both hands free, he pulled his phone out of his pocket and watched me expectantly.

I had one last chance to back away, be a good girl like my parents told me, and keep my future safe by sacrificing my present. Unfortunately, in my present, Sam stood eight inches taller than me, smiling down at me. One dark curl played back and forth on his forehead in the hot breeze.

I gave him my number.

"Texting you." He pocketed his phone. A second later my phone sounded in my purse, signaling my pact with the devil.

"And one last thing," he said. "Try to look twenty-one."

I remembered him telling me I looked eighteen. Then I realized what he really meant. "Oh, will we get in trouble for playing in a bar underage? I never tried." That was exactly the kind of trouble that would make my parents' heads explode.

He shrugged. "Different places have different rules, depending on whether they serve food and what time it is. I haven't asked this place. If it doesn't come up, we're not breaking a rule, right? I don't want to give anybody an excuse to tell me no."

This was one more warning that playing with this boy was bad news. Once more I chose to ignore it. I asked him, "Is that what the stubble is for? You're trying to look older?"

He grinned and ran his hand across his jaw. "The stubble is for *style*. See you there before nine?"

"Nine," I affirmed, sliding along the side of my car to the driver's door.

"*Before* nine," he repeated. "Not right at nine. When everybody isn't there on time, I tend to have a stroke."

I thought of a song as he was walking away. As soon as the idea hit me, I wished he would walk away faster so I could get it down in my notebook. I didn't want him to see me scribbling. Months earlier, Toby had taken my notebook out of my purse and read my lyrics in a sneering voice. I'd always kept my songs to myself, fearing that he'd ridicule the thing I loved most, and true to form he'd confirmed my worst fears. Thank God he couldn't read music. If he'd tried to sing to me, I would have hated my own work forever.

In my rearview mirror I watched Sam walk one row over and put his guitar case behind the seat of a Chevy truck. The truck was older than he was, with a scratched and dented bed, but I knew from experience on my parents' farm that pickup trucks were hard to kill. I could wait to write in my notebook until he drove off, but he was probably already wondering why I sat motionless in the driver's seat. I started the ignition, drove about a mile toward my granddad's house, and pulled off at a gas station to jot a few lines of poetry and music before I forgot them.

When a song stuck in my head like that, I felt like I was holding my breath until I got it down on paper. Finishing, relieved, I looked up and noticed everything I hadn't noticed initially about the gas station: the people going in and out of the building, the riotous colors of the beer advertisements in the windows, the sweeping noise the traffic made on the nearby street. My whole trip here hadn't registered with me, either. I'd driven the car and navigated the road, but my brain had waited until now to start processing again. Even driving away from Sam hadn't registered.

I thought of him bending over to put his guitar behind the seat of his truck, big biceps moving underneath the sleeves of his T-shirt. His father had been nowhere in sight, which must have meant they'd driven to the mall separately. Maybe Sam didn't even live with his dad anymore. He had more and better friends than I did, potential roommates, and the second he'd graduated from high school, he'd moved out.

But as I pulled back onto the street and puzzled through Sam, I decided he more likely was stuck with his dad like I was stuck with my family. He relied on his dad for the job like I relied on my granddad. I could tell from his enthusiasm that nothing had ever been more delicious to him than the taste of his own gig tonight. It took a lot for a big guy like him to give the impression of a wide-eyed puppy.

I felt like that myself—about the gig, and about him. I couldn't wait for *before* nine.

I pulled up to my granddad's house and walked through the front room, which he'd converted to a workshop and showroom. Most of the time even his living space in the back smelled like sawdust and varnish. At the moment it smelled like steam and spaghetti. He was a pretty good cook for only having learned ten years ago when my grandmom died, and I was hungry. My stomach growled, and my heart leaped. I missed sitting down at the dinner table with my whole family, but I still looked forward to eating with my granddad.

"Hi," I called, popping into the kitchen.

"Hey," he said, turning around from the pots on the stove with a spatula in his hand, wearing my grandmother's apron over the denim shirt and jeans he worked in. When we were younger, Julie and I had made fun of him behind his back for cooking us dinner in the frilly apron. My mom had told us sternly that he missed her mother, and not everything in life was fodder for cruel little girls.

His eyes lingered for only a second on my asymmetrical hair—it seemed that in a year, he'd never quite gotten used to it—before he asked, "How was work?"

"This was probably the best day all week." At least, the day sure had looked up after work was over. "I got invited to play another gig tonight."

"No," he said, shaking his head.

Stunned, I stared at him with his sauce-covered spatula in the air. Technically, I was forbidden by my parents to play any gig at all. But my granddad had gone out and gotten me the first one, so I'd thought he would agree to the second one, too, if I presented it the right way. I'd rehearsed my speech all the way from the gas station, and he'd just cut me off.

This couldn't be happening. Not when Sam was involved. I took a deep breath, kept my cool, and started again. "This gig is in the District—"

"Even worse," my granddad interrupted. "In a bar? You're underage. And you're more likely to attract attention playing in the District. That's exactly what your parents said to keep you away from. I didn't see the harm in the mall job, no matter what your parents thought, but even I can see you shouldn't be playing in the District, like you're trying to get your own recording contract. Julie's record company asked us not to talk about you because they don't want the public to hear she used to play with you. What if the record company found out?"

I stared at him a moment more, this rangy, white-haired man in a woman's apron, controlling my life. He was the one who'd gotten me into this mess, in a roundabout way. He'd taught my mother to play guitar. He'd taken her and her brothers to blue-grass festivals. That's where she'd gotten the idea that a drive for musical fame was fun for the whole family. My granddad still had one toe in the music industry. He might not have caught the bug that badly himself—he'd never seemed to crave the spotlight—but he was ultimately responsible for all our obsessions with it. And he was the one taking this gig away from me. If he wasn't my ally against my parents anymore, I didn't have a friend left.

He watched me uneasily for a moment, then added, "I'm just doing what your grandmother would have done."

At his mention of my grandmother, I felt a heavy shroud of failure descend across my shoulders. I wouldn't argue with him when he invoked my grandmother. He loved her too much, living his life as if she were still around. She'd been dead since I was eight, but I remembered her as a lady who liked pretty things and proper girls and never clapped loudly enough when Julie and I performed for her, as if music wasn't what she was after.

"Dinner's ready," he said. "Why don't you sit down at the table, and you can tell me about work."

Usually I helped him with dinner when I came in. If he was offering to serve me, he felt bad about forbidding my gig.

I wasn't sure how far I could push him, though. We were close, but I still couldn't pitch a fit to him like I had in the past to my parents. Getting angry and rebelling against my granddad because he wouldn't let me play a gig, which I wasn't supposed to play anyway, was another in a long line of reasons my parents could give for pulling the plug on my future.

"You know, Granddad . . ." There was no way I could sit down at the table and eat with him now. But I wanted him to know I appreciated the dinner, and I was sorry he seemed so lonely without my grandmom. All I could manage was, "Not hungry," as I ducked out of the kitchen, rounded the banister, and jogged up the stairs. I felt like a bitch—because I was one.

As I burst into the room we pretended was my bedroom, I had an urge to chuck my fiddle, case and all, as hard as I could into the bookcase laden with sheet music and festival awards nobody had cared about in thirty years. The adrenaline rushed to my fingertips.

Face tight with an expression so ugly I could feel it, I closed the door behind me, carefully set my fiddle case on top of the dresser, then fished my phone out of my purse to call Sam.

First, though, I quickly scrolled through the texts from Toby that had accumulated while I was at work. Since spending Memorial Day at the lake, he'd been sending me insults when he was drunk, and apologies and pleas to see me after he'd sobered up. I'd thought about blocking him. I'd already written my fill of songs about him, and I didn't need more material. But now he had the power to take away my college education if my parents thought we were still together. Keeping tabs on Toby seemed like the best way to avoid him. Fear of him had consumed big parts of my week, but I'd obsessed about him less today, since I'd met Sam.

And now my night with Sam had gone south, too. I texted him. Seconds later, my phone rang in my hands.

"What do you mean, you can't go?" He sounded outraged.

"My granddad doesn't want me to play a gig in the District." That was as much of the truth as I could tell him without explaining way more about my sad life than I wanted to reveal to a guy I would never see again, except at the mall.

"What about your parents?" he insisted.

"I'm staying with my granddad this summer. Look, I can't go. I'm sorry, Sam." I clicked the phone off.

At some point while I'd talked to him, I'd sunk to the floor with my back against the bed. Now I looked around the room that wasn't mine, used as a bedroom so long ago and piled with so much impersonal junk that I honestly wasn't sure whether it had once been my mother's room or one of my uncles'. The time was almost seven and the room had grown dusky, but by comparison the windows looked bright with daylight. The twilight seemed infinite in Nashville this time of year, like summer in Alaska, one day merging into another in an endless wash.

An hour must have passed—now it was the fireflies I noticed out the window rather than the sunlight—when a knock sounded on the door.

I didn't feel comfortable enough with my grandfather to have a *talk* with him. I didn't want to see him right now or discuss how I deserved this. I'd already done that once with my family. But I was living in his house, and he'd gotten me the job. After a resigned sigh, I called, "Come in."

I heard the door open, but I kept my eyes on the old wooden floor, feeling hungry and sick to my stomach at the same time. I couldn't think of anything to say that wouldn't be ironic and therefore pathetic. I saw myself as he must see me, a punk sitting on the floor, a defiant girl utterly beaten by an old man and a "no."

When the seconds stretched and he didn't say anything either, I looked up. It wasn't my granddad in the doorway. It was Sam.

He squinted into the dark room, unable to locate me. But I saw him perfectly, his dark hair shining and his face bathed in the softest light from the windows. Maybe he thought he'd come to rescue me, but I knew from the way my heart pounded at the sight of him that I'd never been in more trouble.

4

He flicked the light switch on and saw me. "Oh, I'm sorry, I—" Embarrassed, I backed against the bed like a mouse in a cage with nowhere to go. He'd already seen the mascara stains under my eyes. I hadn't been crying. My granddad refusing to let me play a gig was nothing to cry about. But I'd been rubbing my eyes pretty hard, something I tended to do when my looks didn't matter. And I hadn't thought anybody but my granddad would see me until next Tuesday at the mall.

Instead of retreating out the door, stammering in embarrassment, Sam stood still with one hand on the knob and the other gripping his guitar case. His face was open with concern. "What's the matter?"

I ran my middle fingers under both eyes at once, assuredly emphasizing my beaten-up look, which is what I got for wearing heavy eye makeup in the first place. It didn't matter what Sam thought of me anyway. I deserved what I got. All I wanted now was to release him with as little further mortification on both our parts as possible. I mumbled, "I told you, my granddad won't let me go tonight. It's not even that. It's just been a long . . ." Week. Month. Year. ". . . day."

Sam looked over his shoulder, as if he could see down the stairs and around the walls to my granddad. Then he walked into the room and slid his guitar case onto my bed.

He'd changed again from his T-shirt into a different color of the same plaid shirt he'd worn as Johnny Cash's son, tight across his chest, with the sleeves rolled up past his elbows like a 1940s farmhand. He'd traded his Chucks for a pair of cowboy boots that looked like they'd seen a few seasons herding cattle. I was pretty sure they hadn't, though. Sam didn't strike me as the cattle-herding type. Sam herded people.

He walked back around the bed and stood right in front of me, gazing way down at me, his boots toe to toe with my sneakers. "You can't wear that," he said. "You're cute, but I need you to pull out some stops for me." He held his hand down to help me up.

The ceiling light behind his head made the edges of his hair seem to glow. I blinked up at him as I put my hand in his. When he pulled me to my feet, I realized how sore my butt had gotten from sitting on the bare floor for an hour.

"What are you doing here?" I whispered. "I can't go."

"This isn't about the gig," he whispered back. "This is about a date. I told your granddad I met you today and found out you were living with him, so I happened by, wondering if you wanted to go see a band with me tonight." He reached over to the bed again, opened his case, and looped his guitar around his neck. He placed my fiddle case in the empty space and buckled the guitar case shut. "I said it was a band I know really well." He beamed at me, pleased with his half-truth.

"And he said yes?" I asked incredulously. It seemed impossible that after I'd agonized for an hour over my death sentence, Sam had fixed everything with a simple lie.

"All he told me was to bring you back in one piece," Sam said, "which sounded to me like he's letting you go. He likes me."

"Really?" I squeaked. I wanted to go—more than anything. But maybe Sam was making this up. He was lying to me about my granddad giving me permission, and he was planning to sneak me out of the house somehow. My granddad wouldn't believe me when I tried to explain later. He would tell my parents, and there went Vandy. There went the hope I'd been clinging to for the past year that I would find myself again when I got out from under this family.

But Sam sounded absolutely sincere as he said, "I've been coming here since I was little, you know."

"Oh," I said, remembering that Sam had guessed who my granddad was as soon as I mentioned my fake last name. "So as long as I'm with you, I can do what I want? That's some power you have over people."

"Isn't it? I've fooled them all! They have no idea their trust is way misplaced." He winked at me.

"Wow! You are one talented guy."

"I don't know. What does it say about me that girls' grandfathers reverse their punishment when I step in the room? That's kind of disturbing."

"He must think you won't lay a hand on me."

Sam's eyes brightened. With a small smile playing across his mouth, he said quietly, "We'll see." He nodded toward my closet. "I'll go back downstairs while you change. Do you have any other charges you want me to get you out of while I'm down there? Parking tickets? Bank robberies?"

I looked down at my T-shirt. "What do you want me to wear?"

"I believe in you. Just give it another try. The band is counting on you. And don't forget to bring the guitar case down casually, like, 'Hey, Sam, you totally left your guitar case upstairs! It's totally empty and not suspicious at all!'" He backed out of the room, then paused. "By the way, your granddad told me you were upset with him and you hadn't eaten your dinner. You need to eat. I'll be working you hard tonight." He flinched as he heard his own words. "That didn't come out quite right." He pulled the door shut.

I stood there stunned for a moment, not believing what had happened. In the past year I'd gotten used to bad shit happening out of the blue. This was good—the best—and I wasn't convinced it was real until I heard Sam's footsteps headed down the creaky wooden staircase.

I sprang into action, running for the tiny closet with a tinier space cleared out for my dress bags, which I'd lifted whole from my closet at home, lacking the energy last weekend to pick and choose what to bring. Sam had said he wanted me to look older. Facial hair wasn't an option, but I could definitely dress like a college student. I ripped through one of the bags for the dress I had in mind, black sprigged with red rosebuds. I'd worn it at a festival and Julie had worn a matching one. At the time they'd looked countrified. Now, though, the dress could pass for sexy vintage, especially since I'd gained another half a bra cup size.

I pulled the dress on over my lacy black bra. As I'd thought, I had actual cleavage, not imitation cleavage that Ms. Lottie constructed out of tissues stuffed into my Dolly costume. My bra straps showed underneath the thin straps of the dress. Back when Julie and I had worn the dresses as costumes, she hadn't needed a bra at all, and my mom had bought me a strapless bra. She never would have let me out of the house with my bra straps showing like this— but she wasn't around.

I stepped into the red cowgirl boots I'd worn with the outfit back then. They still fit. I slipped on dangling red earrings and bracelets faceted enough to sparkle in the dim bar, but lightweight enough that they wouldn't clank up and down my arms when I played fiddle. Then I went to peer at myself in the bathroom mirror. My mascara hadn't smeared as badly as I'd thought, and I cheered up even more now that I knew Sam hadn't seen me looking like a heroin addict. I cleaned my eyes up a bit, adding glittery highlights underneath my brows, and applied another coat of blood-red lipstick. I removed my contacts and slipped on red horn-rimmed glasses I'd chosen on a whim at my last eye exam a couple of years ago. My mom had said they made me look like a granny. Power surged through me as I put on this accessory my mother specifically and vocally disapproved of. So there.

Looking at my reflection, I decided that if my mom wouldn't let me go out with my cleavage and bra straps showing, my granddad, though unlikely to say something to me directly, would mention it to my mom the next time he talked to her. I pulled a black shrug out of the closet and buttoned it over the neckline of the dress. I'd worn it on some cooler nights at festivals up north. Now it would get me out of the house.

Then I disentangled Sam's handkerchief from the pocket of my discarded jeans and secreted it in the pocket of my dress.

As I clomped downstairs, lugging Sam's not-quite-empty guitar case in my best imitation of nonchalance, gradually I relaxed, and finally I just walked on through the living room and dumped the case by the door. My granddad wasn't listening for me. He was doubled over at the kitchen counter, holding his sides.

I was alarmed at first that he was having a heart attack, but he was just laughing, harder than I'd ever seen him laugh, at something Sam had said. He'd lost my grandmom's apron at some point. Sam chuckled, leaning against the kitchen counter, spinning his fork on a plate to snag the last bite of spaghetti and sautéed zucchini. He glanced up at me, reached behind him, and handed me a full plate, as though he'd cooked it himself. He probably *had* scooped the food out. He seemed to have taken over my granddad's house.

He placed his own empty plate in the sink as he said, "But baggage claim found it eventually. Want to see? It's held up great." He grabbed his guitar from the kitchen table. As he turned around, he caught my eye, twirled his first finger, and glanced pointedly at my plate, telling me to hurry.

He extended the guitar toward my granddad, who ran his thumb across the "Wright" inlaid on the head. "This is the most delicate part," my granddad said. "If it held up here, it held up everywhere." He nodded toward me. "Bailey did the shading on that inlay, you know."

Sam gaped in astonishment.

My mouth was full, so I just shook my head and gave my granddad a perplexed look. I'd seen him burn wood inlays to make them look three-dimensional. I hadn't burned them myself. The most complicated piece of equipment I'd handled at his shop in the last week was a wring mop.

"It was a selling point," my granddad scolded me, "and you were supposed to go with me on this." He grinned at Sam. "I guess not everybody can be a salesman like you and me." He put the guitar strap around his own neck, then plucked the strings, ran his hand along the bottom curve of the body, and launched a fast series of chords. He wasn't thinking, just testing, more by the feel of the guitar under his hands than the sound of it, from what I could tell. Over the music he asked Sam, "Are you playing anywhere these days?"

"I'm playing with my dad at the mall," Sam said, "which is of course where I met your beautiful granddaughter today."

I rolled my eyes, which he didn't see. He was schmoozing with my granddad, not talking to me.

"Other than that," Sam said, "no way. I'm going to college on a music scholarship, but my dad says I have to switch my major to business and get a good job before it's too late. My dad says a band would be a terrible distraction."

My granddad grimaced. "I think your dad's probably right about that." He pulled the strap off over his head and handed the guitar back to Sam.

"Oh, yes sir," Sam said with a straight face. "My dad has me totally convinced."

With Sam giving me the hairy eyeball, I ate in record time, then grabbed his guitar case and escaped out the door while he carried his guitar separately. No, this did not look weird at all. I held my breath as I descended the ancient cement stairs down the hill that passed for a front yard, waiting for my granddad to call me back. He didn't. We placed the guitar case behind the seat of Sam's truck, on top of his electric guitar case, with his actual acoustic guitar on top of that. My granddad just grinned to us and waved from the front porch.

Sam kept his cool a lot better than I did, but he didn't waste any time starting the truck and speeding up the shadowy street. At the stop sign, I looked in the rearview mirror and noticed he did, too. My granddad wasn't running up the dark sidewalk after us.

I fished in my purse for my dark red lipstick and reapplied it in precise strokes. Then I unbuttoned my shrug, shimmied out of it, and dropped it out of sight behind the seat.

Sam had started to press the gas and drive on through the intersection. When he saw me move, he stopped again, looked me up and down, and smiled. "Now, see? You acted like you were so clueless about what you should wear, and you had me worried, when all along you knew *exactly* what I was talking about."

"Oh, this passes muster?" I asked archly. With lipstick on, my lips felt stiffer, like somebody else's lips. I liked that.

"You know it passes muster." Sam's voice had been honey sweet since I'd met him, but this time I heard a darker tone as he met my gaze.

My pulse quickened. Maybe his claim to my granddad that he was taking me on a date was more than just a ploy to get me to the gig. Maybe it was wishful thinking, on Sam's part as well as mine.

He winked at me, then reached behind the seat and produced a cowboy hat, which he settled on his head.

Now I didn't know what to think. Did the wink mean he'd been kidding when he implied I looked hot? We'd just met—if you didn't count that one festival years ago when I was completely smitten with him—and I had no idea how to read him. I'd grown so used to Toby and the other people I'd hung out with senior year, whose cardinal rule was to suppress enthusiasm. I didn't know what to do with this excitable guy with a lust for life and music, who might or might not have had a lust for me.

"What's wrong?" He glanced over at me as he drove. In the shadows between streetlights, I couldn't see his face clearly, only his dark hair mashed beneath his hat and curling around his ears.

"I just . . . I don't know." Finally I exclaimed, "I can't believe you flat-out lied to my granddad."

"Your granddad is wrong," Sam said simply. We'd turned onto a wider boulevard through town. He slowed to let a car flashing its blinker slide into the lane ahead of him. After a few seconds of thought, the guilt I'd been feeling seemed to register with him, too, because he went on the attack. "You mean to tell me that you're eighteen years old, you just graduated from high school, and you never in your life lied to your grandparents or your parents about where you were going or what you were doing when you got there? A lot of girls *are* squeaky-clean like that, more power to them, but you don't look like one of them."

I gaped at him. "What is *that* supposed to—"

"And don't even start with that," he insisted. "You look the way you do on purpose. You know exactly what I'm talking about."

I blushed—not the reaction I would have had if I'd ever been able to achieve the screw-you attitude I'd *wanted* to achieve. On a sigh I admitted, "I did have some pretty wild nights in high school. I just never lied about them." In fact, now that I thought about it, I'd felt morally superior because I might have been, at various times, a drunk, a pothead, and a bit of a slut (according to girls) or a tease (according to boys, describing the same series of events), but never a liar.

Until now. Sam didn't even know my real name, and though I hadn't lied yet about how famous my sister was about to become, I knew I would do it if he asked me a direct enough question. That made my stomach twist. I'd done a lot of bad things, but somehow I retained one fingerhold on this crazy code of honor. I was about to lose even that.

Sam repeated what he'd learned about me that afternoon: "You learned to play fiddle on the bluegrass festival circuit with your sister."

I nodded. "From the time I was seven years old until last year, that's pretty much all I did. No Girl Scouts, no sports, no . . ." I stopped myself before I said it, because I would sound pitiful. Then I couldn't think of anything else to say instead, which made me seem addled. I finished, "Friends."

"No boyfriends?" This time when he looked over at me, I could see his face clearly in the streetlights. There was no lust there, or jealousy, only curiosity. He wasn't romantically interested in me. He only wanted to use me for his band. I was okay with that. I just needed to get that message through to my fluttering heart.

"Well, not then," I admitted, "and not now. I dated in the past year." *Dated* was a term I used loosely to mean getting drunk at Farrah Nelson's Halloween party and letting Liam Keel and then Aidan Rogers feel me up in the guest bedroom. And then, of course, at a party several months later, Toby.

I realized I'd been staring at the dashboard in miserable silence when Sam leaned over to see where I was looking. Putting his eyes back on the road, he asked, "What made you quit the bluegrass circuit in the past year? Does it have something to do with why your granddad won't let you out of the house?"

"No," I fudged, "that's just because he didn't want me playing at a bar."

Sam wasn't buying it. "Fess up. It's more than that. He was acting like he wouldn't have let you out of his sight if he hadn't known me and I hadn't been so charming."

"And if you hadn't bought a guitar from him before," I said dryly.

"There's that." He glanced over at me, looked at the road, eyed me again. As he drove, his face and his soft brown eyes brightened under a streetlight, then faded into the darkness. "You're sure you're eighteen?"

"Pretty sure."

"Why does an eighteen-year-old let her granddad treat her like a child? Why is he so strict?"

I turned away from Sam, letting my gaze settle out the window. My granddad's house was south of downtown, near Music Row, a quiet neighborhood where all the major record company offices were nestled. He lived so close to them, in fact, that some days this week I'd thought I could smell the smoke from the shriveled souls and dashed dreams burning in the record companies' incinerators out back, wafting a few streets over on the morning breeze. Now Sam and I had steered out of the tree-framed streets and hit West End Avenue through the Vanderbilt campus, where stylish stores and hip bars lined the sidewalks.

Girls and guys strolling hand in hand were dressed a lot like me, and like Sam without the hat. They'd lingered after exams were over, or they lived here full-time because they'd broken away from their parents and no longer spent the summer at "home." I would be one of these people in August, God willing. Sam was right. It made no sense that my parents had collared me like a dog and tied me to the side of my granddad's house with a bowl of water and a dirty rawhide bone.

I sighed harder than I'd meant to, then stopped myself right before I rubbed my eyes and smudged my mascara. "I got in some trouble after graduation last Saturday night."

"Uh-oh. What kind of trouble? Trouble, like, you sprayed Silly String all over the high school auditorium? Or trouble, like, the police came?"

"The police came."

After the bright college campus, before the even brighter downtown, Sam drove into a darker section of Nashville. Here, decaying factories and crumbling houses waited on the edge of urban renewal. I could tell he was looking at me again only by the way the silhouette of his hat changed shape as he turned his head. He asked quietly, "What did you do?"

"*I* didn't do *anything*. That time." My nausea over the whole incident lay exactly here. I was being punished unfairly for doing nothing. Yet I *had* done something that deserved punishment in the past, so maybe I deserved it now.

"I just—" I grabbed my wrist with my other hand and forced my fingers away from my eyes again. I needed one of those rubber dolls whose eyes bulged out when you squeezed it, anything to keep my fingers busy when I wasn't playing fiddle. "I went to a party after graduation, like everybody. I didn't drink because I've kind of stopped doing that, and my parents were home for once, and I didn't want to get in trouble." With my hands I made boxes and graphs on my thighs. "Note all of the ways I was trying to stay *out of trouble.*

"The crazy thing is, this time last year, I wanted so badly to get in trouble. Every time I tried, I didn't have the heart. I smoked a joint and I was so paranoid about what it was going to do to my singing voice, on the off chance I ever needed it again, that the high turned bad on me."

"Yeah," Sam said. "I haven't gotten that far, for the same reason."

"Don't. It was unpleasant. I got drunk a couple of times when my parents weren't coming home until later and wouldn't find out. But before I go to bed at night, I always . . ."

I was about to admit to him that I wrote songs, but I stopped myself just in time. He'd already dragged me on this adventure I wasn't sure I wanted to join, just because I played fiddle. If he knew about the songs, I might get myself in deeper trouble with him.

"I always write in my journal," I said, which was sort of true, if a notebook printed with music staffs could be called a journal, "and I have time for myself. I need that every night. This time my brain didn't work right. I missed my brain. Whenever I drank, I walked around the whole next day wishing I had those hours back. The more I tried and failed to be a bad girl, the angrier I got. The final injustice was that my parents had ingrained the desire to be a Goody Two-shoes so deeply in me that I couldn't even shake it at a party after my own high school graduation. I was aware of this and scared of being caught at this crazy party, totally absorbed in myself." My usual state of mind lately. "I had no idea my boyfriend was high as a fucking space station. And when I rode home with him, he wrecked his car."

Sam didn't make a supportive comment like I'd thought he would. He sped on down the boulevard, which was nearly empty in this sparsely populated section of town with no open stores. The driving should have been stress free, but he held the steering wheel tightly with both hands.

Finally he asked quietly, "Was your boyfriend killed?"

"No!" Maybe I shouldn't have said this like the idea was so ridiculous. We *could* have been killed, as my parents had said over and over.

"Was anybody hurt?"

"No. Well . . ." As the fluorescent lights of a gas station flashed by out the driver's side window, I pulled up my dress to show him the ugly green bruise on my right thigh. It was some grade school instinct to show off a nasty scar. As I was doing it, I realized I shouldn't be showing my upper thigh to a guy I'd just met, or my unattractive bruise to a cute guy no matter how long I'd known him.

He peered over at it. "Ouch!" he exclaimed. "Why did you say no at first? You said nobody was hurt."

I flipped my skirt down. "Well, you meant was anybody *else* hurt, right? You were asking if he'd run into anybody. He only drove into a pond and totaled his car."

Sam gaped at me.

"I know," I said. "We had to wade out, and there was a big scene. Get this. He was high on coke and he didn't even tell me." I started laughing, remembering how shocked I'd been. I'd tried so hard to be bad in the past year, but even *I* couldn't fathom snorting coke. The more I thought about it, the harder I laughed, until my sides hurt. I shut myself down with difficulty. It was strange that Sam hadn't said anything the whole time. I prompted him, "Have you ever *heard* of such a thing?"

Sam wasn't looking at me now. He was staring at the road like the San Andreas Fault had just opened up in the middle of West End Avenue. "Well, yeah."

"I mean, I know you've *heard* of it. Have you *seen* it?"

"Yeah."

He said this so flatly that I suspected there was more to the story. "Have you *done* it?"

"No. I don't . . ." He shook his head, suddenly looking way too serious for his lighthearted cowboy hat. "My father is an alcoholic. Sometimes that's genetic. I might be one, too. If I never have a drink, I'll never have a problem. Same goes for drugs. If you inherit that addictive personality, that problem with obsession, you're going to have a harder time kicking than your average Joe. I'm like, live and let live. I don't judge people. I'm just not going to do it myself."

"You don't judge people, except your dad." And me, for being involved in this crash. Sam's smile, his animated body language, every-thing I'd liked about him had shut down the instant I mentioned it.

He and I had seen eye to eye on so much already. I'd assumed he would understand what had happened to me, too, and sympa-thize, if only I explained it right. But he looked truly horrified—at the wreck, okay, but his horror seemed to extend to me, and the coke, though I'd told him I wasn't the one at fault.

He didn't believe me, I realized with a sinking heart.

Nobody did.

What was new?

He pulled to a stop at a light, checked in the mirror and saw nobody was behind us, and turned his whole body to face me. I expected a lecture, and I was going to have to tell him where to go. This was what I got instead: "Bailey. You're not still dating that guy, are you? You said you weren't dating anybody, but now you're referring to this shit as your boyfriend."

"No," I said rather desperately. The idea gnawed at the back of my mind that I'd unintentionally lost Sam before I even had him. I wasn't ready to give up yet, and I didn't want him to think Toby and I were still together. "Definitely not. My leg really hurt at first. It seems stupid now, but I thought it was broken. Water was seeping into the car. Toby wouldn't get out. He wouldn't let *me* get out. He tried to convince me to take the fall for him."

"What?" Sam glanced up at the green light, then over at a car dealership, as if considering whether to pull into the lot and grill me on this further. Then he checked his watch, saw we didn't have much time before the gig, and kept driving. "Take the fall how?"

"Tell the cops and his parents and my parents that I was driving. That's when he admitted to me that he was high, which explained why he'd been so hot to leave the party all of a sudden, and so paranoid out of nowhere that the cops were coming to break it up. It was also the reason he'd wrecked the car and then screamed at me not to leave it. I was hurt, and he was scaring me. And then he said that I had to take the fall for him because he had everything to lose, a baseball scholarship to Vandy, and I had nothing to lose by taking the blame for the wreck. I was just a washed-up ex-musician." *And you're never going to amount to anything. You're just going to sit around and bitch about your sister like you have for the past year.*

"And you agreed," Sam said, "and lied to the cops, and that's why you're in so much trouble?"

"Oh, no. I was halfway considering it, honestly, because it would have pissed off my mother. Toby knows me pretty well by now. But then he made me mad with that crack about me being worthless. It's one thing to think you're worthless, and quite another for somebody else to tell you that you are. I'm like, 'Fuck you,' and I proceeded to ascertain that the car was not in fact sinking, and I called 911."

Sam frowned out the windshield. "What an asshole," he muttered.

I nodded slowly, like I was still puzzling through it. "Pretty much."

"You're lucky you didn't give in," he said. "Besides all the trouble you would have been in for wrecking his car, the cops would have figured out you were lying to them. If they'd investigated at all, they would have seen that the bruise on your thigh matched up to the handle on the passenger side of the car, not the driver's side."

"I hadn't thought of that," I admitted. "Impressive. You're always thinking, aren't you, Hardiman?" I tapped my temple with one finger. "Spoken like a true criminal."

He laughed uncomfortably. Possibly he was realizing this outlaw chick he'd picked up was more genuine than he'd bargained for. "Did that guy get his ass handed to him by the cops?"

"No. They didn't take him in. His parents got there before the cops did, and I didn't tell anybody what he'd tried to pull, because he just would have denied it. I heard that his folks have already replaced his soaked Toyota. You know, some parents cover their eyes and would rather not know what their kids are up to. It's only my parents who look forward to me screwing up so they can scream, 'I told you so.'"

Sam nodded. "So why *are* you in trouble with your parents? You didn't screw up."

"It's partly because I'd been at this wild party. A couple of other people who'd been there got in trouble, too, later that night.

The parents started texting each other frantically. The party became infamous. And my folks are like, 'How could you be hanging out with these people?' and I'm like, 'I've been hanging out with them for a year and you didn't notice.' They don't enjoy hearing the truth about that sort of thing. And then my sister told me that since I clearly don't have any respect for myself, she doesn't respect me, either. She hasn't spoken to me since."

I'd been able to talk about my parents' misplaced anger with a dry tone and an eye roll. But as I talked about Julie, my chest felt tight. I wished I'd never given Sam this window into everything that was wrong with me.

"Oh, Bailey." Coming from any other teenager I knew, these two words would have been sarcastic, imitating an old person commenting on a terrible shame. Coming from Sam, they sounded sincere.

Swallowing, I went on. "Honestly, I think a big part of why my parents lost their minds over this was that they had to leave town the next day. They didn't have time to stand over me and make sure I was sorry. Instead of letting me stay by myself at home, they made me move in with my granddad. And if I get in any more trouble this summer, they won't pay for Vanderbilt."

"You're going to Vanderbilt? I'm going to Vanderbilt."

He said it lightly. I wasn't sure whether he meant we could hang out together there.

Anyway, to me it was still a long way to Vanderbilt, with no guarantee. "I'm not going if my parents find out about this gig."

"Right, the bar thing."

No, it was not the bar thing. I wasn't supposed to play any gig at all. But that wouldn't make sense to Sam, so I only nodded.

"I'm not trying to get you in worse trouble with your parents. . . ." He frowned at himself. "Okay, I guess I'm asking you to play in a bar and that would seem pretty bad to them, plus lying to your granddad. I'm guilty. But besides getting along with them, what would it hurt if they decided not to pay for Vandy? I certainly don't have perfect pitch, and I got a full scholarship from the music department. I can't believe you didn't."

I shrugged. "My grades were good, but I didn't do any extra-curriculars or community service work when I was in high school. None. I told you. I never did anything but tour bluegrass festivals."

Exasperated, he opened his hands on the steering wheel. "Yeah, but didn't you audition? Didn't they *hear* you?"

"No. If I auditioned and got a scholarship, they'd want me to major in music or at least be in the orchestra, and I don't want to do that."

"You don't want to major in *music*? What is the *matter* with you?"

A loaded silence settled between us. The truck zoomed on through the night. He watched the road. I couldn't give him my go-to-hell stare effectively when he wasn't looking.

Then he glanced over at me and let out a huge sigh. I hadn't realized how tense he looked, hunched over the steering wheel, until his broad shoulders relaxed. "I've been giving you hell, Bailey. I have no right to do that. You just caught me off guard. I had a good friend who died driving drunk last year."

"Oh!" In my own short exclamation I heard surprise, sym-pathy, and relief that he *was* as much like me as I'd thought when we talked at the mall. He only acted different because he'd gone through something lots worse.

He cupped my bare knee under his hand—just long enough for fire to shoot across my skin—and took his hand away. "I'm really sorry. The third degree about your boyfriend—"

"Ex," I reminded him.

"—and your family, and Vandy . . . I'm sorry. That was none of my . . ."

Business. It was none of his business. If he didn't finish the sentence, I would finish it for him.

No, I didn't have the heart. He'd seemed so driven when we played at the mall today, when he upstaged his dad, and when he came to my granddad's house to rescue me. Now he was still driving toward downtown Nashville, but the fire had gone out of his eyes. He seemed lost.

He shook his head as if to clear it, then flashed me a grin. Just like that, he was back to the glowing Sam I'd met that afternoon. "We're going to have fun tonight, you'll see."

"What's the name of this band, anyway?"

"The Sam Hardiman Band, but don't look at me like that! Believe me, I've already caught plenty of flak for that from the other members. I had to write something down when I sent in the audition video, and we hadn't discussed a name before. We need to think of something else." Pulling to a stop at the next intersection, he thumbed through the MP3 player plugged into the dashboard. When a funky beat began, he drove on. "I wanted to play this for you. Have you heard it before?"

I listened for a second. "Yeah, but it's been a while. Justin Timberlake?"

"Exactly. What key is it in?"

"F minor," I said without thinking.

"Wow," Sam said. "That is amazing."

I didn't think it was amazing. It was more of a nuisance. But after years of my mom telling me my miraculous ear was a hindrance rather than a help because of how much I complained about pitch problems she couldn't even hear . . . if Sam wanted to call it amazing, I would let him.

"Hear the disco violins?" he asked. "The band's been playing this song for a while without that part. It's almost like I knew you were coming. I was hoping you could give the song a listen and pick up those licks after one hearing. I'll bet you can do that, can't you?"

"Yeah," I acknowledged.

Admiration evident in his voice, he said, "Like a machine."

Yes, that's exactly what it felt like.

5

Parking in downtown Nashville was always crazy, but the biggest country music event of the year, the CMA Music Festival, was coming up next week, and the tourist area was even more crowded than usual. We parked near the riverfront in a dark deck that I would have thought twice about if I'd been alone.

"There are Ace and Charlotte." Sam lifted his hand to an African-American guy driving by in a minivan that looked brand-new. "Good. They've unloaded Charlotte's drum kit and the amps at the gig already." Watching the van search the packed deck and finally stop in a space several rows over, he said, "I know this is kind of awkward, but if you would act like we don't like each other very much when we're around them, that would really help me out."

As we pulled our instrument cases from behind the seat of the truck, I said, "Okay. Around my granddad, I'll act like we *are* on a date, and around your band, I'll act like we're *not*." I eyed Sam closely, wondering which scenario he thought was the truth.

"Great." He flashed me a conspiratorial grin, revealing nothing. Then he took a few steps across the concrete to bump fists with

Ace. Gesturing to me, he said, "This is Bailey Wright. She's going to play fiddle with us tonight." He turned to me. "This is my bud Ace Hightower."

"Nice to meet you." I shook Ace's huge hand, looking way up into his deep, melty eyes.

"Pleasure," Ace said. Maybe Sam had given him the speech about looking older, too, but unlike Sam's shadow, Ace's beard was carefully groomed into a goatee. If he was supposed to look like a rockabilly hipster, like Sam and me, he hadn't gotten that memo. But if Sam was counting on a female record company executive discovering his band someday, between himself and Ace, they probably had that base covered. Ace wore tight jeans that hugged his muscular thighs and a tight red T-shirt with a chemical formula on it, a joke for nerds who'd paid attention in high school and forged a career path.

No, he hadn't grown the goatee for the bar's benefit. He'd had it for a while. I recognized this guy, and his last name. "Your dad owns the car dealership."

"He does," Ace acknowledged with a wry smile.

"You've been in some of the TV commercials."

"So have I!" Sam called, waving.

Ace told him, "You were dressed up as a dinosaur." Ace turned back to me. "Sam was convinced that if we put him in a commercial, he'd get discovered, and somebody would hire him for their big-time band."

"I was kidding about that," Sam protested. "Nobody would discover me if they hadn't heard me sing and they hadn't seen this face."

"Oh, Lord," said the girl standing behind them.

Sam looked around at her like he was noticing her for the first time. "And this is Charlotte Cunningham," he told me.

She was a tomboy, a fierce one. She wore high-top Chucks and baggy cut-off jeans that came down to her knees so there wasn't even anything Daisy Duke about them, with her drumsticks protruding from one back pocket. Her plain black tank was tight, showing off her cute figure and toned drummer's arms, but she covered up her cleavage as best she could with her long hair, parted in the middle and placed in front of each shoulder. Her hair was medium brown and had a little wave in it—not curly enough to be stylish and not straight enough to be flat-ironed, like that was how it came out of the shower and she hadn't bothered to have it cut since February.

She wore no makeup, which arguably she didn't need because her skin was porcelain and perfect, her eyes an arresting blue-green. But the fact that she was a chick my age without makeup made her look aggressively plain. I got the impression she was trying to give off the same vibe as me—*leave me alone*—only she was coming at it from the opposite direction. I cared very much how I put my look together. I suspected she did, too, but the look itself was supposed to say that she didn't give it any thought at all.

I was about to step forward with my hand out to this girl. I stopped myself when she said flatly, "Hi," and then turned a pouty face to Sam. "I thought you wanted to make a big push to get a gig on Broadway while all the industry bigwigs are in town for the festival."

"I"—Sam's eyes slid to me—"do."

"And suddenly you invite somebody else?" she insisted.

He grinned at her. "This is just for tonight, to see how it works out." When she continued to scowl at him, he set down his guitar case, wrapped both arms around her, and pulled her into his chest. "Now, Charlotte. You're the beauty of this operation. I'm the brains. Let me do the thinking."

"Wow, if you're the brains, we are in *trouble*." She pushed him away. Both of them were laughing. Ace stared across the garage and huffed out an exaggerated sigh.

Sam scooped up his guitar again. Turning as one unit, he and Charlotte headed for the stairs down to the street. With no other choice, Ace and I fell in behind them. Charlotte asked Sam in a lower tone, "How's your dad?"

"Sober." Sam held up his hand with his fingers spread.

"Five days!" Charlotte exclaimed. "That's great."

I'd been thinking again how calculating Sam was, and how careful I needed to be not to lose my heart to him when he only wanted me for his band. But listening to him and Charlotte talk, I got the feeling there was a lot more depth to him. He obviously had real problems with his dad, if his friends knew about them, too. And I could tell from the concern in Charlotte's voice and the way her eyes never left his face as they entered the stairwell how much she cared about him—even if the relationship was, as I suspected, one-sided.

I nodded toward her as I asked Ace, "How do y'all know Sam?"

"We went to the same high school," Ace said. "Sam and I played football together."

I refrained from saying, *That explains a lot*. It explained why Sam and Ace had chests like trucks. It also explained why Charlotte was trying so hard to stake her claim on Sam now that a new girl had arrived. I hadn't even known Sam a full day, and I was already getting myself tangled up in his drama. I reminded myself that none of this was worth my college education.

But as Ace and I emerged behind Sam and Charlotte onto the street, I changed my mind. A singer wailed one of my all-time favorite country songs from the stage in the first restaurant we passed. Before her voice had faded, the voice of the singer in the next bar competed with it for my attention and affection. I loved that song, too. I loved the music and I loved Nashville. I was walking down the street toward my first gig on my own, without my parents controlling my every move. If my granddad found out what I'd been up to tonight, I'd be in big trouble whether I went ahead with the gig or not. Might as well.

"How about you?" Ace asked, startling me out of my thoughts. I'd gotten so lost in the neon lights on the dark, crowded street that I'd almost forgotten he walked beside me. "How'd *you* meet Sam?" he asked.

"At the mall today. I played in a trio with him and his father."

"No way," Ace said. "Were there groupies? A lot of times girls from school follow him around. Pisses his dad off."

"Not today," Sam said, turning around, my first clue that he'd been listening to us. "It's the weekend after Memorial Day. They're probably still at the beach. Oh, man, it smells like a strip club."

Ace laughed, but I thought that was a weird thing to say. Sam was pretty desperate to change the subject. Then I caught a big whiff of the air being forced out of the next bar and onto the street: stale cigarette smoke and air freshener. I tried to breathe more shallowly.

Charlotte turned to Sam. "And how do you know what a strip club smells like?" Her tone was light and teasing with a hint of ugly jealousy somewhere at the bottom, like a dirty film nobody ever scrubbed off the strip club floor.

Sam said simply, "I had a gig."

"In a strip club?" Charlotte shrieked.

"I'd forgotten about that," Ace said, and chuckled. "He was the pride of the ninth-grade football team."

"How old were you?" I asked Sam, trying not to sound like a shocked church lady, but ninth grade?

"Fourteen," he said. "Fourteen when I started, and then fifteen. It was my longest gig to date."

"How could your parents let you do that?" Charlotte pressed him.

I thought: *They weren't paying attention.* Like my parents. In my case, my parents were gone. In his case, maybe something had happened to his mom—I was afraid something had, since he hadn't mentioned her—and his dad was drunk.

"Oh, it was my dad's gig," Sam said.

I couldn't hide my shock anymore. "And your dad took you into the strip club with him?"

Sam spread his hands. "It was a gig!" As if that explained everything.

"The strippers were very nice to him," Ace offered.

I looked to Sam for confirmation. He nodded at me. "They brought me Cokes. One of them wanted me to go out with her daughter."

"Ew!" Charlotte shrieked.

"Strippers aren't *ew*," he scolded her. "It's just another way to make a living." But he turned around and winked at me, like he'd enjoyed the strippers more than he wanted to let on to Charlotte. And like I understood something about him that she didn't.

"How was the band before us?" he asked Ace.

Ace shrugged. "It's never a good sign for a band when they ask a waitress to take the lead for a couple of songs. I don't think we're following a whole lot."

"Depends on how good the waitress was," Sam said.

"She wasn't as good as you," Charlotte said. Sam grinned at her and chucked her gently on the chin. I wanted to throw up.

"That's positive, right?" Charlotte insisted. "We'll look great in comparison."

"It could be bad," Sam said. "Nobody's softened up the crowd for us."

We walked past the one District club I'd been in before—Boot Ilicious, which pointedly flashed a cowboy boot in the middle of its sign, between the "Boot" and the "Ilicious." It was an eighteen-and-up club Toby had taken me to a couple of weekends in May, right after my birthday. He'd bitched at me before because I wouldn't go out of my way to find a fake ID. Once inside, he was skilled at acquiring drinks without a wristband. This would have impressed me at the beginning of the school year, but now it seemed immature and lame.

Which didn't explain why I felt so relieved that we weren't turning in at Boot Ilicious, or why I held my head down as we passed, hoping he wouldn't recognize me if he happened to be hanging in the doorway. Toby had made me feel like my talent was something to be embarrassed by. Worse, I half believed him. For some reason, I was concerned about what he thought of me even though I hated him—just as I'd been disappointed to learn I wasn't the only fiddle player Elvis wanted in his back pocket.

Leaving the club behind, we reached the intersection with Broadway. We were on the lower, less crowded end of the street, so it wasn't far to the river, with the Titans football stadium on the other side. I leaned around Ace to look up the hill. The sidewalks along Broadway were packed with tourists, country music overflowed onto the street, and neon signs flashed in the shape of cowboy hats and boots and guitars all the way up the sidewalk. The real action was near the top of the hill, in the three or four bars famous for hosting acts that got discovered by record company executives who wandered into the audience, scouting their next star. I felt better just gazing at it—redeemed, like a girl in a country song who stuck to her guns and made it big, despite the stories her boyfriend told her about herself.

The light changed, and we stepped into the crosswalk. Sam was looking up Broadway, too, with his eye on that far corner.

As we crossed the street, I thought I spied the bar where we were headed, only two storefronts down—not a bad gig. But we kept walking right past it, past abandoned and crumbling historic facades, to a building that stood by itself because the buildings all around it had been torn down. A couple of people sat on the sills of the plate glass windows in front, smoking. At least we knew smoking wasn't allowed inside, and that there were some customers. Two, to be exact. An enormous muscled bouncer stood in the doorway of the building, checking the IDs of some guys wanting in.

Beyond that, the block diminished into businesses that were closed at night, then a slummy area of deserted shells, ending in a huge construction project that wouldn't be finished for years. I turned around and looked behind us. A few pedestrians peeled off Broadway and ventured down this side street. Very few. The lights of Broadway seemed far away.

If the location bothered Charlotte, she didn't let on. She still talked animatedly with Sam like he was the only friend she'd ever had. She probably didn't even notice her surroundings because her eyes had stayed glued to him since we'd left his truck.

"Careful," Sam told her, pointing out a hypodermic needle lying in the weeds next to the sidewalk.

"Do you want me to carry you?" Ace joked to me.

Honestly, I was tempted to say yes. "No, thanks," I said instead. "I feel safe with my needle-proof cowgirl boots on." As I followed Sam through the door, I held my head high in an effort to fake the bouncer out and make him think I belonged here. Nothing would be more embarrassing than to be the one singled out as not looking old enough, especially after Sam had made such a big deal about it.

The bouncer didn't pull me out of our little line or ask me for ID, though. I stepped across the threshold.

The music blasting over the speakers, filler between the live bands, was another country song I loved, but that was the end of my reasons to feel comfortable here. I'd been with my parents to the Station Inn, the most important bluegrass concert hall, which had looked so nasty that I'd been afraid to touch anything. This place made the Station Inn look like the Grand Ole Opry.

The walls were filled with framed and signed photographs of country stars from decades past—names I knew because I'd walked the edges of the biz for years, but these stars weren't famous enough for someone to impersonate them at the mall. Instead of posing carefully for publicity photos, they closed their eyes and opened their mouths like they were singing their hearts out in front of an audience. The implication was that they'd been photographed *here* at this very bar, but the photos could have been downloaded off the Internet for all I knew. I didn't think so, though. Every facet of the frames and every curve of the little 45-speed records strung from the ceiling was coated with a layer of filth like the place hadn't been dusted since Elvis died. The dim lights and spotlights in blue, green, and pink didn't quite disguise the dust.

Despite the bar looking deserted on the outside and unsanitary on the inside, quite a few customers pushed past each other to the bar or the restrooms. Sam held up his guitar case like the prow of a ship that broke through the ice pack in the arctic. I hugged my fiddle case. As we wound through the crowd, middle-aged tourists and Vandy frat boys glanced up and down my body, curious what a fiddle player in a rockabilly band looked like up close.

The entrance was a short ramp from street level to the level of the room. At the end of the ramp, Sam stepped three feet up to the tiny stage and pulled me up after him. After being surrounded by people taller than me like I was down in a hole, it was a relief to be saved from the throng. From this vantage point I saw that there were actually two small stages, one to the left of the entrance and one to the right, both of them backed up against the windows onto the street. Charlotte's drum set took up one stage, and Sam and I balanced on the other, with Ace climbing up behind us. He and Sam both opened their guitar cases in the corner.

I could also tell from up here that the building had two levels. The back was elevated so those customers could get a better view of the band. They were already lining up against the guardrail that separated the upper section from the lower one, staking out a good vantage point for viewing the band—for viewing *us,* I realized in a sudden moment of disorientation and pure joy.

After plugging his guitar into an amp and setting it in a stand, Sam pulled out his phone and thumbed the screen. He stepped closer to me and spoke in my ear so I could hear him over the music. My skin buzzed with the sensation of his breath on my skin. "Do you have your phone with you?" he asked.

I nodded, pulling it out of my purse.

"I'm texting all of you the playlist for the first hour." He eyed me. "Uh-oh. I've transposed some of these songs from the key they were in originally. I'm just trying to find the best place for my voice. Is that going to mess you up?"

Yes, it would. I could play a song in a different key from the original, but I would hear the ghost of the first key in my head, an annoying niggling that was as near as I ever came to schizophrenia. I was a professional musician, though, so I said, "I'll deal with it. You start and I'll figure it out after a few notes." My phone vibrated in my hand with his text.

I endured a delicious tingle as I felt his breath in my ear again.

"One more thing," he said. "The band gets some money from the bar, but we get a lot more in tips. We keep playing while one lucky member strolls around the room with the tip jar." He pointed to the large glass jar on the far corner of the stage. The faded and peeling "Pickled Eggs" label still clung to it, but "Tips" was written across the label in marker. He grinned at me.

"Oh, *hell* no." I looked around the room at the crowd watching us, clinking their beer bottles together, bending their heads to talk about us and size us up before we even started.

"They're friendly," he promised me, "and not as drunk as you think. They just want to hear some good music. And by the time you pass the jar around, if we're lucky, there will be brides."

"Brides?" I asked dubiously.

He nodded. "Bachelorette parties. They tip great."

"But, Sam." I *really* did not want to dive into that crowd again. "If you're so keen on the brides, why don't *you* carry around the tip jar?"

"Because you're a lot cuter than I am." His words were flirtatious but firm. He wasn't backing down.

Charlotte stood at the edge of the opposite stage. She waited for a break in the crowd pushing up and down the entrance ramp, then stepped across the gap between the stages and extended her phone toward us. Her glance flitted from him to me and back to him like he wasn't technically allowed to whisper in my ear. "Hey, what's this third song on the playlist?" she shouted over the crowd noise. Needlessly, I thought, because if the three of them had played all these songs before, she could figure it out. She just wanted to break things up between Sam and me.

Ignoring her, I told Sam, "If I'm a lot cuter than you, so is Charlotte. This is a girl thing, right? You think people will tip a girl better. If she carried the tip jar before, she can do it again."

He stared at me a moment. I knew he'd heard me. But he turned to Charlotte, took her phone, and peered at it. "It's the Cyndi Lauper song. Sorry, I can't spell." He handed her phone back and turned away, dismissing her. He told me, "We've never played with you before. It'll be easier to play without you than without Charlotte."

"Oh, fuck that," Charlotte broke in. She sneered at me. "It's because you're prettier than me."

Sam took Charlotte by both shoulders and spun her to face him. Looking straight into her eyes, he told her firmly, "Stop."

Charlotte stared up at him with her lips drawn down and her strange blue-green eyes big as the sky. I thought I saw tears forming at the edges of her lashes, and as I watched, goose bumps popped up on her forearms. Her fingers were splayed in midair, her fingernails scribbled with a type of nail polish I'd never seen before, translucent black. The embrace, or the scolding, or whatever it was, lasted so long that I got uncomfortable as a spectator, like they were involved in a round of PDA.

Ace must have felt the same way. "That's enough," he said, looming behind Charlotte. He punched Sam in the shoulder— gently, but I wouldn't have wanted to be punched even lightly with that meaty fist.

Sam blinked at Ace and dropped his hands from Charlotte's shoulders. He glared at me. And then he placed his cowboy hat on the head of his guitar, and jumped down from the stage. He walked out the front door of the bar.

Charlotte retreated behind her drum kit like this was normal behavior for all of them. Shaking his head, Ace took a few steps backward, too, into his position onstage. I was left standing there with my hands out and pleading like I wanted to give my violin and bow away to the next person who walked by.

Exasperated, I called to Ace, "Is Sam coming back?"

"Yeah. He has to 'focus' before gigs." Ace made finger quotes around *focus*. He turned his ear to his amp and thumbed one of his bass strings, twisting the tuning peg.

I wasn't sure I believed Ace. I looked from him to Charlotte to the expectant crowd watching us—watching *me* more than any of us, since I was the one out front. I'd complained about my tip jar duties. I'd hesitated to let Sam drag me into this gig. But now I was here, and I'd be damned if I let this opportunity go.

Depositing my fiddle and bow in my case—and *closing* the case because my parents had taught me to be more careful with my fiddle than my own body—I sat daintily on the edge of the stage and stepped to the floor, avoiding giving the crowd an eyeful of my underwear. I followed Sam out the door.

Either the bouncer read the panicked look in my eyes, or he was used to band drama. Before I could say anything, he pointed. I walked in that direction, around to the side of the building. Sam stood with his back against the brick wall, between two metal joints sticking out of the mortar where the building next door used to be. His chin pointed up as if he stared at the stars, but his eyes were closed.

Boots crunching in the broken cement and glass, I stopped so close to him that he must have heard me even over the music booming from inside. He didn't open his eyes, though.

"Sam," I said.

"What." He wasn't bending over backward to sweet-talk me anymore. He sounded angry and impatient with me—like Toby.

"What the hell is your problem?" I hated that my voice climbed into shrill fear, but I couldn't believe I'd gotten so close to this gig, only to have it yanked out from under me because previously ador-able Sam had unadorable stage fright.

"It's Charlotte," he bit out. "I can't have that negative emotion in my head before a gig. Charlotte knows that. She's a great drummer and a good friend, but if I ever fire her, it's going to be for fucking with me before a gig."

"She wasn't fucking with you. She was expressing her insecurity about her relationship with you and her position in the band, and she was asking you to tell her she was wrong. You didn't do it."

Now he did open his eyes. He stared me down like I'd just awakened him from a long winter's nap.

"Sorry!" I exclaimed. My tone let him know I wasn't sorry at all. "Am I fired, too?"

"Maybe," he grumbled. "Why were you giving me all that guff about the tip jar? You're the one who got Charlotte started in the first place."

"Oh, no. All this between you has been going on for a long time. You neglected to tell me before you dragged me here."

"The point is the gig," he said impatiently. "I'm in the wrong mind-set for the gig. Now I've got to turn this thing around somehow." His dark eyes, warm beneath his long, dark lashes, slid to meet mine. I realized by degrees that he wanted me.

Self-conscious, and trying not to be, and not a hundred percent sure I was reading him right, I held his gaze, waiting for him to make the first move. When he did, tingles raced up my arms. He took my hand and tugged me closer. "Come here."

I held back, not stepping forward until the strength of his pull overcame the gravity rooting me to the spot. But when I did give in to his momentum, I led with my chest and dropped my shoulders so he could catch a glimpse down the front of my dress.

He looked where I wanted him to look as we stood as close to each other as we could get without embracing. In the warm night I could feel the heat of his body through his shirt and my dress.

Slowly he raised his eyes to meet mine. "Would you mind helping me get in the mood?"

"I thought we were supposed to act like we don't like each other."

"Around Ace and Charlotte." He lifted his thumb to stroke my lip. Through the coating of lipstick, his touch made me shudder. "Let me kiss you just this once," he said.

Just this once was a refrain with him. He was the devil in disguise, the handsome but low-down, no-good sneaky guy from a thousand country songstresses' revenge plots. Yet there was no way I was turning him down, any more than I could have turned down playing this gig. Ace and Charlotte weren't peeking around the corner of the building at us—too frightened by Sam's sudden and insistent exit, I thought—and there were no windows on this wall that they could spy through. Anyway, the two of them were Sam's concern, not mine. We were on the side of the building facing the deserted end of the street, not Broadway, so there was nobody at all to see us.

I said coyly, "Boys don't make passes at girls who wear glasses."

He gave me a small smile, then solved the problem by carefully sliding my glasses off and folding them into his back pocket. His other hand never left my mouth.

I opened my lips, letting his thumb dip inside.

His dark eyes widened and he watched me for a moment, like he'd expected to get slapped, not invited, and now he wasn't sure how to proceed.

Only for a moment. His thumb slid from my mouth down to trace my jaw. He cradled my chin in his hand and lowered his lips to mine.

His mouth was unexpectedly hot, like he'd been drinking coffee, or I was even more thoroughly frozen than I'd thought. But he didn't force the kiss into a big production like Toby had during our first encounter. His mouth pressed mine almost chastely, until I felt the very tip of his tongue rub along my bottom lip.

I felt like gasping with pleasure and shock, but I didn't want him to know how he was affecting me, in case he didn't feel the same way. I kept my mouth on his and inched forward instead, slipping my hands around his waist. Except for a few brushes against him at the mall, this was the first time I'd touched him. I'd thought, and Ace had confirmed, that Sam was an athlete. I still wasn't prepared for how solid he was underneath my fingertips.

I shouldn't have worried that he wasn't enjoying this as much as I was. As soon as I touched him, he inhaled sharply through his nose, pressed his hand more firmly around my jaw like he never wanted to let me go, and wrapped his other arm around my back. The stubble on his cheeks pricked my face. He kissed me more deeply—still taking his time, but eagerly enough to let me know the feeling was mutual. We took turns leading each other down a dark spiral.

He pulled away, blinking at me like he wasn't quite sure what had happened. He glanced at his watch. "We have to go in and get started." Then he looked into my eyes with an intensity that let me know there was nothing he'd rather do less.

After a year spent feeling worthless, and several months with a boyfriend who treated me like he was making do with me until he found someone better, I was really enjoying Sam. I knew I was being ridiculous, and I half thought he was setting me up and faking the whole thing, because he was too cute and the situation was too perfect. Maybe I was about to get cut down, but as good as I felt right then, I was willing to take the chance.

Surging with more power than I'd felt since I could remember, I rubbed my thumbs down toward the waist of his jeans before I let him go and drew back. "Is that what you needed?" I said in a teasing voice I didn't know I had. "Are you in the right mind-set now?"

"Uh-huh," he affirmed, eyes still wide on me as if he couldn't quite focus. He acted like kissing me had blown his mind. It was adorable. "Wow. Yes. I wish we had a song about this on the playlist. Or maybe we do."

Seeing a strange shadow across his mouth, I drew his handkerchief from my dress pocket. "Uh-oh, lipstick."

He chuckled as I cleaned him up. "Not my best look?"

"What about me? Am I smeared?" I pursed my lips and lifted my chin to give him a better view.

"You're perfect." He pulled my glasses from his back pocket, unfolded them, and set them across my nose. Brows drawn together like he was deep in thought, he took my hand and tugged me around the corner to begin our gig.

6

I expected Sam to drop my hand as soon as we entered the building so Charlotte wouldn't see us and pitch another fit. But he
didn't, for whatever reason—maybe because he thought he might
lose me in the crowd that had packed the place while we went
missing. The sidewalk outside the bar had been just as empty when
we walked in this time as when we first walked in. I had no idea
where these people were materializing from. They crowded the
floor and overflowed onto the ramp we struggled up.

I was happy to walk behind him. Happy, for the first time in a
long time. I felt my cheeks glowing with pleasure that he was still
holding my hand. I loved looking at the back of his head. Everything about him seemed perfect and positive. I was going insane.

He hopped up onstage and pulled me after him. Settling his
hat on his dark waves again, he surveyed the crowd as he said in
my ear, "The natives are restless. Let's get tuned up quick and get
going. I'm not going to try to butter them up with a 'How're you
doing, Nashville?' I'll just jump right into it and hold Alan Jackson
in front of me like a shield. I signal Charlotte and she starts first, so
listen for her."

Nodding, I knelt and opened my fiddle case against the wall and plugged my pickup into the available amp. While my back was turned, I heard Sam hollering over the noise, but I couldn't make out anything he was saying except "Perfect pitch." When I stood, Sam and Ace both crowded me and tuned their guitars to my long, low E. Then Ace backed up all the way to the window onto the sidewalk.

I set my bow against my strings, ready to start, and looked over at Sam for the signal. I shifted uncomfortably with my elbow against the wall. Even with all the room Ace was giving us, Sam was too close on my left side. I wouldn't have room for full strokes of my bow. If it came down to it, the lead singer was a more important member of this band than I was. I would give him my place and stand on the floor, and possibly be groped by the frat boys currently leering at me and inching closer to the stage in the hope of seeing up my dress.

Glancing over at me, Sam saw me shifting and solved the problem. "I'll go over here," he said, making one wide step to straddle the space between the stage and the end of the bar. He shifted from a wash of blue light into a flood of bright white. The bar waitress only glanced casually up at him like he wasn't the first lead singer to arrive at this solution. Ace waited until a couple of newcomers passed by, then handed Sam's amp across the space to him, then his mike stand, then his guitar. Ace acted like this wasn't the band's first concert in cramped quarters, either. As Sam and the bar waitress got the cords situated, I wondered what the facilities had been like at the Lao weddings.

I half expected Charlotte to give me a dirty look for holding her boyfriend's hand and stealing her tip jar and existing generally. She only had eyes for Sam, though, and this time she wasn't gazing at him moonily but watching him closely with her sticks raised, an experienced drummer with her head in the game, waiting for her signal.

The music on the loudspeakers suddenly diminished and died as the bar waitress dialed the volume down. Voices swelled, and someone whistled. Every face turned to us.

Sam looked over his shoulder at Ace to make sure he was ready.

He looked at me. I winked at him like I played gigs in bars every night of the week. Adrenaline flooded my arms and made my fingers tingle.

He glanced over his shoulder at Charlotte.

That must have been his signal to her, just meeting her steady gaze. Before he'd turned back around, her drums burst into life, Ace played the bass line and Sam the melody, and I was waiting for a place to jump in, feeling like I was running to catch up.

I found my slot and laid into my lick exactly as the audience burst into applause and cheers as they recognized the song, an oldie that pleased the moms in the audience, but popular enough that the college girls up front knew it, too, and raised their bottles and whooped. I couldn't laugh. My chin stayed glued to my fiddle to keep it steady under the sawing of my bow. But I wanted to look over at Sam and exchange a chuckle with him at the appreciative response of the crowd to such a hokey old tune.

Sam was smiling, too, but not at me. When he pulled off a complicated riff and the crowd clapped, he beamed at them like he was a kid on Christmas and they'd just given him exactly the toy he'd always wanted.

That was all before he started to sing.

After the first few words, a cheer went up again as the audience expressed their relief that Sam wasn't just a pretty face and he had the chops to go with the hat. As I began a few measures of staccato notes, backing him up with chords in the verse until I bowed along with him in the chorus, I had time to look out at the crowd. The college girls stared up at him on the bar in awe. I could tell from the occasional hand raised above the crowd that someone behind the rail on the upper level was doing the Texas two-step. Everyone was smiling.

Including me. My jaw was aching already. I tried to relax it and return my expression to my usual neutral. I couldn't have my face sore when I needed to secure the fiddle with my chin for the next two hours.

But it was hard not to smile when the crowd seemed so enthralled with us. I glanced over at Ace to see if he was as wowed by the experience as I was. He hadn't smiled at me before now, but he flashed me an understated grin that let me know the big football player was moved. Thick fingers nimbly picking the metal bass strings, he closed his eyes and lost himself in the groove. Sweat along his neat hairline glistened in the blue light. On the other tiny stage, Charlotte was a whirling dervish of drumsticks and arms and brown wavy hair, such a flurry of energy that it was hard to reconcile the crazed sight of her with the precise beat she was putting out.

We sounded good together, I was realizing. The first song was a bit early to hand down a verdict, but so far we sounded like we'd been playing together forever. The groups at the mall had sounded like that, too, since we were all seasoned musicians, more or less interchangeable. But at the mall, we'd been imitating something great and bygone. Right here, right now, Charlotte and Ace and Sam and I might have been playing a cover, but we weren't imitating anybody. *We* were the young, hip thing to see in a Nashville dive on a Saturday night.

As the song drew to a close, I knew what was coming. There was a money note at the end, and I was afraid Sam wouldn't be able to hit it. It seemed too high for him. But he made it, as if he'd calculated the key of this tune carefully to play up his voice to advantage. After the abrupt ending, there was a half second of silence before the crowd screamed. Now Sam did ask, "How're you doing, Nashville?" in an exaggerated drawl worthy of the most down-home, country-fried musical savant. The audience didn't have time to respond with another howl before he took a quick look behind him at Charlotte and she kicked off the next driving beat.

Sam had engineered this song, too, transposing it into exactly the right key to make his strong voice sound as good as it could without going over. During the first verse, he glanced over at me, pointed at me, and touched his mouth. I assumed he meant I should sing the prominent harmony on the chorus. If the band had been performing this song in the past—and they must have been, since they sounded this good now—they'd been doing it without the harmony. Now that Sam had me, he wanted me to make the song sound more like the original.

I obliged, watching Sam for the precise timing, never once thinking about the harmony itself. I could sing harmony automatically, which was why I'd sung it above Julie while she sang melody. Record company scouts assumed she was the stronger singer and that's why she was the center of attention, but really she was on melody because she had trouble with harmony. She lost her way. I never did. When every other facet of my life was a mess, music stayed true as math. My notes slipped into their predetermined places above Sam's voice in the chords.

My harmony ended along with the tune. Sam and Charlotte started a new groove before I caught my breath and brought my fiddle under my chin. We played song after song like that. The crowd grew happier. The bar grew hotter. Long tendrils of Charlotte's hair stuck to her face as she whipped it around in a frenzy of rhythm. Sam pulled his handkerchief from the pocket of his tight jeans, removed his hat, mopped his brow, and put his hat back on, like a young farmhand on the prairie.

When I'd glanced around at Ace between songs, I'd noticed his face was covered with a sheen, too, and he was taking long pulls from the bottle of water that had been handed from the bartender to Sam to me to Ace. The next thing I knew, college girls were rushing to my feet with their eyes up and their hands out, reaching past me. When I looked behind me again, Ace had taken off his chemical formula shirt and was wiping his brow with it. It must have shown the formula for pheromones, the way these chicks were acting. Charlotte seemed to feel it, too. She craned her neck to get a better look at Ace's bare chest around her high hat cymbals.

"Throw it!" one of the ladies shrieked to Ace.

"I can't. I'll need it later," Ace said, laughing heartily now, his unamplified voice sounding dead against the ceiling.

"Maybe we need to let *you* pass around the tip jar," came Sam's voice over the mike. He was grinning at Ace. The women screamed enthusiastically. Sam swept his eyes over them. I could almost see the wheels turning in his head, calculating the exact moment when the joke had played out and we needed to move on.

He turned around to signal Charlotte. For once, Charlotte didn't see him. She stared at Ace with her lips parted. Sam reached toward her and snapped his fingers. Startled, she blinked at Sam and immediately started the song.

Only a moment later, it seemed—but when I thought about it, we'd played seven songs in the interim—Sam looked pointedly at me, tapped his watch, and stuck out his pinkie and thumb to make an old-fashioned phone receiver. I'd been checking my own phone periodically for the playlist, but I hadn't even glanced at the time, or thought of Julie at all. For the first time in almost an hour, my guilt came rushing back.

I slipped my phone into my pocket, quickly packed my fiddle into its case against the wall, and grabbed the big glass jar in the corner. Ace balanced his guitar with one hand and helped me down from the stage with the other. The smiling college-age girls who liked Ace so much were the ones surrounding me, but I felt a little like I was being lowered into the lion habitat at the zoo.

"Ladies and gents," Sam said into the mike, "we're passing around the tip jar now. Please tell us with your generosity whether you like what you see."

Asking the crowd whether they liked what they heard would have made more sense, but he was playing to the women in the audience, I thought. He knew how good he looked. I glanced up at him, intending to roll my eyes. He *was* eye candy, but I didn't want him to know I was such a pushover.

When I looked over at him, though, he was watching me, his eyes traveling down the line of my dress as though he'd meant people liked what they saw in *me*. I grinned at the idea. I loved that he kept telling me how good I looked tonight, and that I was beautiful and perfect and exactly what he'd had in mind. My outfit might be time-warped country cosplay, my makeup too heavy, my hair a color not found in nature, but I'd never felt prettier—or sexier. With new confidence I waltzed around the room to the beat of the band wherever the crowd parted for me, holding my tip jar high and pausing when hands sought it with folded twenties. I smiled brilliantly at them whether they were leering frat boys or old men with loosening skin, and I feigned nonchalance over the bills piling up in the jar.

The song ended with a crash of Charlotte's cymbal. "Thank

you for your kindness. We'll be right back," Sam said before the crowd could drown him out with a "Woooooo!" I handed the tip jar up to Ace, who was in the middle of putting his shirt back on, and clomped down the ramp.

As soon as I passed the bouncer and stepped into the night air, I realized I'd gotten just as hot as the rest of the band, and I probably looked it. My sweat cooled on me as I glanced toward Broadway. If I walked that way with my phone, Julie would hear the music from the other bars, and she'd know I was out. She'd been on the road constantly for the past year and, up until she stopped taking my calls, was often backstage at a concert when we spoke, or at dinner with Mom and Dad and record company bigwigs. I could always hear her voice, but the ambient noise threatened to drown it out. If she caved and answered the phone, it would be just my luck for her or my parents to hear the music from the bar and ask me where I was. I didn't want to tell them and forfeit my college education. I didn't want to lie, either.

The volume turned up on the canned country music and leaked through the door of the bar. The pop-goes-country song with a throbbing beat seemed to vibrate the broken glass under my boots. I couldn't stay here. I headed in the other direction on the sidewalk.

A girl at the corner of the building yelled into her own cell phone. Passing her, I heard her say, ". . . can't believe y'all want to go to that place. You'll stand in line on Broadway for two hours before you get in. I'm telling you, this place has *no* line and the lead singer is *hot*. You should have heard him singing a hick version of Justin Timberlake. Sheila may be marrying David in a month, but on their big night, she'll be staring at the ceiling, thinking about this guy." The girl was silent for a moment, listening. She burst into laughter.

As I retreated down the sidewalk and her laughter faded, I wanted so badly to turn around. I'd gotten only a glimpse of her before I'd heard her talking behind me. I wondered how old she was, and therefore how old her friend likely was. That is, I wanted to know how far away they were from *me*.

I hadn't pictured myself getting married anytime soon, especially when Toby was all I had to choose from for a husband: shudder. But a couple of girls I'd graduated with were getting married in the next few weeks. One was pregnant. The other had signed a contract at her church that she wouldn't have sex until she got married, rumor had it. She needed to get married ASAP so she could finally do it with her dork boyfriend.

I tried to imagine shackling myself to a loser just because I couldn't wait any longer for one big night, then discovering someone like Sam a day too late. The best way to prevent that from happening, besides not getting married, was never meeting someone like Sam.

Half a block away from the bar, I finally looked back. The girl gestured wildly with her free hand while she talked into her phone, but I couldn't tell how old she was. She was too far away. The bar seemed small, isolated in a sea of abandoned buildings, pitch-black behind their barred windows.

The music was still loud enough for someone to hear on the other end of my phone, so I kept walking, even though I didn't feel safe here. Nobody was around. A single car swooshed by slowly, stopped at the traffic light at the corner, and moved on without backing up to kidnap me. I kept walking to the next streetlight and stood under its glow, as though the light were a force field that could keep me safe. The problem was, I couldn't see clearly beyond the brilliance.

I scrolled through my phone—three new drunk texts from

Toby—and hit Julie's number. She'd waited for my call nearly every night this year. My face had flashed on her screen, and she'd picked up before the phone rang on my end even once. Not this time. I listened to one hollow ring, then two.

As I stared into space, waiting, a tall figure appeared around the corner across the street. I couldn't make out colors or details outside my pool of light. He could have been a college student coming to my concert at the bar. He could have been anybody. The first thing I noticed about him that alarmed me—besides the fact that he'd been lurking in an empty lot—was that he stepped out into the street without looking both ways for traffic. Granted, there wasn't any traffic and he wasn't in danger, but most people would have looked all the same. And if he'd been headed for the bar, he probably would have walked down the sidewalk on his side of the street first before crossing. He wasn't headed for the bar. He was headed for me.

I didn't panic. Julie's phone still rang in my ear, and there was a chance she'd pick up any second. As the figure drew closer, I could see that he was an older man, not a college student. He had a full beard. His clothes were shabby and looked way too warm for this hot night. He was homeless, maybe, but I had no way of knowing that. And even if he were, that didn't automatically mean he was racing across the street to assault me. This is what I was thinking. I knew I ought to be alarmed and I also knew if I was alarmed I was making a lot of baseless assumptions.

Meanwhile, I should have felt a spike of adrenaline—he was coming closer, he was running now, he'd reached the center line in the street, I could see his face, his eyes on me—but I didn't feel a thing, just watched him coming and thought this was how I would die.

"You've reached Julie Mayfield!" Julie's voice mail chirped. "Shout out!"

As the man loomed in front of me, I still didn't run. He would catch me. I just wanted to click my phone off before Julie's voice mail beeped and recorded what happened next, so she wouldn't have to listen to it. My thumb hit the button to end the call. The man entered the glow of the streetlight, his face dark with dirt and shining under sweat. I could smell him just before he reached out one hand to touch me.

"Back off!" Sam shouted, shouldering himself in front of me, knocking me so hard that I nearly dropped the phone. He was between me and the man now. Down by his side I saw the flash of a knife blade. I meant to cry out or pull him back to stop him, but the man had seen the knife. He backed into the street, again without looking, then spun around and ran.

Sam returned his knife to his pocket. Breathing like he'd dashed all the way here from the bar, he watched the man until his shadow disappeared behind a temporary wall around the new construction at the end of the street. I'd thought all day that Sam's young face belied the old beard he was trying to grow, but at that moment, dark eyes narrowed against danger, he looked as world-weary and tough as Johnny Cash himself. He scanned the area, turning in a slow circle—something I hadn't thought to do. If a second man had wanted to attack me from behind, I never would have seen him.

"Walk," Sam barked, giving me a little shove on the small of my back. I started down the sidewalk in the direction he pushed me, toward the bar. Normally I would have protested being pushed around, but he still looked furious. As he walked beside me, he demanded, "What were you doing?"

"Making my phone call, like we discussed."

"Did you have to walk to Georgia? You were calling your boyfriend, weren't you?"

"My boyfriend?" I repeated, confused and disgusted at the

thought of running out of a gig with Sam to convey some breathless secret message to Toby. "No."

Sam was jealous. This registered with me on some level, blank as I felt.

But the next thing he said made me think he wasn't jealous after all, only wary that I was manipulating him. "You called someone who you didn't want to hear the music," Sam insisted. "Someone you didn't want to figure out where you are."

"It was just my sister." I caught the pointed toe of my boot on the broken sidewalk and tripped. Sam saved me from falling with a hand on my elbow. He held me for a few seconds while he looked over his shoulder again in the direction the man had gone.

Several minutes too late, the little good sense I usually possessed came rushing back. I began to realize how close we'd both come to tragedy. I squealed, "Were you going to knife that guy?"

"No," Sam said firmly. "I was going to *show* him my knife and get you away from him. Which I did. Were you going to let him grab you?"

I didn't know. Now that I had my wits back, I couldn't quite puzzle out what I'd been thinking when the strange man stalked like a shadow into my bright circle.

"You *were* going to let him grab you," Sam said incredulously. "Do you have some sort of death wish?" As we walked, he looked behind us, then to our right at the empty lots, then to the left across the street, ahead of us at the bar, and behind us again.

"Me!" I exclaimed. "He could have turned that knife around and used it on you. Why are you walking around with a concealed weapon, anyway? Is this neighborhood really that unsafe?"

"I didn't expect you to walk a mile down a deserted road to make a phone call," he said testily. Then, glancing sideways at me and looking almost sorry, he said, "I didn't know it wasn't safe.

I think it *would* be safe if you hadn't wandered in that direction alone." When I glared back at him and didn't give in, he sighed. "Okay." He pulled his knife out of his pocket to show me. I drew back in surprise before I saw it was his shiny silver guitar slide covering his entire middle finger.

"Oh." As relieved as I felt that he wasn't actually brandishing a knife, my heart went out to him. When he'd seen that guy coming for me, he could have watched the shit go down and called 911. Instead, he came for me, armed only with sleight of hand. He might as well have threatened to slay a dragon with a banana. I was overwhelmed with warmth for him, and somehow unable to tell him so.

"Yeah, lame." He examined the slide ruefully, turning his hand over to look at it from both sides. He deposited it back in his pocket. That was that, until somebody needed him to use a guitar pick to disarm a bomb.

I still wasn't sure how he'd found me in the first place. "Were you watching me?" I asked.

"I just wanted to make sure you were okay." He turned all the way around and walked backward beside me for a few steps, satisfying himself that the sidewalk was empty and the man wasn't coming back. Then he put out one hand and touched my shoulder, stopping me. "Bailey. Are you okay?"

"Yeah," I said lightly. Maybe later I would think back over what had happened and feel the terror I knew I should have felt at the time. My heart *had* finally sped up, but only at Sam's sudden appearance. *That* I hadn't quite gotten over, and I was still panting shallowly. "Are *you* okay?"

He nodded, squeezing my shoulder. Then he seemed to shake the whole incident off, refocusing himself to sing.

"Do you need me to help you get in the mood?" I asked hopefully. I really wanted *him* to get *me* in the mood. I wanted my heart pounding for a different reason.

He didn't bother to take off my glasses this time. He put both arms around me and pressed his mouth on mine, sweeping his tongue inside.

Initially surprised by the depth of the kiss, I recovered to meet him passion for passion, opening my lips for him.

As suddenly as it began, it was over. He let me go and took a shuddering breath.

I sidled forward and put my hand in the pocket of his jeans. Feeling warm as his eyes widened, I shoved my fingers as far down as they could reach into his tight jeans and fished out his guitar slide. I placed it on his middle finger and lifted his hand to my eye level so I could see my tiny, rounded reflection, then brought my lipstick out of my own pocket and reapplied it.

He laughed. "You have style, Bailey."

"I ain't nothing but class," I agreed.

We waved to the bouncer and walked up the ramp again. Ace sat on one of the tiny stages with his legs hanging off the side. If I'd been sitting there—which I would not, because the stage was sticky—I would have been afraid of being crushed by the even larger crowd now. But Ace, while mild mannered, cut an imposing figure. Nobody would get close enough to him to crush him. Charlotte sat beside him, alternately cupping her hand over his ear, shouting above the throbbing music, and flashing the evil eye to girls who walked past them. Charlotte thought she should have not just one boy, not just the other boy, but *all the boys*. I hated to break it to her, but if girlfriend truly wanted to start a collection, she needed to do something about her hair.

They stood when they saw us. Sam stepped onto my stage and helped me up before grabbing his guitar and hat and returning to his place on the bar. We were clearly still messing around and tuning, and Sam took a moment to text us a playlist, but a cheer went up when the audience saw us. From my vantage point three feet above the floor, I spotted a white veil that hadn't been part of the crowd before. In a white T-shirt with "Bride" bedazzled across her boobs was a girl flanked by a group of her friends wearing matching "Bridesmaid" shirts. To the bride's left I spotted the girl who'd made the phone call outside the bar. The bride was very young and I had a fleeting wish that she wouldn't settle for David, that she would wait for her Sam to come along.

But not *my* Sam. The girl was whispering in the bride's ear as they both lifted their eyes to him.

And he was after *me*. "I've never tried to impress a girl with yodeling before," he said into the mike.

"Nobody has," Ace yelled across the aisle.

The people who'd been in the bar for our first set laughed at this exchange. The newcomers didn't know what to make of it and tittered impatiently. Sam sized them up with one sweeping glance from wall to wall. "'Long Gone Lonesome Blues,'" he murmured. He glanced back at Charlotte. The crowd's whoop was cut off by the sudden two-step beat of the drums.

After the intro, I settled into my usual staccatos for the verses. But as he entered the chorus and started yodeling, I decided to stick with my short chords for that section, too. He didn't need anyone competing with him, for one thing. And I wanted to hear him.

Sam's Hank Williams imitation wasn't so much of a yodel as a very controlled falsetto. I could tell he had practiced this. Depending on how early he got the idea to tap me for his band, he must have been punching the air and yelling *Yes!* internally when I mentioned Hank that afternoon, because he had this song ready. The fake Hank at the mall had been off-key. The real Hank had howled like a stray dog, which was his appeal. He was a poor boy from Montgomery who spent too many nights boozing on an Alabama lake, and he looked it. Sam's voice was rich and full, a bad imitation but a great interpretation, and the crowd loved it. He nodded to me so I would take a solo. During the first few measures, I could hardly hear myself over the cheers for Sam.

I didn't think, just let the bow flow over the strings to the rockabilly beat with a hint of funk, Hank's original modernized by Ace and Charlotte. At the end of the solo I glanced down the body of my fiddle at Sam. He briefly took his finger off his strings and twirled it in the air: *Go again*. I kept fiddling. The crowd grinned up at me. On the second level in back, the Texas two-step had resumed. Sam twirled his finger with an offer of another solo. I moved my head shortly: *No*. The music was for the audience, not me, and they would get restless. I'd had my turn.

Because of Sam's expert yodeling, the song ended with much louder applause than we'd gotten in the whole first set. But when his "Thank you, thank you" finally broke through the crowd noise, he added, "Miss Bailey Wright, ladies and gentlemen." I felt the force of their cheers in my chest.

"Thank you," I said into my own mike, grinning and taking it all in and not quite believing my luck. At the same time, "Miss Bailey Wright" echoed in the back of my mind. For the first time, I was glad my parents didn't allow me to have social media accounts for fear of what I might post about Julie. If I had, and I'd had the poor foresight to label myself Bailey Wright Mayfield, these folks might have searched for me and found me and posted pictures of me on my own page for my parents and Julie's public relations team to see. As it was, I was caught between feeling safe and exposed, between wanting the crowd's praise and wishing I could squeeze into my fiddle case to hide.

Charlotte started the next song before I was ready, which broke me out of my downward spiral. We played country megahit after hit, interspersed with funk classics that I thought were strange choices until I saw how the crowd loved them. Sam motioned for me to pass around the tip jar earlier in the set this time. He'd been right: while I pasted a confident smile on my face, which was so much easier wearing makeup and a dress that felt like a costume, nobody treated me disrespectfully, not even the drunks. And the bridesmaids tipped *great,* twenty upon twenty tumbling into the jar.

Back onstage and about ten songs in, I thought we must be nearing the end of our night. I didn't want to stop. Sensing my sadness, maybe, or reacting to his own, Sam announced a slow song that hadn't been on the playlist, then looked pointedly at Charlotte and Ace to make sure they'd heard him. He looked at me.

From under the shadow of his cowboy hat, his dark eyes lingered on me a little too long for this to be a signal between bandmates. He was asking me if I was having the best night of my life.

I mouthed, "Yes."

He glanced at Charlotte, who launched the ballad. If yodeling had been an obstacle course for Sam's voice, the ballad was his weight-lifting competition, just him and the song with his every weakness exposed. But he had a strong voice, a little husky, a voice anybody could pick out on the radio and say, "That's a Sam Hardiman song." He might need me to get attention for his band, but he didn't need anybody if he ever wanted to get voice work for himself. I bent my chin to my fiddle and enjoyed the last few minutes as the set closed down. My bow stroked the strings and sent the rough vibration through my body. Sam's voice filled my ears.

Done. "Thank you," Sam said into the mike. "Y'all have been kind." With that understatement, ignoring the wild "Wooooooo!" that erupted, he simply handed his guitar and mike across the aisle to Ace and jumped down from the bar, holding his hat with one hand.

I was surprised by the band's sudden bustle, but of course they'd done this many times before. Ace packed up his bass and slipped out the door—to fetch the minivan, I assumed. Charlotte and Sam took turns, one carrying an instrument case or piece of equipment or drum from the stage out the door while the other waited with the pile on the sidewalk. I joined in. There was a lot to clear away and some pressure to hurry because the next band was already unloading their own van in the street. But as I muscled a tom onto the sidewalk where Charlotte was waiting, I realized Sam was gone.

Reading my mind, she said flatly, "He disappears like this. He doesn't care as much about us as you think."

"Uh-*huh*," I said, not wanting to get in a fight with this damaged girl, and not wanting to betray Sam by agreeing. I let her sit there on her drum stool while I went back for Sam's guitar. Inside, the crowd milled from bathroom to bar again. Way back on the second level, Sam stood at the rail, talking to a man with a full gray beard. He could have been anybody—especially since Sam probably knew as many losers on the Nashville music scene as I did.

I'd made a few more trips, with Charlotte now watching me contentedly and making no effort to trade jobs with me, when Sam bounced outside, beaming. There was no lead-up in Sam's world, no "Guess what?" He immediately burst out, "They asked us back!"

"Dude!" Charlotte exclaimed, raising both fists.

Sam looked at her, then at me. I think he would have hugged me or her if he'd been with either of us alone, but he sensed that something was broken out here and he was not going to step into the middle of it.

Luckily Ace drove up then, his athletic physique an ill match for his pristine mom-mobile. While Charlotte and I each picked up a drum, Sam opened the passenger door and leaned inside to shout to Ace, "They asked us back!" I couldn't make out what words Ace used in response, but I could hear him crowing. I wished I could see his excited reaction, because it seemed about as typical of Ace as driving this van.

"When's the next gig?" Charlotte asked as Sam deigned to walk back and help us pile the drums in the van.

"Tomorrow night," he said. "Cool?"

"Cool," she said.

I waited for him to ask me if it was cool, and I didn't know what I would say. I wanted to say yes. I needed to have this night again. I ought to say no, because every night I played put my future in jeopardy. A gig this good couldn't last forever, and then I would have thrown away college for nothing.

The new band started with a blast. "In," Sam said, gesturing with his head to the van. We all closed ourselves inside so we could hear each other. He took a wad of cash out of his back pocket—what the bearded bar owner had given him, probably—and then dumped out the tip jar on the seat between us. I helped him flatten and count the money. He handed a stack of bills to me, one to Charlotte, one to Ace, and stuffed one back in his pocket.

I didn't say anything because I didn't want to seem unseasoned or unprofessional, but I had never. In my *life*. Seen so much money.

Of course, I'd never actually gotten paid for a gig before.

I folded the bills into my fiddle case rather than my purse. If the scary man came back and I was mugged on the street, I would give up my purse and let him steal my license and credit card and identity before I let him get my fiddle.

"Bailey and I will walk back," Sam told Ace. "See you same time tomorrow." He and Ace bumped fists. He gave Charlotte a high five.

"Good night, Bailey," Ace called as I rolled the door open. "Nice work."

"Same to you." I opened my mouth to acknowledge Charlotte, but she was staring pointedly out the window.

Deposited on the sidewalk, watching the van drive toward Broadway, Sam and I picked up our cases and headed in the same direction. "Do you mind walking?" he asked. "I just wanted to talk to you."

"You just wanted to stay in the District a little longer," I accused him. But I didn't blame him. As we reached the intersection, the excitement was palpable. Happy barhoppers swayed up and down the sidewalks, and music poured from every door.

We stopped outside a bar that seemed particularly rowdy. As on the stage we'd just left, the drummer and the bass player were backed up to the window. Between songs, the bass player looked over his shoulder at us like he was just as curious about the people staring as they were about him. He locked eyes with Sam and lifted one finger off the neck of his guitar in greeting. Sam gave him a little wave.

"You sound better than them," I told Sam.

"*We* sound better," he corrected me. "And you sound better than everybody. The tips prove it."

"You told me this was your first gig in the District," I reminded him. "You don't know what the tips would have been like without me."

He lowered his dark brows at me. "It's a compliment, Bailey. Take it."

"No," I joked. But I really did wish he wouldn't say things like that. So far I'd done a fairly good job of enjoying the night without thinking about the consequences or the future.

His brow wrinkled with confusion, just for a moment, before clearing to its usual pleasant default setting. As we crossed Broadway, I watched the road ahead of us, knowing he was looking up the hill at the promised land.

Safe on the opposite sidewalk, I commented, "Ace and Charlotte are really good."

"I know," he said appreciatively. "I can't tell you how many bands I've tried to put together over the years. This is the first one that's stuck. Ace and Charlotte have been in bands before. They just needed a new place to call home, you know? Ace was playing R & B until now. You can really hear it in his bass line."

"Yes!" I said, realizing only after I'd exclaimed that I'd sounded way more enthusiastic than I'd intended. Sam smiled at me like I'd just given away a secret. The truth was, I used to have nerdy conversations about music with Julie. It had been too long.

I cleared my throat and said more calmly, "I noticed Ace was adding a seventh sometimes that wasn't in the original."

"So cool, right?" Sam asked. "It makes the whole game more interesting to watch, like throwing an elbow. And I rescued Charlotte from our high school jazz band. She has a lot of experience playing for the local middle schools and old folks' homes."

"This is a good thing?" I asked.

"Yes, because she's hungry. She lives in an apartment. She can't practice at home because the neighbors complain. It's not even her drum set—it's her set from the high school band, and she's just neglected to give it back yet. That driving beat she gives us comes from a lot of years in the marching band. But you can also hear how much she appreciates having a place to play and people to play with, and how bad she wants to keep doing it."

I felt guilty about every uncharitable thought I'd had about Charlotte that night. But as I worked through it, I felt a little less guilty because Sam was *trying* to make me feel guilty.

Or was he? I'd suspected over and over that he was manipulating me, yet his delivery was so honest and guileless that I was never quite sure.

However, I was sure after what he said next. "And then there's you, miss 'I don't want to be in a band right now,' miss 'I don't want to major in music when I go to Vanderbilt.'"

"Oh, boy." Why couldn't he let me live another hour in my fantasy world, starring him, where I didn't need to answer questions?

"If you're not majoring in music at Vanderbilt," he pressed me, "what's your major?"

We were passing the strip club again. I pretended I was holding my breath to avoid breathing great lungfuls of smoke and air freshener, but really I was hoping a piano would fall out of the second story of one of the bars, changing the subject. Sam wasn't going to like my answer.

After several moments, when the piano crash was not forthcoming and Sam continued to watch me with an "I told you so" expression, I conceded, "Biomedical engineering."

He gave me a sideways look like I'd said I was majoring in the literature of Antarctica. "Biomedical engineering. Like, inventing new cancer drugs?"

"More like working on one tiny part of one chemical that might someday be a component of a cancer drug."

"Mm-hmm," he said in a tone that sounded like I'd proven him right. "So you'd work in a lab."

"Or a cubicle, at a computer."

"That sounds like fun." I heard no sarcasm in his voice, but I knew it was there. "Did you pick the major that was as far away from music as you could get?"

"No, the guidance counselors at our school gave us a personality test and matched us with professions we'd be good at."

He nodded. "Your personality is analytical."

Intellectual, unemotional, cold. "Yes."

He held open the door to the parking deck for me. After it squeaked shut behind us, he said, "You're so analytical that you would turn your back on a profession you love just because a standardized personality test told you what career you should have." His voice echoed around the stairwell.

"You're doing it again," I said quietly.

"Right," he said, opening the door at the top of the stairs and watching me as I passed under his arm. We wound through a couple of rows of parked cars to his truck, then deposited our instrument cases and his hat behind the seat and got in. All this time he didn't say a word—which is what I'd wanted, for him to leave me alone. But now that I had my wish, I missed his nagging. His brows were knitted and his lips were pursed as he stared out the windshield of the truck with his keys in his hand, slack on the seat. Thinking hard didn't suit him.

His eyes shifted to me. I never forgot how handsome he was, but when he looked straight at me, his brown eyes fringed with long, dark lashes gave me a shock. A guy should not be this handsome when a girl wanted desperately to keep her boots on the ground.

"Do you want me to take you home now?" he asked in his husky voice, barely above a whisper.

I licked my lips. "What are my other choices?"

His intense gaze never left me as he asked, "Do you want me to kiss you?" His normally expressive mouth quirked into the smallest smile. He'd worn the same look that afternoon when he held open the door of Borders for me. I had something he wanted. He was going to convince me to give it to him for free.

I didn't want him to feel like he'd gotten the better of me.

There was something about his question that put the responsibility for kissing on me, not him. But even with that smug look on his face, he was so handsome with the dim glow of the parking deck lights shining in his dark waves and glinting in his friendly eyes. The responsibility was only a little one, negligible, casual, like picking up a lipstick at the drugstore.

I said, "Yes."

7

I expected him to lean forward immediately, but he didn't. His lips parted and he watched me like he wasn't sure he'd heard me correctly.

He was a lot shyer than I'd thought. Either that, or he suspected I wasn't serious and I would hit him. Either way, I decided I'd better take charge. I leaned toward him and to the right, aiming to start with his ear.

He crashed into my forehead. It took me a second of seeing stars to realize he'd started forward in the same direction, and we'd bashed heads.

"Oh, God," he said, covering my forehead with his palm. "Are you okay?"

My face turned white-hot. I was blushing, and I knew it, which probably meant I didn't have a concussion. "Yes." I put my hand on his forehead, too. When he dipped his head, my fingers slipped back through his waves. "Are *you* okay?" I asked.

"Yeah. I'm sorry. I *have* done this before." His hand slid down to cradle my cheek. "I'm going this way."

"I'm staying still," I assured him.

Now his thumb traced down my chin. My heart sped up at his touch, but I told myself he was trying to get better traction so I wouldn't unexpectedly jerk and cause us to bash heads again.

That's honestly what I was thinking. I could take the sweetest situation and make jokes out of it. If I expected nothing, I was never disappointed. But as he moved toward me, there was a point when our eyes locked. He looked so sincere that in that moment, I believed him. I believed *in* him. I believed anything he wanted to tell me.

His gaze slipped down to my lips. I closed my eyes.

His lips touched mine, a tickle on one side of my mouth, then a pressure that sent tingles down my neck and across my chest. My instinct was to slip both hands around his waist and pull him closer, but he wasn't some guy from school I was making out with at a party. He was special.

So I didn't push him. And he didn't push me. We kissed like that for a long time, exploring each other's lips and nothing else, while electricity ran along my skin and set my fingertips on fire.

Finally he pulled back. I couldn't read his expression clearly in the dusky truck, but I thought he looked almost frightened, his dark eyes hooded and his brows drawn into a worried crease.

I whispered, "What's wrong?"

"Nothing," he whispered back. "Absolutely nothing."

I gasped as his fingers slipped behind my neck and into my hair.

His hand stopped. His eyes widened with concern. "Okay?" he asked.

More than okay. I nodded.

He watched me carefully for a moment more like he wanted to make sure I wouldn't change my mind. Then his fingers slipped farther into my hair, tangling themselves so I couldn't have gotten away, and his palm tightened on the back of my neck. Now I understood why he'd asked permission. Things were about to get serious between us. I hadn't known when I'd said yes that this was what I was in for.

His lips met mine again. His tongue gently parted my lips and slipped inside my mouth. This time I couldn't help my hands creeping around his waist and grabbing handfuls of his shirt to pull him closer.

"Mmph," he said, because we both were facing forward and twisting sideways to kiss. Now he took my hands on his waist as my agreement that he could rearrange me. He never stopped kissing me as he pulled my leg across his thigh so that I straddled him. Then he put his hands over mine on his waist, reminding me this was what I'd wanted, as he scooted forward. Through his jeans and my thin dress, I felt how hard he was.

I'd always thought kissing was sweet, whereas anything having to do with a guy's pelvis was some kind of threat. Now, for the first time, I understood how a guy getting hard for me was sweet, too— maybe because his hands in my hair and his mouth on mine were making me lose my mind.

He broke the kiss and looked out the driver's side window of the truck, then the passenger side, making sure nobody was watching. His labored breaths sent a new shiver down my arms every time a puff passed across my cheeks.

He faced me again. He was a lot taller than me, but because I straddled his thighs, our eyes were even. He leaned forward until our foreheads touched, still gazing at me, so close and so dark that I could hardly see him. I felt his breath in my mouth as he traced down my neck with his middle finger, callused from holding his guitar string down, and unbuttoned the top button of my dress.

As I watched his fingers, I remembered that my mother had dragged Julie and me to the fabric store to pick out the material for this dress. I had protested and said that rather than red rosebuds on a field of black, we should have the dresses made from the bolt printed with saguaro cactuses and horse heads, so appropriate that it circled back around to become ironic. I'd been tired of playing dress-up, one; and two, I was tired of matching Julie. I'd loved playing with her, but the matching outfits had seemed unhip and old-fashioned, something we would have worn on stage in my grandmother's time.

He reached down to undo the second button of my dress. Suddenly I was the one huffing a surprised breath into his open mouth. He pushed through the opening he'd made in my dress and slipped his fingertips beneath the cup of my bra, across my bare breast. He stopped at my nipple, rolling it gently between two fingers. I squirmed on his thighs. It felt like there was a nerve stretched directly between my breast and my crotch.

I had made out with boys before. Boys had felt me up before. They had gotten my bra off me at parties. But they'd wanted to see me, or grab me, more for bragging rights than for their own pleasure. *My* pleasure never entered the equation. Sam was different. He teased me, tested me, touched me gently and watched my reaction with his depthless eyes. Ms. Lottie had warned me he was a heartbreaker.

"There should be a country song about this," I whispered.

"I'm pretty sure there is," he whispered back, sliding his whole hand into my bra to cup my breast.

There wasn't, though. Plenty of tunes sung by men comically recounted everything they'd gotten away with in their trucks when they were teenagers. No songs sung by women rehashed how much they'd enjoyed it. But they should have. I could be the one to write that anthem.

Abruptly he withdrew his hand, lifted me off his lap, and set me back in the passenger seat. I was disappointed that he'd decided to end this. Then he put his hand behind my head, pulled me down to flatten me along the seat, and rolled on top of me. "Is this okay?" he asked.

It was more than okay. In answer, I bent one knee so my pelvis was closer to his and I could feel more of him through my dress. I wasn't prepared to go all the way and I didn't think he would ask me to, but as far as I was concerned, Sam Hardiman could position me any way he liked on the seat of his truck. I ran my hands back through his waves and gently pulled his head until I could reach his ear with my mouth.

"Ahh," he sighed. His breath quickened, but he held very still to savor the experience. I knew exactly how he felt. As I tickled his earlobe with my tongue, I concentrated on the sensation of my body coming alive. I'd gone through all of this before, but never with a guy this beautiful.

Suddenly a car chirped. Headlights blinked somewhere in the deck. The noise sounded so close that I stiffened under Sam.

It wasn't my imagination that the noise was suspicious. Sam pushed himself off me, propping his elbows on the seat. He craned his neck to look out the window.

The door jerked open. The man from the deserted street must have followed us here. I screamed.

A rough hand smothered my mouth. But in the next second, I saw it was still Sam who held me. He uncovered my mouth and looked outside the truck again. "What the fuck, Charlotte?"

"Hey!" Charlotte exclaimed. "This is exactly how you got *me* to join your band."

My heart was still throbbing from the scare. Now it hurt from being broken into pieces. Sam had made out with me so I would join his band. He had touched me that way, kissed me all night, made me fall for him, just so I would stay in his band. He had done it before, with Charlotte.

When another girl came along, one with more talent and better style than me, he would do it again.

"Sorry," Sam murmured in my ear. He hefted himself off me, momentarily crushing my arm—"sorry, sorry, sorry"—and pulled me after him so we both sat upright. Then he bailed out of the driver's side of the truck and slammed the door.

Charlotte peered through the open passenger door at me. Blinking innocently, she said in a superfriendly voice, "When you first showed up tonight, did he tell you to act like the two of you weren't into each other?"

Sam had rounded the truck and reached her. "Could I speak with you privately for a moment behind that Audi?" He shoved her along in front of him until they disappeared around the next car.

Ace stood with his arms folded in the empty space next to Sam's truck, looking over his shoulder in the direction Sam and Charlotte had gone.

Buttoning my dress, I called to Ace, "Well, that was awkward."

"Sorry," he grumbled.

We could both hear Charlotte's increasingly shrill voice: ". . . just bring her into the group, Sam, without asking anybody's opinion? Like we don't even *matter*?"

I couldn't make out any of what Sam said in response. I could hear only his stern tone. It must have worked, because she replied with indiscernible words, and then he stalked back toward the truck.

When Sam drew even with Ace, he stopped and gave him a glare. Ace just raised one eyebrow at him.

Sam threw up his hands in frustration, closed my door, rounded the truck again, and slipped behind the steering wheel. As he started the ignition and backed out of the space, I thought about opening my door and flouncing away. But I would have no way home. The last thing I wanted was to make a phone call to my granddad to rescue me from the District. I stayed put, watching Charlotte come from behind the car to meet Ace in the empty parking space. Their heads turned to follow us as we drove off.

"I'm so sorry about that," Sam said quietly, his face blinking pale and then dark again as we passed under fluorescent lights spaced along the ceiling. "I should have warned her I was bringing you tonight. She was comfortable with the band the way it was, and she never accepted we needed to add somebody new. She won't act that way to you again."

She certainly wouldn't, because I wouldn't be around. She would be reacting exactly the same way to the next girlfriend Sam brought in.

But I didn't say any of that. I owed Sam nothing, not even a fight about it. I stared out the window as we exited the parking deck, onto the side street. The lights of the District grew fewer and farther between until they faded into the neon wash of the larger city.

Sam's voice broke the silence. "The gig is at the same time tomorrow night. Want to tell your grandpa we're going on another date, and actually grab a bite to eat beforehand? If you're not busy earlier, maybe we could spend the afternoon together."

"I'm not playing the gig," I said flatly.

"You're—" he burst out, then pressed his lips together, controlling himself. He'd been afraid I would say this, and he'd only been pretending he thought I might not mind what Charlotte had told me. He said, with admirable calm considering how upset he must be, "But they asked us back."

"But *you* didn't ask *me*."

"No," he said. "Wait a minute. I *told* you that they asked us back, and you didn't say you wouldn't play with us. You've decided this

only now, after what Charlotte said. Listen, Charlotte is a great girl
and I love her—"

He kept talking. My brain paused here like time stood still. He
loved Charlotte. And he glossed over it. This was a warning to me.

"—but she's a few bricks shy of a full load about some things."

"About you," I accused him.

"We dated," he acknowledged carefully. "I did not date her just
to get her to join the band."

"Did you tell her to act like you weren't into each other when
you brought her into the band with Ace?"

"Maybe," he said, meaning *yes*, "because Ace would *think* I was
dating her just for that. But I wasn't. And I definitely was not doing
what I was doing with you just now to get you into the band.
You're already in the band."

"I most certainly am not," I said. "I never agreed to that.
Charlotte may be a few bricks shy of a full load about you, but
I'm not."

"Bailey!" he exclaimed before I'd quite gotten all of this out of
my mouth. "You can't turn this down. We already have a gig. We
scheduled another gig with you in it."

I shrugged. "Go back to the bar owner and say your special
guest star won't be joining you, and ask if he still wants you."

"He *won't*. That's been the whole point of this, Bailey. I can't do
this without you. If I could, I would have done it last week."

I wasn't sure that was true. He'd gotten the first gig without me.
I was quickly learning that Sam said what he needed to say to get
people to do what he wanted. Judging from the force behind his
words, maybe he'd even started to believe them himself.

"Look," I said with a sigh, "I told you from the beginning that
I can't be in your band. I'm not allowed."

"You're not *allowed*?" he asked incredulously.

"No."

He grimaced out the windshield, considering this idea. "That's why you walked to Georgia to phone your sister. Or whoever you were calling."

"It *was* my sister, and yes."

"That's why your grandpa didn't want to let you out of the house. Why aren't you allowed to play a gig, Bailey? That's insane."

I nodded my agreement. And I had to explain the insanity to him, or he would never leave me alone. "I'm staying with my granddad because my parents are gone with my little sister. They all came home for my graduation, which was when I got in so much trouble about the wreck. For the past year, usually one of my parents has been home with me, physically, because they don't trust me. But when they're here, their minds are with my sister."

"Doing what?" he asked quietly, like he was sure by now he didn't want to hear the answer.

"Touring with her while she opens for bigger acts, and letting her get a lot of practice."

His mouth dropped open. "She has a development deal with a record company?"

Of course he would guess. He might even understand more about the music business than I did. I said, "Yeah."

"Is it working out?" I could see in his eager expression that he hoped it was working out, like Mr. Crabtree was eager for another Elvis song to play at the mall, a dog waiting for someone to throw a ball. If Sam had his way, he would network with my parents and my sister, around and then right over me. And he would ruin me in the process.

"So far, so good," I said, understating by several hundred thousand dollars.

"Did she get discovered on the bluegrass festival circuit?" he asked.

"Yeah."

"But you were on the circuit, too."

I swallowed. "Yeah."

"So she got discovered, and you didn't."

"I don't want to talk about it."

He sighed in frustration and gestured with his hands on the steering wheel as he exclaimed to the broad, dark street, "Too late. We're talking about it, and you owe me an explanation."

I almost said, *I don't owe you shit*. But I thought back to my week at the mall. The anticipation I'd felt before I played with a group for the first time in ages. The way my hopes had been dashed when the group didn't measure up to Julie. The elation I'd circled back to when I discovered Sam. The way the roller coaster had crashed to the bottom again when he and his father fought.

I knew how excited he'd felt when the band came together tonight. I'd felt that excitement myself. I was dashing his hopes now, as mine had been dashed repeatedly. I shouldn't have agreed to play with him in the first place. I should have refused like a good girl and let his hopes lie there in the dust. So I *did* owe him an explanation now.

"The record company agreed to sign Julie," I began.

He nodded his acknowledgment, face tight with barely controlled anger.

"My parents tried to get the company to sign me, too, and keep us together as a duo. The company flat-out refused. Single teen girls with pop crossover potential are what's selling right now. But Julie and I had been playing together forever. We'd never played apart. The record company thought it would be terrible for their public relations, and for Julie's, if it got out that they'd snatched her from an inseparable sister duo and shunned me."

"It would." Sam's grimace had relaxed a little. He was beginning to see where I was coming from.

Not that I cared. I was offering him this explanation to detangle myself from this mess, not to involve myself further with a manipulative playboy.

"The record company told my parents I should disappear. They didn't want Julie to mention me in any of her interviews, because reporters might come looking for me and discover that ugly past. They made me get off social media so I couldn't post stabs at Julie that everybody in the world could copy and paste. And they specifically said they didn't want me to pursue a music career that might distract from Julie's, or embarrass her, or advertise the fact that they'd left me behind."

Turning off the broad street and onto Music Row, Sam looked like he was squinting into the streetlights, but I could tell he was really thinking hard, coming up with a way to talk me down. "You say the record company wanted *you* to do this stuff. But their contract wasn't with you, surely. It wasn't even with Julie. She's too young to sign a contract. Their deal was with your parents, so how can the record company tell *you* what to do?"

"They can convince my parents to say that if I get in any trouble, I can't go to college."

"Oh," he mouthed, but no sound came out. He recovered from his shock to say, "And by trouble, they mean a gig."

"They also mean going to a drunk graduation party and getting into a car with my tweaked-out boyfriend, who drives into a lake." I was back in my parents' kitchen, talking with them around the table rather than in the more comfortable den, because I was still wet from the lake and my mother didn't want me dripping on the carpet. My thigh throbbed and swelled, the discoloration visible below the short hemline of my sequined dress. I hadn't complained about it, and my parents hadn't asked. They told me I had better be damn glad this had happened now. What if it had happened a week from now, on the day Julie's first single dropped? Did I think the tabloids wouldn't be all over me like stink on shit?

Julie had stared at me from the kitchen doorway, her face contorted with an expression so anguished that I couldn't even read it. Julie and I loved each other. We were there for each other. And she walked away from me.

I caught myself rubbing my eyes and forced my hands down. "But yeah, gigs are included in the bad behavior, too. My granddad said he would work on my parents so I could keep playing at the mall. He is *not* going to work on them if he finds out I played this gig in the District tonight after I lied to him. I shouldn't have let you talk me into it. This has to be the end."

Sam pulled to a stop in front of my granddad's hill of a front yard. I hoped I could just bail out of the truck. No such luck. Sam wasn't done with me. He turned off the ignition and placed one hand on my knee.

"Here's what I don't understand," he said. "Your parents put you and your sister on the bluegrass circuit and tried to get you a deal. They got one for your sister, and they kind of gave up on you."

No, that wasn't right. I clarified it for him. "They *totally* gave up on me."

Without lifting his hand, he shifted his whole body toward me. The soft light from the porch touched his hair but left his eyes in darkness as he asked, "Why have *you* given up on you?"

"Because *they* did," I said shortly. "Everybody did."

"*You* are part of everybody," he pointed out. "As long as you have faith in yourself, you still have someone's support."

He sounded like the tail end of a TV gospel show, or a fortune cookie. "That is cockamamy."

He squeezed my knee. "You have *my* support."

Done with him, I knocked his hand away. "Of course you're going to say that. You want me in your band."

"Why would I want you in my band if you weren't good?" he protested. "I'm not operating a charity mission here. You *are* in my band. *Our* band. You heard how good we sound together. No professional musician would walk away from that."

"I guess I'm not as professional as you thought." I opened my door, slid out of the truck, and waited for him to slide out, too, so I could retrieve my fiddle.

He stared across the seat at me. I still couldn't see his shadowed eyes, but I could read the outrage on his parted lips. I thought he might refuse to move, holding my fiddle hostage.

Slowly he slid out and even bent the seat forward for me. But as I reached in for my case, he said, "This has to be about what Charlotte said to you. There's no way you would turn this gig down unless you were mad at me. Come on, Bailey. You have to be bigger than that."

Jerking my case free, I shoved the seat back into place and slammed the door, then backed a few paces to stand on the concrete staircase up the hill. "*I* have to be bigger than that?" I shouted at him over the roof of the cab. "*You* should have been bigger than that when you decided to make out with both of us. Unlike you, I don't take just any gig I'm offered." I whirled around, the thin skirt of my dress failing to make as dramatic an exit as my heavy circle skirt that afternoon. I jogged up the stairs.

As I fished the key out of my purse and opened the front door, all my attention was on Sam's truck behind me. I listened for him to rev the engine and tear off down the street, but he didn't. Maybe he wasn't as mad as he'd seemed. He'd only feigned anger to try to get what he wanted, but he didn't care as much about having me in his band as he'd claimed. Tomorrow night he'd be feeling up another fiddle player in the parking deck.

More likely, he had no place for negativity because he was too busy thinking, plotting out how to manipulate me next. I'd met Sam half a day ago, but already I knew when he wasn't done with me.

I closed the door behind me. Only then did Sam's truck start and move down the street.

As the noise faded, my alarm grew. I'd been so focused on Sam that I'd completely forgotten about my granddad. All the lights were on in the living-room-turned-showroom with shiny finished instruments hanging in rows from the ceiling. I was totally exposed with my bra straps showing—my shrug must have been behind Sam's seat, crushed under two guitar cases—and I was holding my forbidden fiddle. I'd just taken great pains to walk away from the dangerous lure of my life's goal, only to get busted.

But as I paused and listened, I heard my granddad snoring softly in his bedroom. I hadn't asked him what my curfew was, if I had one, but it was way past midnight and he wasn't waiting up for me.

I slipped off my boots at the bottom of the stairs so I wouldn't wake him with my clomping. Then I walked into the kitchen and opened the pantry. My grandmother's mason jars were still there, though she hadn't been alive to can tomatoes from the garden in ten years. I unscrewed the lid of one, opened my fiddle case to extract my share of the night's wages, and plopped the bills inside, where they unrolled and expanded against the glass. It seemed like a fittingly redneck place to keep the money from a rockabilly band.

I lugged my boots and fiddle and the jar to the top of the stairs. In my room, I slid the jar onto the dresser, collapsed on the bed, and stared at the money. It was *so much money*. I'd made it all from playing my fiddle for two hours. I couldn't quite believe it.

Yet Julie with her high-powered contract made that much money every second.

I stayed in that strange in-between place for a long time, wanting to be ecstatic that I was a professional musician, not wanting to be jealous of Julie, saddened all over again that the two always walked hand in hand. I thought about hiding the jar in a drawer so I wouldn't see it constantly and feel that wash of jealousy over and over again. But the sense of accomplishment was too good and too strong. When I received my first paycheck from the mall next week, I could deposit it in my bank account, but I knew I would cash it and stow it in the mason jar like an idiot hiding money in the mattress, just so I could see it.

And I knew that, angry as I was at Sam, and much as he probably hated me right now, we would be playing with each other again tomorrow.

Pulling my music notebook and colored pencils from my purse, and rubbing my eyes to my heart's content, I sat down at the desk and wrote a song about that.

8

The next afternoon, my granddad and I rocked in chairs on his front porch, lazily playing our instruments. He strummed along with me, agreeing to whatever sleepy oldie popped into my head, while I tried to enjoy the sound of my fiddle, the touch of the bow against the strings, the way those sounds seemed like a natural accompaniment to a breezy summer day.

I tried and failed. I played songs as familiar to me as my own fingers, but different possibilities cropped up stubbornly in my mind, places these tunes were never intended to go. I could add a seventh to the bass line in my head. I could slide from a bluegrass tune straight into a startlingly similar R & B standard. I was awake and alert and out of my comfort zone. Sam had done this to me.

"Phone's ringing," my granddad said.

I stopped fiddling and listened and sure enough heard my Alison Krauss ringtone, faintly. At least my granddad wasn't in danger of losing *his* hearing anytime soon.

"Probably Sam," he added unnecessarily.

I gripped my fiddle tightly to keep from flinging it away as I jumped up from my chair, leaving it rocking wildly. I ran through the showroom, dashed up the stairs, and shoved my hand into my purse. But the number on my phone wasn't labeled.

Not Sam.

"Hello?" I snarled.

"Hey!" a girl said brightly. "It's Charlotte."

I felt my nostrils flair in distaste.

"Cunningham," she added when I didn't say anything. "The drummer."

"Uh-huh." Whatever message she'd called to deliver, I was going to make it as difficult as possible for her. "How did you get my number?"

"Sam asked me to convince you to come back to the band."

"I was never in your band," I said.

"Whatever. Sam is mad at me. He thinks you dropped out because of what I did last night. I just wanted to apologize. I shouldn't have dragged Ace back to Sam's truck and opened the door. I knew what was happening, but you're a big girl, and I should have just let it happen. And I didn't mean what I said." Her tone was super-friendly and, therefore, ironic, just like last night.

I started to rub my eye, then quickly pulled my hand away. Charlotte wasn't worth rubbing my eyes over. "Yes, you did mean it," I told her. "Girls don't say 'This guy is making out with you like he just made out with me' without meaning it. That's pretty specific."

"Well." Stumped, she took a deep breath. "Look, I wasn't trying to be rude. I just felt like you should know what was going on. Sam has had a different girlfriend every week this year. He has literally had, like, fifty-two girlfriends. He wears his heart on his sleeve. He will make you feel like the world was made for the two of you while he's with you. He'll convince you to do anything he wants, and he'll make you think it was *your* idea. With Sam, two and two doesn't always equal four. Depending on what he's trying to convince you of that day, two and two might equal five. He's so convincing that sometimes he seems like he doesn't know himself that he's manipulating you.

"And then, when he's gotten what he wants out of you, it'll be over. You'll be having the week of your life, and out of the blue he'll say"—she switched into a lower voice that was supposed to be Sam's—"'I'm messed up right now, and I can't give you what you deserve.' And then he's on to girl fifty-three. Wait, this isn't convincing you to come back to the band, is it?"

I let the silence fall between us, like a security gate rolling shut over a storefront at the mall. Surely she could hear how passive-aggressive she sounded. But as the seconds dragged on, I decided she might be so socially inept that she *didn't* understand her own passive-aggression, or the meaning behind my silence. I said, "I don't know what your plans are for higher education, but you should probably rule out law school." I hung up.

The triumphant feeling lasted about two seconds, and then I was alone in the quiet room that wasn't really mine, listening to the breeze in the oak trees outside, staring at the phone in my hands and feeling numb.

I was determined to stay strong and put an end to my relationship, such as it was, with Sam. From the very beginning, I'd suspected him of something like what Charlotte had described. It was hard to turn my back on him. Better now than later, when his claws had sunk further into me.

But I couldn't help a little flight of fancy, the memory of his hands on me. I put one hand up to cup my breast and thought of the way he'd touched me. The most endearing thing about him had been the way he seemed bowled over by me, like he'd never met a girl so sexy and beautiful. Was it good to treasure the memory of a few perfect hours together? Or would I have been better off never meeting him?

I wasn't getting married, but I was as bad off as that girl Sheila at the bar last night, marrying David and thinking of Sam while she stared at the ceiling.

There was definitely a country song about this.

I pried my hand away from the phone and galloped back downstairs to my granddad. We had just launched "Wildwood Flower" when he said, "Phone's ringing. Y'all can't bear to stay away from each other?"

"Nope." It was probably Charlotte again. It definitely wasn't Sam. Even if it *was* Sam, I wasn't excited about talking to him. Yet strangely, I made it up the stairs in record time. The number wasn't labeled. Not Sam. "Fuck," I said, then clicked the phone on. "Hello?"

"Hello, Bailey. It's Ace."

I sighed heavily, directly into the phone so he would hear it, and didn't say anything.

After the silence stretched on, he added, "Hightower. The bass player. From last night?"

"Hello, Ace," I said, letting him know from my tone that I understood why he was calling, and it wasn't going to work. But even as I unleashed that sarcastic barb, my voice faltered. I thought I heard Sam singing, like he was serenading me. I walked over to my windows. Nothing was beneath them but grass dappled with sun and shade.

"Listen," Ace said. "Sam asked me to convince you to play with us again tonight. We're all so sorry about what Charlotte said to you. She and Sam dated before, but it was nothing serious. Just a week. She's not quite over him, I think—"

"You think?" I interjected.

Ace went on as if I hadn't interrupted. "—and she wanted me to drive back to the parking deck last night and find you with him. I knew I shouldn't have done it, but I did it, and I'm sorry."

I couldn't concentrate on a snappy comeback. I still thought I heard Sam, and he was drowning out Ace's apology. It was like talking to Julie every night for the past year, asking her to repeat herself again and again over the din of the entourage surrounding her. "Where are you?"

He paused between it's-none-of-your-business and what-would-it-hurt-to-tell-her. "Broadway."

"Sam's singing on Broadway?" I exclaimed. He'd finally gotten the gig he wanted! And he hadn't needed me after all. My heart raced with elation and pain together.

"Oh," Ace said. He realized that I could hear Sam, and he should have walked to Georgia to make this call. "Well, he's busking."

"What?" I exclaimed. Lots of musicians hung out between the clubs on Broadway, playing whatever instrument they had with their cases open for passersby to throw bills into. Usually these people looked only marginally better groomed than the man who had almost grabbed me last night. "Why is Sam busking?"

"He does this a lot," Ace admitted. "If he doesn't have a gig, he makes one."

This I had to see. And hear. "I'm coming down there." As my words popped out, I was inching closer to giving in to Sam's demand that I play with his band. At the very least, I was giving away how far I'd fallen for him. But no matter what, I was not going to miss the spectacle of Sam busking.

"You can't come down here." Ace almost sounded like he was having an emotion, and it was desperation. "You saw how he was last night. He needs to be focused when he sings. Fights with girls mess that up."

Nice. Way to make me feel special. "I'll be secret," I said. "I won't let him see me."

"You're hard to miss," Ace said. "No. I shouldn't have told you where he is. He's already mad at me, Bailey. Come on."

"See you there."

My granddad must have assumed that a second date with Sam was inevitable. He accepted it without complaint. I slid my fiddle from the seat of my rocking chair, buckled it into its case, and took it with me, hoping that it looked natural. When my granddad eyed me suspiciously, I told him I wasn't sure what Sam and I were going to do that night, but we might jam together. It was true.

Preferring not to park in a dark parking deck by myself, even though it was still daylight, I trolled the upper part of the hill near Broadway for a space. It wasn't long before I spotted Sam's old truck in a pay lot. Behind it sat not Ace's minivan from last night but a brand-new SUV with the Hightower car dealership insignia on the back. I stopped behind that.

With my fiddle case in one hand and my purse slung over my shoulder, I stepped out of my car in high heels, stylish shorts, and a crazy blouse layered with necklaces. Broadway was exposed to the slanting sun, and my usual Goth-wear was heavy for this heat. But if wearing shorts took some of my power away, I hoped the killer heels gave it back.

As I reached the corner and scanned Broadway down the hill, I headed for the biggest crowd. I could picture Sam drawing a crowd all alone with his guitar. As I moved closer, I didn't hear him playing or singing, yet nobody in the crowd was moving on down the sidewalk like they'd heard enough. They were staying put. I could picture Sam convincing people to stay put.

I tried to push through to reach him and show him I wanted to play with him before he started his next song. That would smooth over everything we'd said to each other the night before. I wouldn't give in and join his band. I couldn't. I wouldn't start a relationship with him, either, if he asked. That was crazy. But we could play on Broadway every Sunday afternoon for a while, until Julie got famous and somebody recognized me as her sister. Before that happened, I would get my fix of playing with him. We would do fine if we could just play together and never had to speak.

But before I could find a hole in the crowd, the strains of his mellow acoustic guitar glided above the heads of the crowd. I would have thought from the intro and the chord progression that he was attempting Alan Jackson's "Remember When," which was in G, but he was in C.

The next second he was singing "Remember When" after all. He'd smartly taken the key up half a scale because his voice was higher than Alan Jackson's. One thing I had to give Sam: he knew his own voice and how to box his weight.

While his voice urged me forward, the lyrics of the song gave me pause. The narrator was a teenager, losing his virginity with the girl he loved. I backed through the second row and then the third, my hand going sweaty on the handle of my fiddle case.

In the next verses, he and the girl got married. Their parents died. They fought. There was supposed to be a guitar solo here with a gradual modulation from the key of G to the key of A, which in Sam's version went from C to D. The original song was full of expressive violins, and he could have used me here. But he didn't have me. To his credit, he didn't try to replicate that slow solo but marched quickly through the chords to land at his destination, never losing his audience, and resumed his lyrics. In these verses, he and his wife had children and mellowed out. They grew older and their children moved away, but they vowed never to have any regrets about their lives coming to an end because they were so in love.

At this point tears stung my eyes. For once I hadn't been concentrating on Sam's notes and whether he was in key. I'd been listening to his words. The people all around me had, too. Middle-aged women's eyes filled with tears. Men put their arms around their wives' shoulders, all for a song so vague that it applied to everyone—everyone in a joyful relationship, that is—because even the happiest couple experienced sadness as time passed. And all this was sung by an eighteen-year-old who couldn't possibly know what he was talking about, and who was treating this public street and free audience as practice. Yet I was moved, and so were they.

I wanted to listen to the rest of his performance, but I couldn't stay there in the crowd. His song ended and only a handful of people moved away down the street. The rest would leave eventually, though. The bodies in front of me would shift, and he would see me. I didn't want that anymore.

I ducked into the nearest bar, which doubled as a restaurant during the day and didn't start ID'ing until later. I ordered an iced tea—I meant to pay for it, but the bartender nodded to my fiddle case and told me there was no charge. He must have been a down-and-out bluegrass reject himself. Then I headed up the stairs to the open-air balcony, empty in the late afternoon. Sliding into a seat at a table overlooking the sidewalk one story below, I watched Sam. His cowboy hat was gone. His plaid shirt and cowboy boots, gone. He wore a T-shirt and shorts like an eighteen-year-old headed for the mall, dressed to be himself.

He never looked up at me. But on his third song since I'd sat down, I noticed someone leaning in the shade of a nearby building, waving. It was Ace, saluting me. I put my finger over my lips.

He pushed off from his resting place and headed for the specta-tors. I hoped he wouldn't call Sam's attention to his admirer with a deck seat. Ace skirted the edge of the crowd and disappeared under the building where I was sitting. A few minutes later he reappeared with his own tea, coming toward me across the second floor of the restaurant.

He slid into the seat facing me, surprisingly nimble for a huge guy, not even swaying the ice in my drink as he tucked his knees under the table. He didn't disturb me, either. We watched Sam cycle through another impeccable performance of an old favorite, then look up at the crowd in astonishment at their applause, like he'd forgotten all about them.

"I feel better if I come with him," Ace said quietly. "He ought to be able to take care of himself. But sometimes he forgets where he is and what he's doing. A sociopath would kill him over the couple of hundred dollars in that guitar case right now."

I nodded. "Is that why you want to be in the band? Because he wants you to be?" I was fishing for information about myself more than Ace. I knew I couldn't be in Sam's band, but I desperately wanted to be. And after Charlotte's warnings, I wondered whether this was an idea that Sam had put in my head, a conclusion I never would have reached if he hadn't kissed me.

Ace poured a packet of fake sweetener in his tea and stirred it with his straw. "Like I told you last night, Sam and I played football together." I recognized this phrase as boy code for *We are very close friends.* "I used to play bass for my brother's R & B band, but after he moved to Chicago, I put it away until I happened to mention some of my past gigs to Sam at football practice. He got all excited and wouldn't leave me alone until I agreed to jam with him. And we sounded great together. Sam would sound great with anybody, really, but he made me feel like I was holding my own. It was this really strange mix of James Brown and John Denver, but we made it work, you know?"

I nodded. Just like I could make it work when some crazy old lady wanted me to play Reba McEntire.

"Sam and I played with anybody who wanted to start a band in high school," Ace said, "but most guys aren't serious about it. They want to be in a band so they can impress the ladies, but they don't want to practice, and the band lasts a week. Then Sam started dating Charlotte."

He took a sip of his tea. It was just a pause in his story, and after swallowing he would go on with the story of Sam dating Charlotte. But he drank and drank, the seconds stretched on, and most of his tea was gone in one pull.

He dabbed his lips almost daintily with his cloth napkin and went on as if he hadn't strangely stopped. "They didn't date long. Ever since, we periodically have these knock-down, drag-outs about whether Sam decided we should all form a band because he was dating Charlotte, or whether he sought Charlotte out and started dating her so that she would join his band. I don't know the answer to that myself."

"It sounds like you've given it a lot of thought," I pointed out.

Ace's face wasn't expressive—he was the opposite of Sam in that regard—but now that I knew him a little, I could tell from the slightest tightening of his jaw that he was upset. "Charlotte asks me about it all the time. She comes up with a new theory, a new angle, and wants to discuss it with me. You're not helping."

Without meaning to, I sat back in my chair. I didn't like being blamed for this. Whatever problems the band had, they'd definitely had them before I showed up last night. I'd only brought them to a head.

"Sorry," he said, holding up his hands in a show of truce. "It's not your fault. Anyway, they were still dating when Sam came to me with this idea of a band. I did not want to be in a band with Sam and his girlfriend."

"Because he's had fifty-two girlfriends this year," I guessed.

"Oh," Ace said, shoulders sagging. "Charlotte said that to you."

With my stony silence, I told him yes.

"It hasn't been fifty-two," he said carefully. "That would be one per week. Don't get me wrong. There have been a lot. Maybe more like twenty-six."

"Now you're just rubbing it in," I said, hinting that it would be okay if he shut up about this now.

He eyed me uneasily, thrown off by my protest, and unsure where to take this argument from here. He said awkwardly, "Well, so, and, Charlotte was girlfriend number twenty or thereabouts, so he was pretty far along in this pattern. I knew they were going to break up in a week or two, and then I'd be in a band with Sam and his *ex*-girlfriend."

"And besides the awkwardness anybody else would expect, that was a special problem for you, because you were in love with her."

I don't know what made me say it. I'd suspected she had a thing for him—besides her more obvious thing for Sam—by the way she'd sat protectively beside him onstage last night and watched other women jealously as they passed. I'd thought he had a thing for her because of the way he watched her flirt with Sam without ever commenting that he was tired of it or it was gross, just taking it with a carefully composed blank face. I'd deduced the feeling was mutual because they'd ridden to the gig together. Who'd set that up, and what excuse they'd used, I didn't know, but they'd both allowed themselves to be assigned to that minivan together, and to work as a team against Sam when he seduced a fiddle player later in the night.

I could have stayed quiet. Should have, maybe, if my goal was to get *out* of this band. But the longer we'd talked and listened to Sam singing below us, the more resigned I'd become to the fact that I was probably stuck with them, at least for tonight. At least until I got my fill. And I needed Ace's confidence now, because that way he might help in my exit strategy later.

"I was *not* in love with her," he said so loudly that several people at the very back of the crowd around Sam looked up at us curiously.

"I see," I said smoothly. "You only had the worst kind of crush on her, then. You felt guilty that you had a thing for your best friend's girlfriend. Then they broke up, and you and she became friends, and the crush only got worse, and you fell in love with her more gradually, later."

"We've ridden together to all these gigs for months, and we *are* friends, and that's all," he said self-righteously. I didn't believe him, and I was pretty sure he knew that, but there was nothing he could do about it but brush it off. He sat back in his chair and tried his best to relax his shoulders so I wouldn't notice how antsy he'd gotten. Too late.

"To answer your question," he said, "no, I didn't want to be in this band just because Sam wanted me to, but that's part of it. He's had a really hard year."

Because of the fifty-two girlfriends? Poor baby.

Ace went on, "Anybody who knows him, even all the girls, will tell you he's a great guy, and they'll do anything for him, right up until they want to kill him."

I nodded. We were on the same page there.

"He literally got down on his knees and begged me to be in his band. I'm sure he'll do this to you, too, at some point, if he hasn't already. In public. When he did it to me in the football locker room, I said yes. And now . . . God, we're all fighting like cats and dogs, but I can't imagine *not* playing in this band. I mean, I loved playing in my brother's band. But the bar last night had an energy, you know?"

"I think that was from the bachelorette party."

He eyed me like he didn't believe me, waiting for me to admit the truth.

After a long pause, I admitted, "Fine. I felt it, too."

Watching me over the rim of his glass, he drank the rest of his tea, then glanced at his watch. "It's time for Sam to wrap up. I have a family reunion to get to."

"Oooh," I said. "Good food?"

"You got that right." He stood as carefully as he'd sat, stirring not a single wave in my tea. "Do you want me to tell him you're up here?"

Applause broke out below us. Sam had ended a song. He said a brief thank-you and started the next tune as if impatient with the crowd's response. All he wanted to do was play some more.

I said, "Yes."

Ace returned to his post next to Sam, and I passed another quarter hour there by myself, listening to Sam's voice, contemplating how little he needed me and how long it would take him to realize that whatever I contributed to his band wasn't worth the trouble. Finally he nodded to the crowd and started to scrape and stack the money from his open guitar case into his pockets. Ace glanced up at me once more. They both disappeared under the deck where I was sitting.

I made my way back down through the building and onto the sidewalk, where Sam was waiting for me.

"Hey," he said, half smiling.

"Hey," I said.

He nodded to my fiddle case. "Why didn't you come play with me?" Immediately he rolled his eyes at himself. "That's not what I meant."

I didn't point out that if he was constantly hearing double entendres in his own words, he had a dirtier mind than he wanted to let on. Sam having a dirty mind was okay with me. It was adorable, actually, as long as his mind was on me. "You didn't really want me to play with you. You were a soloist today."

He shrugged. "I didn't have to be. I always like company. I always like *your* company." He leaned down and, before I could protest or remind him I was still mad at him, kissed my cheek. "You look beautiful."

I smiled demurely and said, "Thank you."

"I hope you're not planning on wearing that to the gig tonight, though. You look like L.A., not Nashville. Where are you parked?"

Without a word, I pointed up the street toward both our cars. I didn't really think he assumed I was playing with him tonight. He just hoped so. He thought that in saying it, it might come true. Now that I hadn't protested what he said, he would use that against me later. And I didn't care. His arguments worked on me only if I let them.

Seeming to sense that he'd overstepped his bounds, he eyed me as we moseyed up the sidewalk. "Ace said you talked a few minutes ago. He said you might play with us after all."

"Hm," I said noncommittally.

"Charlotte said she called you, and that conversation didn't go over as well."

"Hm," I said again, finally relaxing my hauteur to glance over at him. Beads of sweat balanced at his hairline. To make him sweat a little longer, I changed the subject. "Charlotte said you wear your heart on your sleeve."

He craned his neck to peer down his arm and lifted his sleeve up with the other hand as if to get a better look.

"You sang all those songs this afternoon with such emotion."

"Thanks," he said, as though I'd complimented him on his confident stage presence or the mellow tone of his voice, something he'd worked on.

"I was confused by that," I said. "Those songs were about getting married. Getting divorced. Stuff that older people have been through and you haven't. Take 'Remember When,' for instance."

He looked surprised. "You were listening that long?"

I brushed his question off. "What were you thinking about when you sang that? You said last night that you had to be in the right mind-set to sing. I didn't *think* you were saying that just to sneak a kiss."

"Hm," he murmured, imitating me. The longer I was around him, the smarter I was afraid he was. I'd thought I was making him sweat a little, but it might have been the other way around.

"When you sang Alan Jackson," I went on, "you weren't remembering getting married, obviously, or having kids."

A crowd blocked the sidewalk ahead. They were listening to a banjo player and a guitarist who stood on the front steps of a saloon, playing a mini-set to entice people inside. Automatically, Sam took my elbow as I stepped from the curb down to the street in my high heels, but he was looking back over his shoulder at the musicians. The banjo player gave him a little nod.

Supporting me as I stepped back up on the sidewalk, Sam said, "I guess I was thinking about Alan Jackson himself. Being him. You know, he dropped out of Newnan High School south of Atlanta and married his high school sweetheart. His wife was working as an airline stewardess when she saw Glen Campbell and gave him Jackson's demo tape, which is truly how Jackson got his start: through luck and a lover."

"Right." I knew this story. Everybody in Nashville did. It was why we dreamed of playing the bars on Broadway, where a country legend might drop in and change our lives with one phone call. It was why my parents had instructed me to share the stage with anyone who asked, on the off chance it might be Shania Twain.

"Jackson dragged his wife to Nashville and eventually made it as a country star," Sam said. "So when I sing his song, I'm thinking about the fact that they fell in love with each other way before he was famous. How hard it was for them at first, and how easy it is now. What a relief it must be that they can pay for their kids to go to college instead of crossing their fingers that their kids are smart enough, or good enough at music, to get a scholarship."

"So you think he wrote the song about his real life?" I asked.

"I don't know where else it would come from. Some of the details aren't right, though. In the song, they aren't getting along, but then they have kids and everything's all right again. In real life, having a baby doesn't solve anything. It just causes more problems." He sounded so high-and-mighty that I was about to ask him exactly how much he'd been watching those reality TV shows about teen pregnancy when he went on, "If you're an alcoholic, the last thing you should do is get your wife pregnant. You should go to rehab instead. Let your wife make a clean break and leave you. Don't try to charm her back to you. She can live happily ever after and have a baby with someone else. The baby won't know the difference. He'll probably be a lot better off."

"Wait. You lost me. Alan Jackson is an alcoholic?"

"No. Sorry," he said, waving away the idea with his free hand not carrying the guitar case. "I'm talking about my dad. I wear my heart on my sleeve, remember?" He said this pleasantly as ever, but he plodded up the hill a little more quickly after that.

I wanted to change the subject as much as he did. So I teased him, "Speaking of which. Did I hear your voice break a little at the beginning of that song, when you reached the lyrics about making love to your girlfriend, how you were each other's first?"

I'd meant the question as a flirtatious ribbing. I never meant for him to look over at me with his dark eyes wide with horror. He muttered, "I don't think so," quickly checked both ways for traffic, and stepped into the street.

I trailed him on my high heels, wondering what can of worms I'd opened. My first thought was that he was horrified at my flirting—and the very suggestion that he would make love to *me*. But that didn't seem right. He was shocked because he'd thought I was bringing up something I knew, something that had happened to him. And it stood to reason that he'd lost his virginity with one girlfriend or other, seeing as how he'd had twenty-six of them.

"Sam," I called.

"What," he answered without turning around.

"My car's back down there, and so's your truck."

"I am so sorry!" he exclaimed, turning around. "I forgot you're dressed like L.A. in your . . ." His voice trailed off as he eyed my high heels, then let his gaze travel up my legs. Forcing his eyes to my face again, he said, "I just need to go right up here to deliver something, but you don't have to come with me."

"I'll come with you." When I caught up with him and we turned to resume our trek, I asked, "If you want to make it in this business, why don't you try out for one of those singing reality shows? You'd win."

"Those contracts are too restrictive," he said immediately. He'd thought about this a lot, and probably got asked this a lot, too. "You're only successful if they decide you're going to be. Kelly Clarkson was the first. She wrote a lot of her own songs, so she had a leg up. But when she decided to do something different for her third album, the record company dropped their support. She had to struggle back. If you go on those shows, you have to agree ahead of time to whatever contract they offer you. You have no control over the exposure you get or the songs you sing, at least at first, so you really wouldn't have any control over your own career. If you're going to get no support from the company, you might as well not sign a contract. You go from your name meaning nothing to your name being a joke. I'll bet we can't even recall today who most of those winners have been."

In protest, I named the winner who'd become a household name in country music: "Carrie Underwood."

"Exactly," he said, pointing at me, "and what song did she get?" He gestured to the church we'd reached on our hike up the hill. "'Jesus, Take the Wheel.' That is a great song. It has a good melody and a good story hook, plus Jesus. Country music fans love their Jesus. If all she'd had was 'Some Hearts' or 'Good Girl,' I don't know that she'd be as big today, but the record company saw fit to give her Jesus." He turned and walked up the sidewalk toward the church's front door.

"So you might not get the Jesus tune with the great hook," I acknowledged, following him, "but somebody would be feeding you songs. At least you'd have a chance. You're so talented, Sam." Out of the blue, I was pleading with the back of his T-shirt, wanting him to be successful, wanting him to pursue that without threatening my college career as collateral damage. "You could make it big with your band, or more likely as a solo artist. I honestly don't see what you have the band for."

"Help me out here." He shoved his hand in the pocket of his shorts and pulled out his handkerchief, which he gave to me. "The thing is, I don't want to be this big head." He curved his hands around either side of a wide imaginary circle to show the potential for his big head, possibly on an album cover. Then he pulled an empty plastic bag out of his pocket and put that in my outstretched hand, too. "I want to jam, like last night. I want to look behind me to see if Charlotte's ready, and look over at Ace to see what he's going to do, and point to you for a solo, and listen while you take off."

I understood. I'd always thought of bluegrass musicians as interchangeable, like the tribute bands at the mall, but that's not what he wanted. I said, "You want the band to be like a family."

"The one I have at home definitely isn't working, so, maybe." After a glance around the sidewalk to make sure no scary men were lurking, he pulled wads of cash, his take from busking, out of his other pocket. He dropped them in the plastic bag I was holding out for him.

"The problem with feeling like your band is a family," I said, "is that when you have another kind of relationship within the band and that relationship goes south, the whole band suffers. Ace and I were talking about you and Charlotte."

"That's . . ." Sam was tactful, and I could tell he was searching for a polite way to explain as he shoved his hand deep into his pocket to make sure he hadn't missed any bills. "That's on Charlotte's end."

"No matter whose fault it is, it's there. And for that reason, if you and I are going to play together, I don't think we should pursue another sort of relationship." It pained me to say it, but better to cut us off now than later, when he'd broken my heart.

I expected him to gape at me and then protest there on the church steps, but he only gave me a baleful glance and murmured, "Thank you," as he took the bag from me. Sealing it, he said, "Luckily, you have repeatedly stated that you're not going to be in my band. We can pursue any kind of relationship we want." He turned and stuffed the bag through the mail slot in the church's massive front door.

Now *I* gaped at *him,* then shoved the door, then jerked the large iron ring that served as a handle. The door was locked. "Sam! How much money did you just give to that church?"

He blinked at me, then lifted the mail flap and peeked through the slot. "I didn't count it. Why?"

"I didn't peg you for a religious person."

"I'm not."

"Or a giving person."

"Thanks."

"I just mean—"

"That you'd expect me to buy a new amp with it?" He shrugged. "I'm cheating a homeless person out of panhandling money. This is my way of giving it back. The church feeds them sometimes. You're not supposed to give cash to the homeless in case they buy booze with it. Come on." He took my hand.

I didn't pull away. We really *were* playing with each other, toying and testing. I let him swing my hand a little as we made our way back down the hill toward the lot where we'd parked.

"You have a great voice, too, you know," he said. "It's not very strong, but if that was your goal, you could take lessons."

This wasn't what I'd expected him to say. I walked beside him in stunned silence. His hand around mine now seemed ironic.

"That didn't come out right," he said. "I didn't mean to insult you."

"You're not taking it back, either."

He turned to me as we walked, watching me silently.

"Wow. Nobody ever told me that before." With a few words from him, I was reevaluating everything that had happened between Julie and me. "I guess the record company picked my sister because her voice was stronger. And here I thought it was just because she was the one singing melody and getting the attention—and that was only because she got confused when she sang harmony. Nobody ever sat me down and said, 'Julie is a better singer than you.'"

"You have the ideal voice for harmony, high and sweet, and you have perfect pitch. I would kill for perfect pitch." He squeezed my hand. "Just because she got a development deal doesn't mean anything is going to come of it. A lot of those deals never pan out. The singer drags herself back to town with her tail between her legs."

That was not going to happen to Julie. Her development deal had panned out just fine. And the instant I said this to Sam, he would never leave me alone about using her as a door into the industry.

As we walked down Broadway hand in hand, I felt the strangest sense of peace. *Resignation* might have been a better word. Sam hadn't meant to insult me when he said my voice wasn't strong, and he hadn't. He'd opened my eyes. I was seeing everything, including myself, more clearly than I had in a year.

And my relationship with him was the clearest of all. In the next few days he would start hearing Julie on the radio and find out exactly what her development deal had turned into, and how successful she was about to become. Everything would change then. For now, Sam was mine, and I would enjoy this moment.

He dropped my hand and put his arm lightly around my shoulders. "Bailey, you've been avoiding the subject, but please come play with us tonight. I want to play with you. And I just want to be around you. You're the only person I know on Earth that I can have a conversation about songwriting with who doesn't have sideburns." He reached around to touch my other shoulder and stop me. "Be my friend and play with me, please." He wore a pitiful face with his bottom lip poked out. "Just this once."

"Just this once," I mocked him. "That's what you said last night. Repeatedly."

"It *is* for just this once," he insisted. "Every time. It's like a movie rental at one of those kiosks. There's no contract to sign or membership fee. I'm not asking you for anything beyond tonight."

"Okay," I said.

His lips parted. He was ready to argue with me. He didn't seem to know what to do with my agreement. Finally he repeated, "Okay," and we rounded the corner to our parking lot.

He glanced at his watch. "The gig isn't for hours. What say we grab some dinner? Then I have to keep a promise. It won't take long. You can come with me. And then we can swing by your place and let you change." He nodded to my shoes.

"What about you?" I gestured to his regular-guy, not-a-country-crooner-wear.

"Normally I wouldn't go in this," he said, looking down and brushing an imaginary piece of lint from his T-shirt, "but nobody's going to be looking at me anyway." He unlocked his truck and opened the door for me. "They're looking at you."

9

After twenty minutes on the interstate pointed south of town, we pulled off and stopped at a meat and three that looked a bit dubious to me from the outside. Sam said he'd eaten there a million times, though, and the nearly full parking lot indicated he wasn't the only fan. As it turned out, he was right and I was wrong. We stuffed ourselves with black-eyed peas and collards and sweet potatoes like candy.

Between bites I asked, "Is there something going on between Ace and Charlotte?"

He seemed surprised. "Not that I know of. Why?"

"They rode to the gig together last night. I got the impression they're used to doing that."

He shrugged. "She doesn't have a car. He can have any car he wants on loan, anytime. They can get her whole drum set in the back of a minivan. My truck bed is open. We couldn't stop anywhere if we wanted to. We'd be in trouble if it rained." He sipped his tea, eyeing me over the rim of the glass. "Do *you* think there's something going on between them?"

"I think Ace has a thing for Charlotte, and Charlotte has a thing for you."

He grimaced. "I don't want to hear it."

I nodded slowly, thinking about the near-date we were on, and everything Charlotte had warned me about. "I hear you've had fifty-two girlfriends in the past year."

He rolled his eyes. "I wish people would stop saying that. I don't know who started it, but it's an exaggeration. I doubt I've dated half that."

"So, more like twenty-six?" I echoed Ace.

Sam shrugged noncommittally, then busied himself with scraping the last forkfuls of food off his plate. He changed the subject to a new song we'd heard on the country station as we drove down here . . . and in midsentence a tune came to me, and lyrics using the trope of the twenty-six girlfriends. I pulled my notebook out of my purse. Angling it carefully so he couldn't see the staffs, but holding my body casually enough that I hoped I didn't look like I was trying to hide anything, I scribbled this idea. The illustrations in colored pencil would have to come later. "Just writing something down," I said defensively when he spoke, though I hadn't registered what he'd said.

"Bailey." He put his hand on my shoulder. Looking up from my notebook for the first time, I realized the restaurant crowd had thinned. He was holding a to-go box like he'd had time to go all the way through the buffet line again.

"Still hungry?" I laughed. Quickly I flipped my notebook closed and slipped it into my purse.

"I promised my mom I'd pick her up some dinner." When we got back in the truck, he handed me the foam box to balance on my bare knees. "I could tell she felt down when she went in to work today. She's worked a month straight at the car plant without a day off."

"What?" I exclaimed. "Why?"

"They have a lot of orders. The opposite problem is that they get laid off because they don't have enough orders. This is hard, but trust me, it's better."

"I don't get it," I said. "I thought auto workers had unions to protect them from that kind of thing."

"They have unions up north, in Detroit. But the car factories moved to the South to get away from the unions. Maybe the workers don't need them anymore. I mean, yeah, my mom has to work all the time, but she gets paid for it. She gets time and a half and sometimes double time, and I guarantee you no hourly worker in Tennessee has ever seen base pay like this before."

He slowed down and waved to the uniformed man in a guardhouse, who grinned. He parked in an open space on the fringe of the largest parking lot I'd ever seen. The asphalt gave off waves of heat and scent as we hiked across the lot toward the vast factory building. Out front, workers in jeans and uniform polo shirts smoked cigarettes or played peekaboo with visiting toddlers or accepted dinner from family members. As we approached, a tiny, pretty blond lady who looked nothing like Sam left her chat with a group of workers and came toward him with her arms out.

He hugged her without embarrassment and kept his arm around her as he pointed her toward me. "Mom, this is Bailey Wright."

"Oh! Very nice to meet you." She shook my hand. Her eyes drifted to the right and took in my asymmetrical haircut. Immediately she turned back to Sam. I knew what she was thinking. She wanted to be nice, but she saw no need to invest time in getting to know me, because I would be replaced next week. I was Girlfriend Twenty-seven.

"You know that job your father wanted you to get?" she asked him.

The smile never left Sam's lips, but he wasn't smiling with his eyes anymore. "Yeah, I know that job my father wanted me to get."

"Jimmy says he has an opening for you on the loading dock, but you have to come in for an interview tomorrow or Tuesday. He wouldn't grill you or anything. The interview just has to be down on paper. The Japanese want things done a certain way. It's not like a Ford plant."

Still smiling, Sam nodded. "I have something else to do tomorrow and Tuesday and every other day Jimmy is available to interview me."

His mom gave him a warning look. "You have to do something this summer, Sam. Your father thinks this job would be great experience when you switch your major from music to engineering." She grinned, a joke, and showed him her crossed fingers.

"If my father thinks working on a loading dock would be such great experience," Sam growled, and I took a step back because I'd never heard this angry tone from him before, "my father should come interview with Jimmy tomorrow or Tuesday. I'll bet he's not busy."

His mom looked hurt, like he'd insulted her as well as Mr. Hardiman. Her gaze slid to me, then back to Sam. "Seriously, Sam. He's going to make you get a job or get out. This wouldn't have anything to do with the music career you're not supposed to be pursuing, would it?"

Sam took a deep breath through his nose and let it out slowly. Then he leaned down, kissed her cheek, and took the box of food from me to hand to her. "There's banana pudding."

"Oh, baby!" she exclaimed. "Bless your heart! Thank you, Sam."

He gave her a halfhearted wave as he turned, and we crossed

the parking lot to his truck again. I knew he was in a terrible mood because he went a whole two minutes without saying anything, which was probably a record for him.

We were through the gate, down the road, and back on the interstate toward Nashville before he burst out, "She's as high as she can go in the factory without a college degree. In fact, they've told her they'll pay for her to go to college. But there's no way she could do that, working like she does. She's exhausted. She'd have to quit temporarily. There's no guarantee the job would be waiting for her when she got back. My dad would have to get a real job." He paused. "Which might be good. He wouldn't get to play gigs for a living, but he wouldn't get to drink like he does, either."

I nodded. He was talking more to himself than to me. I stayed quiet and watched the emotions pass across his face.

"Maybe it will be good for my parents when I go to Vandy in August and move out of the house," he said. "Maybe I've been taking up some of the slack for both of them. I've always thought I was helping them out, but I've really just been the glue holding them together when they would have been better off apart all along."

I nodded, but I had no idea. My parents got along great. They were of one mind when they ditched me.

Sam ran one hand back through his dark waves. "My mom was never able to make him go to rehab, but she dragged us all into counseling. My reaction to everything the counselors said was 'No way.' I did *not* make excuses for my dad. I did *not* help my dad hide his drinking. Which is exactly what they said my reaction would be. I thought they were a bunch of smart-asses at the time. But now my dad is sober*er* by a long shot, and still not sober. At eighteen you can see over some walls into other rooms, and you start to wonder whether the adults were right all along. It's disorienting."

"Does that mean you're going to interview with Jimmy for that loading dock job?"

He laughed then. The dark cloud around him lifted. He was happy-go-lucky Sam again, driving his truck through a steamy June evening, into a Tennessee sunset. "I guess we'll swing by your granddad's house now so you can change."

"You know what?" I was afraid to go back. My granddad had let me out of the house with the understanding that I would be with Sam, who seemed to be my carte blanche. I didn't want to push my luck by going back to switch from an L.A. to a Nashville outfit, then coming up with an excuse for the wardrobe change. I hadn't forgotten his suspicious look at me that afternoon when I walked out with my fiddle. "Since we're on this side of town, let's just pop into my parents' house. It's the mother lode of hokey Nashville-wear."

Just a few miles outside the city, my parents' neighborhood was a green and gorgeous series of rolling hills and small farms, a stark contrast to the neon lights of Broadway. I'd always loved it here. After being away for a week, I still thought it was beautiful, but the steam hanging in the air seemed sinister. As we passed, I didn't point out the pond Toby had sunk his car in.

Sam's truck crunched to a stop on the gravel driveway, in front of the newish farmhouse built to look like an oldish farmhouse. As I stepped out, something seemed very wrong, like I was visiting my deserted house again after the zombie apocalypse. Scanning the acres of pasture around us, I realized what the difference was. "My parents weren't going to be here much this year, so they sold all the animals." What had been a cacophony of off-key animal sounds before was now dead silence, save for the hot wind in the trees and the ominous dinging of the wind chimes hanging from the porch ceiling. Wind chimes were the bane of my existence because they weren't tuned to actual notes. I had told my parents this and they had left the chimes up.

I fished my keys from my purse and climbed the wooden steps. "Wave to the security camera," I told Sam behind me. I flashed a hand toward the lens hidden in one upper corner of the porch. "I want them to know I know they know I'm here. God forbid they catch me bringing a boy over here to adjust my wardrobe."

"That is ridiculous," Sam said, following me through the kitchen. "I am Grandpa-approved."

It wasn't until I crossed the den that I realized what a bad idea this had been. Sam was going to find out about Julie's success sooner or later. Then our relationship, such as it was, would be over. I'd been hoping it would happen later rather than sooner. But the trappings of Julie's upcoming career were everywhere. On the sofa tables sat framed photos of country megastars hugging her after she'd opened concerts for them. My mom had even framed the program from her biggest concert so far, as if to say, *I am so proud! My baby got third billing!* My tension mounted until I almost wished Sam would come to the realization that I'd been lying to him, and we could get the awful breakup over with before we were ever really together.

He didn't seem to see the evidence against me, however. He saw photos of *me* with the stars at bluegrass festivals. As we mounted the stairs, he paused at a picture of me posing with my fiddle, decked out in cowgirl hat and shirt and boots and square-dancing skirt, age five.

"Awww," he said, as though I'd been the most adorable child alive. For the hundredth time in a little over a day, my heart opened for him.

I'd told him to wave to the camera so my parents would know our visit was innocent. I'd implied to him that of *course* it was innocent and I never expected anything else to happen between us. But I wished he'd argued with me or at least acted hurt. I walked more slowly than usual up the stairs, making sure he caught up with me, wishing he would "accidentally" bump into me. I listened for his breathing behind me, so focused on his whereabouts that I hardly noticed my own until I'd reached my room. It was silly, but I knew that for the next few nights I would have fantasies about Sam and me getting too close for comfort on that carpeted stairway.

I was hyperaware of what he would see when he walked behind me into my room, but I shouldn't have worried. Except for Julie, I had no secrets from him. My room looked exactly as it should, with the evidence of bluegrass festivals—posters, trophies, and photos—cluttering the room, but it all stopped this time last year. It was like my life had been put on pause.

"You can have a seat," I said casually, gesturing to my desk chair, my comfy reading chair in the corner, and my bed. I walked into my closet and rifled through the remaining dress bags, pulling out an outfit that said *I am the fiddler in a rockabilly band* or possibly *I am insane.* I walked back into the room to show it to Sam.

Instead of sitting in a chair or lounging across my bed like a too-forward boy in a teen movie, he still stood awkwardly with his arms crossed exactly where I'd left him in the middle of the room. I got this vibe from Sam sometimes: deep down he was a gentleman, but he kept getting confounded by his striking looks. Women must throw themselves at him. It was possible the twenty-six girlfriends hadn't been his fault.

For a moment he stared at the dress I was holding up as if he didn't really see it and he'd been thinking hard about something else. He blinked. "Oh. Yeah, that's okay. May I look?"

After doing a quick mental inventory of my closet and finding nothing embarrassing either way—no dolls that looked like I was still taking care of them and laying them down to sleep on their shelves at night, but also no pot pipes—I swept my arm in that direction: *Be my guest.* The closet wasn't big enough for both of us to stand in. I walked over to my desk and looked through the junk mail I hadn't bothered to read the weekend I got in so much trouble.

Because I was about to enter college, theoretically, I received a lot of catalogs trying to sell me college clothes and college bedroom sets. I flipped through one without picking it up from the desk, like it had nothing to do with me. Nice Girls in the photos towed pallets of the contents of their new dorm rooms, all matching in a pink flowered theme or a purple butterfly theme, across the quad. Nice Boys waved to them from the vaulted doorways of what were supposed to be dorms but looked like the original home of the Grand Ole Opry, the Ryman Auditorium, which had started life as a church.

"This," Sam called. He held up a shirt Julie had given me as a joke, printed with a cowboy boot and "NashVegas" in loopy letters, all outlined in sequins.

I took the shirt from him. Closing myself alone inside the closet, I exchanged the L.A. blouse I had on for the Nashville shirt that turned me into Sam's centerpiece. After swapping my heels for shiny white cowgirl boots, I opened the door to show him.

He was staring at the doorway, waiting. "Oh, yeah." His whole face brightened with his smile. "That's it. Do you have a skirt?"

Obligingly I retreated into the closet and came out in a miniskirt with an electrified print that I'd thought fit my image last year but I'd never had the courage to wear.

"Yes, ma'am," Sam said, the admiration evident in his voice. "You should always wear skirts onstage. That should be your thing." He held out his hand to me. "Ready?"

♪ ♫ ♪

It seemed to me that the gig was over almost before it started. I had almost forgotten how time could fly when I was performing. I was tempted to put down the heel of my cowgirl boot to step on the night and anchor it there before it slipped away.

We played completely different songs from the ones the night before. When Sam texted me the playlist and I asked him about it, he said, "It's Sunday. A lot of tourists are here for the weekend. If they liked us last night, they might come back tonight, and we need to be playing something different so they don't get bored. A lot of the bands around here are great, but they've got a tiny repertoire. We have to be better." He glanced up at me, then grudgingly added, "My dad taught me that."

Ace's family reunion came. He had to whisper to one college girl from the night before that he couldn't take off his shirt again because his mom was in the audience, but generally we were under a gag order, forbidden to admit that Ace's relatives belonged to him. We wanted the bar to think we were drawing a crowd because of our actual talent. The ploy seemed to work. Once while I played staccato notes, keeping time with Sam's guitar break, I saw the bearded owner who'd been talking to Sam the night before looking with obvious satisfaction over the whole bottom floor succumbing to a line dance that Ace's aunts had started.

When ten o'clock rolled around and we took our break, I gazed up the street toward the abandoned buildings and new construction, looked at Sam scowling at me, and dropped my phone back into my purse. I couldn't get far enough away from the noise of the bar to make my call to Julie without putting Sam's life and mine in danger. And after she'd ignored my calls and voice mails for a full week, I decided she wasn't worth it. If she wanted to talk to me, she knew how.

We ended the night on a high note, with the crowd clamoring for more and complaining as we vacated the stage for the next scheduled band. The bearded owner asked us back again. This time, rather than dividing the tips in Ace's van and sending him and Charlotte on their way, Sam suggested we grab a bite at an all-night restaurant on the edge of the District. I could tell by the way he glanced uneasily at me that he was concerned his line to me about playing with the band "just this once" was wearing thin.

Ace and Charlotte parked the van back in the lot where they'd already paid for the night. Sam and I walked up the hill and stowed our instruments in my car and his truck. We waited for Ace and Charlotte outside the bustling dive. Just as I spied them hiking up the sidewalk together, a train sounded its horn a few blocks over. I closed one eye and made a face and hoped Sam didn't think I was reacting to the idea he was excitedly telling me about for a new soul cover tune.

He stopped in the middle of what he was saying and stared down at me. "It's the train, isn't it?"

"Yes, ugh!" I exclaimed. The relief in my voice didn't begin to match the relief I felt. Either Sam's own pitch was close to perfect, or he wanted mine badly enough that he'd thought through the pros and the cons. He understood how I experienced loud, inescapable, off-key tritones, whereas everybody else thought I was making my discomfort up.

Chuckling down at me, he placed his warm hands over my ears, shutting out the plaintive moan of the train.

A second before, the sidewalk had been crowded with people passing in and out of the restaurant, and I'd been aware of the diners on the other side of the glass storefront. Suddenly they were all gone. Sam and I were the only two people in the world. I'd felt close to him while we played for the past two hours. We'd flirted with each other for hours before that. But now his dark eyes held mine and lost all their humor. Tingles raced across my skin.

"Poor thing," he said in a low, sexy tone.

And then, as quickly as the moment had come, it was gone again. He slid his hands off me and turned away in one movement. Charlotte and Ace had almost reached us. Sam's body had shielded them from seeing the way he touched me.

I tried not to overthink this as we all took a booth in the restaurant, flanked on one side by a table of tipsy adults who giggled over their barbecue sandwiches, and on the other by teenagers who only wished they could find a way into the Broadway bars. A barbecue sandwich here was as close as they could get. When I slid in beside the window so we could order our own late-night munchies, Sam took the seat across from me, leaving Charlotte to sit next to him. But I didn't honestly think he had a thing for Charlotte anymore. He had a thing for his band. In deferring to Charlotte's happiness by taking his hands off me, he was only trying to keep the peace.

While we ate, I noticed Sam picked at his fries. This didn't make me self-conscious about eating my own. I'd felt so lonely and stressed and skipped so many meals when my mom was out of town during the past year that I figured an extra plate of fries couldn't hurt me now. But Sam's lack of an appetite did make me wonder again what he was up to with this sudden band camaraderie. He finally popped a fry into his mouth, almost as a prop for his casual act, then chewed and swallowed and asked Ace, "Did your dad say the video turned out okay?"

"No, no, no," I insisted, "what video?"

"The picture is a little dark because of the low lighting and the neon," Ace said, eyeing me, "but the sound is perfect."

"What video?" I demanded again.

"I told you," Sam said as innocently as his guilt would allow. "You can send in a video audition for a lot of the Broadway bars. One of them told me to make the band more special and try again."

I nodded, biting my lip to keep from bursting into a recitation of exactly what I thought of Sam. He'd brought me here to break it to me that he'd moved on to the next stage of his plan for the band, whether I liked it or not. He was telling me in the crowded restaurant, with Ace and Charlotte present, in the hope I wouldn't make as much of a scene.

"What part of 'no' didn't you understand, Sam?" I asked.

He eyed me steadily. "The part where you were wrong."

Infuriated, I nodded. "So you'll do anything you want, you'll lie to anyone about anything, if you think you're right and they're wrong."

"Yes!" he exclaimed, exasperated, like this was *obvious*.

"Why do you keep trying to convince me to do this?" I leaned toward him across the table. "I've told you what my parents are going to take away from me." I was half waiting for Ace and Charlotte to gasp and ask about this strange deal with my parents. When they didn't, I knew Sam had already told them.

"Yes, but they're wrong to do that," Sam said levelly, meeting my gaze while he ate another fry.

"Just because you think they're wrong doesn't mean they're

not going to do it." My voice rose. I had a fleeting thought that my parents' ban on misbehaving in public probably included making a scene in late-night restaurants, but I was so angry that I couldn't help it. "God, Sam! I swear the only way you would take anything like that seriously is if it happened to *you*. If it happens to anybody else, for you it's like it didn't happen."

"Nothing's happened, Bailey," he said soothingly—except I knew he wasn't really trying to soothe me but rather to make me feel crazy, because he never stopped eating French fries. "Your parents haven't found out."

"They will," I insisted. "You keep telling me, 'Just one more gig. Just one more gig.' But I know what you really want. It's like you're saying, 'Just let me touch it. That's as far as we'll go.'"

I'd meant it as an angry joke. We were eighteen years old, adults. We could make sex jokes to each other.

He didn't laugh. His eyes widened. He looked cornered, like a tender fourteen-year-old boy overwhelmed by a forward girl. He put his elbow on the table and balanced his temple on his fingers as though he had a headache. Then he cut his eyes sideways at Charlotte, as if she had anything to do with the conversation.

"You obviously know what you're talking about," Charlotte said.

"What?" Sam asked sharply at the same time Ace turned to gape at her.

"Isn't that what she's doing?" Charlotte insisted. "Dressing like that"—she nodded to my tight NashVegas T-shirt—"acting like a tease, just to get a gig?"

"No," I said so calmly I was proud of myself. "You've gotten me mixed up with Sam."

Sam and Ace hardly seemed to notice my attempt to defuse her sharp comment. "Apologize," Sam told her. That rare angry edge had entered his voice, the one I'd heard at the factory.

Her mouth opened and her eyes widened like she was astonished he'd betrayed her. Then she gathered her wits and said haughtily, "It's true."

"Apologize," Ace repeated calmly but firmly.

Charlotte turned to look at Ace. Their eyes locked for a moment. Something passed between them.

She muttered, "Sorry," but she wasn't looking at me as she said it. She was rolling her eyes.

Still glaring at Charlotte, Sam sighed a huge sigh, shoulders sagging so low against the back of the booth that I realized how tight and tense he'd been before. To me he said, "I told you from the beginning that I wanted this audition video. In case the bar calls me, we need to figure out when we're all available to play from now on."

"There's no 'from now on,'" I said instantly, holding my ground. "I told you, I'm not in your band."

"Are you quitting?" he challenged me.

As his dark eyes drilled into me, my adrenaline spiked, and for once it wasn't because of the yearning that took hold of me when he offered me a glance. It was a fight-or-flight reaction to a threat: the threat of never being able to play with the band again. I couldn't keep on playing with them, because my parents would find out eventually. I couldn't stop playing with them, because my heart would shrivel up and die. There was no solution to this problem. The only tool I had was putting off the decision.

"I can't quit the band," I said. "I'm not a member."

Charlotte raised her hand. "I don't like this game." She still wasn't looking at me. This time she wasn't looking at Ace or Sam, either. She stared above Ace's head at the far wall. But in the stubborn set of her jaw and the hard look in her strange blue-green eyes, I saw what I was doing to her. I wanted desperately to play with the band. So did she. She'd enjoyed the comfort of stability with the band before I showed up. I had thrown the band into a tizzy and ruined everything for her.

And I realized she was right. While I was in this limbo, so were they.

Echoing Sam, I sighed and relaxed my shoulders against the back of the booth, directing my gaze above his head at the Hatch Show Print poster of Johnny Cash so iconic that every business in town displayed a copy of it. "I can't tell you when I can play from now on," I said, "but I can tell you for . . ." I held up my hands while I thought about how long I might safely play with them without ruining my future. I was so deep in limbo that I couldn't even answer my own question. If they'd asked me two days ago, I would have said I couldn't play with them at all. The deeper I fell in love with the band's gigs, the longer the safe time stretched.

"A week?" Sam suggested.

I shook my head no.

"Five days?" Ace asked, exasperated. His words moved me more than anything Sam had said. Sam lived life in a constant state of near-exasperation, whereas Ace rarely showed any emotion at all. If even he was exasperated with me, I deserved it.

I owed him better. I owed them all better.

"Four days," I negotiated. Julie and my parents would be coming back to town tomorrow, but I would still be staying with my granddad so he could keep tabs on me, theoretically. They would be busy with concerts and parties for Julie's single release and the CMA Festival. That meant my parents would be even angrier if they found out I'd disobeyed a direct order right under their noses, when Julie's record company was so concerned about her image and theirs.

It also meant my parents would be totally preoccupied with Julie, my granddad would likely go with them to her concerts, and nobody would be watching me. If they cared so much about what I was doing, they ought to be monitoring me more closely. This would serve them right.

But there was one night I wasn't sure about. "Maybe not Tuesday." That was the day Julie's single was scheduled to hit stores. It was also the night of her Grand Ole Opry debut. The venue wasn't the biggest in Nashville. It certainly wouldn't get her as much exposure as her CMA Festival concerts on Thursday afternoon and Friday night. But it was the stage every country musician dreamed about playing on, and Julie had scored it for her single debut day. No matter how big her career got and where her tour took her, she would always remember this concert.

And I was still holding out hope that my family would invite me.

"Today's Sunday," Sam reminded me. "You can't say, 'Maybe not Tuesday.' Either you're in or you're out."

"Okay. Not Tuesday." Clearly Sam wasn't going to let me back out of a gig once I told him I was in. And I couldn't miss Julie's debut if I actually got invited. I could add that to my long list of items I would never forgive myself for.

Sam pushed his plate of fries away and turned his paper menu over. He looked around the table and then asked, "Anybody got a pen?"

I reached for my purse to pull out a pencil—carefully, without revealing my music notebook inside. Before I could open the flap, Charlotte produced a black permanent marker. As she handed it to him, I realized the marker must be how she was achieving the strange see-through effect of her scribbled black nail polish. I decided then that if we ever reached the point that she no longer pissed me off every time I looked at her, I would take her for a proper manicure.

Sam drew a calendar on the menu. "Not Tuesday," he muttered in grudging agreement. "But we already have something for Monday." He scribbled the gig on the calendar, then looked up at me. "It'll be fun. It's a surprise birthday party, a pool party! It's in Chattanooga. Though— Uh-oh."

"What?" Ace asked.

Sam's eyes never left me. "Are you working at the mall tomorrow? Could you get off a little early? Or if you're with Elvis, just walk out on him."

"I work there Tuesday through Saturday," I assured him. "Not tomorrow."

Slamming down Charlotte's marker, Sam put one hand on the edge of the table and one over his heart like he'd just averted a stress attack. Charlotte patted his shoulder in a way that made me want to pinch her.

He picked up the marker and tapped it on the calendar. "We won't get paid as much for the party as we do when we work for tips. And obviously, playing in Chattanooga won't do us any good when we're trying to make a name for ourselves in Nashville. If it helps us pick up more Chattanooga gigs, though, we could use those to fill holes in our schedule."

I stared at him, waiting for him to hear himself. He was doing it again, assuming I would play with the band permanently.

"What?" he asked when he looked up and saw my expression. Then he willfully misunderstood what it meant: "Yeah, you're right. If we're trying to fill holes in the schedule, Memphis would be better than Chattanooga, because there are so many record company connections over there." He looked back down at his calendar and stroked a few more words with Charlotte's marker. "I'm working on something here in town for Wednesday. And now we have the video. With any luck we'll be playing on Broadway by Thursday." It was hard to be skeptical when he beamed at all of us like this Broadway gig was a done deal. "Things are getting serious. It would be nice if we finally named the band something other than the Sam Hardiman Ego Trip." He winked at me. "How about Death Wish?"

"No way," Ace said. "Sounds like a heavy metal group."

Sam shrugged. "Redneck Death Wish, for clarity." As it rolled off his tongue, he grinned even bigger. "I like it!"

"No!" squealed Charlotte, wrinkling her nose.

He pointed at her. "We'll change it if you come up with something better." He glanced at his watch. "I'll give you a year."

Ace put up his hand to high-five Sam diagonally across the table. Charlotte rolled her eyes again, which made me feel a little less like her eye roll while apologizing to me had been an attack. The ice was broken then, and our conversation eased into how our performances had gone the last two nights, and what we could improve for our next three gigs. It was the first time we'd ever talked together as a band. Though the fight-or-flight feeling returned and the hair stood up on my arms, it wasn't as intense as it had been before. I made up my mind to enjoy the band while I had it, because I might never get it again.

At the same time, I wondered what effect my decision to join the band temporarily would have on my relationship, such as it was, with Sam. I'd told him we shouldn't date if we were in a band together. He'd said we could do anything we wanted because I'd insisted we *weren't* in a band together. And now that we were, at least for the next four days, the panicky feeling turned a sinister corner.

I picked up Charlotte's marker from Sam's menu-turned-calendar and reached across the table for Sam's shoulder. He was deep in conversation with Ace about changing the ending of one of our songs, but he offered his shoulder to me.

Using the marker, I drew a heart on his sleeve. I started with the heart itself, then surrounded it with dots and swirls like a henna tattoo, the kind of doodle I drew to decorate the songs in my music notebook that nobody would ever hear.

Sam still nodded at Ace. But as I finished the heart and backed away across the table, he held out the edge of his sleeve with two fingers so he could see it better. His dark eyes locked on me. My panicky feeling morphed into something like the caramel sundae Charlotte had ordered, sweet and irresistible.

Charlotte stayed in the conversation about music, too, but she managed to give me a pointed look up and down, telling me tele-pathically that she might have apologized for her tease comment, but she wasn't really sorry. She reached in front of me on the table and retrieved her marker.

Around midnight we all walked through the warm, heavy night to the lot where Sam's truck and my car were parked. Two abreast, I took the lead with Sam on the sidewalk, but there was no opening for us to return to the personal conversation we'd had while we were alone. The four of us were brainstorming for songs we could add to our playlist. What I really wanted was not just to talk with Sam but to make out with him like I had the night before, twenty-six girlfriends be damned. I would worry about them later.

But as we reached the lot and leaned against Sam's truck, chatting, I came to terms with the fact that it wasn't going to happen. Not tonight. He'd proven to me by now that he wouldn't risk an-gering Charlotte and tearing the band apart by publicly displaying his affection for me. Resigned, I stopped trying to make smoldering eye contact with him and even asked Ace, more than Charlotte, "Do y'all want a ride back to the van?" I didn't *want* to give them a ride—awkward—but I figured I'd better, since Sam's truck would be crowded with the three of them.

"Oh, we'll just ride with Sam," Charlotte piped up breezily. Obviously she looked forward to being crowded between Ace and Sam.

"See you tomorrow, Bailey," Ace said. He pushed Charlotte in front of him as they rounded Sam's truck to the passenger side and got in. I almost thought he was giving me time alone with Sam on purpose—or giving *Sam* time alone with *me*.

Sam squared himself in front of me. Looked down at me. Licked his lips. Turned to look over his shoulder at the cab of his truck, presumably to see whether Charlotte was watching us through the back window. I couldn't tell with the streetlights reflecting on the glass, and honestly I wasn't interested. Sam wasn't going to try anything while Charlotte was anywhere around.

The interesting thing was watching him struggle through it. The diffused lights from overhead softened his features and darkened the stubble on his face, but I clearly saw two embarrassed points of red flush his cheeks as he blinked slowly at me and thought about last night.

"We usually meet at Ace's dad's car lot and all drive together when we have a field trip out of town," he told me. "I could pick you up and take you there tomorrow afternoon."

"Sounds good," I said brightly, as if a gig was all I expected from him.

He lowered his brows at me and hesitated, unsure whether I was toying with him. I wasn't going to clarify. After feeling like I was stumbling around under his thumb all afternoon, I enjoyed finally taking the lead in this dance. My only response was to raise my eyebrows like I wasn't sure what he was waiting for, though electricity raced just underneath my skin because he was standing a few inches away.

"See you then," he said suddenly. Walking to his truck, he looked up at the sky, searching for strength. With his hand on the driver's door, he turned back to me. "You leave first, so I know you're safe, considering your death wish and all."

"Ha." I got into my car obediently, though, and drove off. Stopping at the intersection, I looked in my rearview mirror and saw that both Charlotte and Ace turned toward Sam, probably ribbing him about me, Girlfriend Twenty-seven. Sam stared straight ahead, watching my taillights until I turned the corner.

10

I climbed the steps of my parents' house, toward my room, but Sam stopped me with an arm encircling my waist. "Bailey," he breathed, gently flattening me against the wall. Above us, a framed photo of Julie and me in our bluegrass festival outfits creaked on its nail.

In reality, I was descending the steps inside my granddad's house. After a long morning of sanding guitars and sweeping the floor, my repeated fantasies about what Sam didn't do to me in my parents' house the previous night had become a lot more interesting than my real life. I wondered whether the bride from our gig was doing something similar, fantasizing about Sam while she made love to her David or wandered around her house or drove through her lunchtime commute, titillated in her compact car.

"I can't," I whispered, bracing one hand against Sam's chest to back him away. The hard pressure of his hands on my upper arms and his groin against mine never changed. He said in my ear, "I know you're holding back, Bailey. There's something you don't want me to know. Whatever it is, I promise it won't matter. I want you, and I know you want me, too. Let go and feel, just this once."

I let out a sigh agonized enough that my granddad heard me in the kitchen and asked me what was wrong as I crossed the show-room to the front door. "Nothing," I called back. "See you later."

"Here?" I asked, blocking Sam's hand with mine just before he unbuttoned my shorts.

Sam glanced down the carpeted stairs, then up. "You don't like risk?" he asked coyly.

"I—"

"That's okay. I want you to feel comfortable. Come on." He took my hand and led me up the stairs, away from the last portrait of Julie and me together at a festival. He put his hand on my bedroom doorknob and turned it. And in real life, I pulled open the front door—

—and jumped ten feet in the air, registering only a split second later what had startled me so badly. Sam was standing there with his eyes wide and his hands out to save me.

"Holy fuck!" I yelled at him.

He put his fists on his hips and eyed me skeptically. "Yeah, I get that a lot from the ladies."

"What's the matter?" my granddad hollered, concerned, but not concerned enough to turn off the polisher.

"It's just Sam," I yelled back.

"In my day, the young people didn't greet each other that way," my granddad called. Sam had a mysterious effect on him. He'd never attempted even this lame humor before.

"Bye," I yelled. Stepping out onto the front porch and pulling the door closed behind me, I explained to Sam, "You startled me. I was thinking about you."

He grinned. "I was thinking about you, too. I thought we could hang out before we need to leave for the gig."

"I can't," I told him, hoping he heard the sincere regret in my voice. "I was just leaving for a doctor's appointment."

"I'll go with you," he said.

"No, thanks."

"Why not?" His eyes were suddenly two dark points, his mouth drawn into a small, worried circle. "What's wrong?"

Surprised by his reaction, I put my hand over his heart to re-assure him. It raced under my fingertips. "Nothing's wrong," I said, self-consciously removing my hand again.

"Then why are you going?" he demanded.

"It's my annual exam."

"Then why can't I go?"

I'd just had a similar mortifying conversation with my grand-dad at breakfast. He hadn't wanted to go, but he'd demanded to know exactly where I was going and why. Exasperated, I enunci-ated every syllable so Sam would be embarrassed into backing off. "It's with the gy-ne-col-o-gist."

His face didn't change. He asked suspiciously, "If it's your an-nual exam, what happened a year ago that made you go in the first place? Wasn't that right when you got mad at your parents and went wild?"

I folded my arms. "Yeah, but not like you're implying. You're starting to sound like Elvis at the mall."

I'd intended that comment to shake Sam out of this strange worry and into anger. Anything was better than this intense stare he was giving me, like he knew something terrible had happened and I was keeping it from him.

"I'm a virgin," I blurted.

His shoulders sagged then, maybe with relief, maybe with defeat.

"Right," I said. "My mother wouldn't believe that, either. She's the one who suggested I get on the pill. She was worried I would embarrass the family further and she wouldn't be around to stop me. She made sure I took precautions."

Sam pulled a handkerchief out of the pocket of his shorts, wiped his palms, blotted his forehead, and stuffed the cloth back in his pocket before he told me, "I'm a virgin, too."

"*You're* a virgin? What about the twenty-six girlfriends?"

His dark eyes widened at me again, then slid toward the door. I felt my face flush, expecting my granddad to burst onto the porch to inform us that young people did not mention the V-word in his day.

After several tense moments with no telltale footsteps across the creaking wooden floor inside, Sam cleared his throat and said quietly, "Yes, I'm a virgin, despite the twenty-six girlfriends. It takes more than two weeks for me to make my move."

"Ha." My short syllable carried a huge amount of relief. I'd told myself I didn't care how serious he'd gotten with how many girls, but obviously I did.

"I'm sorry I made you admit that," he said. "I thought . . . I don't know what I thought. I just worry sometimes. Last year I was in counseling for worrying."

I winced. "You were?" Sam was so candid about his dark side, and it always took me by surprise. It was so easy to forget when he sang, and when he smiled. When he'd told me his whole family had been in counseling because of his dad's problems, I'd assumed that was long ago, not last year.

"Yeah. It was a group of sad and depressed teenagers. That's how I knew there was something wrong with you as soon as I met you at the mall. You act like those girls sometimes. It's like you want to laugh, but it gets caught here." He touched my chin. "Or maybe here." He touched the back of my head. Then, because of the way I was looking at him, he slowly put his hand down.

"Are you still in counseling?" I ventured.

"No, I got kicked out. I asked a girl on a date." He laughed. "We weren't supposed to do that. They *said* they'd told us that up front, but I never read the fine print. What kind of crazy group is it if there are girls in it but you can't date them?"

"The world has gone mad," I said.

He pointed at me. "That's what I told them!" He gestured down the steps through the yard, toward his truck parked at the bottom of the hill. "So, I'm driving you to your appointment."

"Oh." I wrinkled my nose. "You're *not* going into the exam room with me."

"Oh, God, no!" he exclaimed. "I would pass out."

"Well, the doctor isn't going to—"

"No," he cut me off. "I'll just be there for you in the waiting room." Walking down the steps in front of me, he hugged himself tightly.

"You don't have to go, Sam," I protested. "You look so uncomfortable right now."

"I like doing things that make me uncomfortable. I try not to have a comfort zone." He stopped on the stairs. "You know what? It might get late, and we need to leave early enough to make it to Chattanooga even if there's traffic. We can't be late to a gig. Why don't you go ahead and get your bathing suit?"

"Bathing suit!" I exclaimed.

"It's a pool party!" he reminded me, exasperated. He leaned in and whispered, "And get your fiddle."

I galloped back inside, tossing to my granddad that Sam was taking me to a pool party. Technically, not a lie. I stuffed my bikini and a towel and my fiddle case into my beach bag together and ran down the steps to Sam's truck before my granddad could get suspicious.

No, *I* was the one suspicious. After I explained where my doctor's office was and Sam started down the tree-lined street, I said, "I have a theory."

"What's your theory?" Sam asked gamely.

"You don't *really* have a burning desire to go with me to the doctor's office. Boys are afraid of anything having to do with the inner workings of girl parts. I've seen them go out of their way to avoid touching brand-new, unopened boxes of tampons. You just want an excuse to hang out with me until the gig tonight."

He gave me a devilish grin. "That's a good theory."

"And it's not because you like me. It's because you're deathly afraid I'll change my mind and I won't show up. You've got better stuff to do than hang out with me, but the gig is worth it."

His face fell. "Bailey. I may be a lot of things, but I'm not a l— Well, I take that back. I guess I *am* a liar." He turned to look at me across the truck cab, sunlight filtering through the leaves of the trees overhead and playing across his face as he drove. "But not to you."

A song popped into my head about that, along with the perfect melody and even an unusual chord structure for the chorus. He was a liar but not to me, or so he said, and that made me feel special. But Toby had lied to me about the drugs he was doing and the girls he was messing around with on the side. I knew I had my flaws, but I didn't make a habit of lying. I was no match for a flat-out liar.

That was the message of the song. The words kept changing, and I worked through them in my head. During the rest of the drive and wait in the doctor's office, Sam kept asking me what was wrong. Every time he spoke, I lost a piece of my song. Finally I asked, "Don't you ever feel the need to practice guitar in your head?" That gave me an excuse to finger the imaginary notes in my lap. Connecting them to my imaginary fiddle helped me remember them.

The nurse called me into the examining room. In the pause between taking off my clothes and talking to the doctor, I snatched my notebook out of my purse, my paper gown crackling on top of me, and managed to dump the whole song onto the staffs. By the time the doctor came in, which usually stressed me out because I didn't want to be touched, I was so relieved and relaxed that I could have taken a nap.

The exam went almost exactly like the first time. The difference was that instead of prescribing the pill, the doctor asked me how I felt on it. But just as before, she made a studied point of *not* letting her eyes linger on my heavy makeup or punky hair. Cheerfully she examined me and then felt me up. She asked me if I was sexually active—I said no, but she hardly waited for my answer, like she didn't believe me anyway—and she made me promise promise promise that if I *did* become sexually active, I would make my partner use a condom to protect us both from STDs because that's not what the pill was for.

I got a little annoyed with the whole lecture. She was acting like I'd learned nothing from watching television. I didn't snap at her, though, because I wanted her to give this speech to other girls. To Julie. *I* had given it to Julie, though the way my parents watched her, she'd probably be a virgin until she was thirty. Regardless, I wanted the doctor to give her the speech again.

I buttoned up and escaped into the waiting room. What with the lecture and scribbling down the song about Sam, I'd almost forgotten about Sam himself. He was curled up in a chair, half his normal size, with his elbows on his knees and his hands in his dark hair. When he saw me, he jumped up and beat me to the door.

"Are you okay?" I asked sarcastically in the parking lot. "You act like *you're* the one who got examined."

He chuckled uneasily. "I felt very uncomfortable. Everybody in there assumed I'd gotten you pregnant. The guys were looking at me sympathetically, giving me the bro nod. The women were accusatory."

"I said you didn't have to come."

"It's okay." He slid his hand along the bed of his truck, then suddenly spread his hand in the air. The sun-heated metal had burned him. "I'll channel that emotion and use it."

I considered him from the other side of the pickup. "You don't look well. Do you want me to drive?"

"Sure." He sighed. We both rounded the truck, switching places.

We had an hour until we were supposed to meet Ace and Charlotte, so I drove to the outskirts of the Vanderbilt campus and led Sam into an ice cream shop. He still looked lost, stuck on something in his head. I almost asked him if he'd gotten a girl pregnant and it had ended badly, but I knew that wasn't the problem. He'd told me he was a virgin, and he'd told me he didn't lie (to me). And I couldn't really complain about the way he was behaving. He looked like I felt when I was writing a song.

I bought myself a scoop of vanilla. I loved the taste, cool and clean with no other flavors or lumps to mar it. I bought Sam one of those junky flavors with everything but the kitchen sink mixed in—pretzels and chocolate and gummy worms. He didn't seem to get my joke about our contrasting personalities, didn't even hear my order, just accepted the cone and followed me until I sat down on a shady patch of grass in Centennial Park.

"Your ice cream is melting," I prompted him after he'd sat unmoving for several minutes.

He blinked, took a huge bite, and made a face as he crunched. Then he swallowed and laughed. "What *is* this?"

"You should pay closer attention." I took a nibble from my spoon. "Explain something to me about the band. Yesterday you said you didn't want to try out for a music talent show because you'd have to take their contract if you won, and you'd lose control of your career."

"Right."

"And part of the control you wanted was picking out your songs."

"Exactly." He licked his ice cream, more tentatively this time, not sure what he would find inside.

"But I don't see how you're putting that into practice, because nobody in the band is writing original songs. Is your ultimate goal to get the band a gig on Broadway, or to get the band a recording contract?"

"A recording contract," he said firmly.

"If that's what you want, that's what you need to act like. A gig on Broadway is a great first step to get attention. Once you get the attention, you need original songs to back it up."

"I know that. I guess I was just waiting for it to happen." He took a thoughtful bite. A warm breeze tossed a curl back and forth across his forehead.

The band's lack of new music worried me. I'd wanted to bring the subject up the night before when we discussed the playlist, but I figured Charlotte would rightfully point out that I was not an official member of the band and this was none of my business. Now was my chance to talk to Sam about it, but he wasn't even here.

"Where are you?" I asked. "Back in the waiting room?"

He looked up at me and chuckled. "Yes, sorry."

"You could write a song about that terrible feeling you had," I suggested. "There's a whole genre of songs about guys getting their girlfriends pregnant and their girlfriends having an abortion. Tim McGraw. Ben Folds."

Sam shook his head. "I can't write songs. All I can do is sing. You remember that gymnast who had to retire when she was twenty years old, before the Olympics, because she blew out her knee snow skiing?"

I squinted at him, thinking. "Shawn Johnson?"

"Maybe. Anyway, if you're a gymnast with a chance of winning Olympic gold, you do not go snow skiing. You don't take the chance of ruining everything for yourself. The only thing I can do is sing. I mean, I can play guitar, but so can every wannabe in Nashville, so it doesn't even count. I wasn't great in school. I wasn't great at football. I can sing, though, and even I am not stupid enough to screw that up."

"I don't see how writing songs would screw up your singing," I said. "Writing songs is supposed to be therapeutic, like any kind of writing. Have you ever tried? It seems like you have something to write about."

He eyed me as he finished off his cone, and not like he was enjoying it. More like he was trying to get rid of it. Wiping his mouth with his handkerchief, he said, "I feel like I've been through a lot in the past couple of years, but I've kept pretty stable. That's because I channel that emotion into performance. I can handle emotion, as long as it's only a song. It works for me, and I don't want to change it. I don't have anything left for writing."

He looked past the swaying limbs of an oak tree, into the empty blue sky—the same stance he'd taken last night and Saturday night when he was trying to gather himself before going into a performance. I was beginning to understand how unstable he might be deep down. I had a hard time escaping my own reality. My only flights of fancy were writing songs and—just today—fantasizing about Sam. I'd wished it was easier to get away from myself, but Sam seemed to have the opposite problem. He got so caught up in a trip inside his own mind that he had a hard time fighting his way back.

"If you're putting your emotional energy into performance," he said, "you're also getting it back out again, right? You're giving so you can receive." He spread his arms wide. "If you were writing songs with it, you'd be holed up in your room in the middle of the night, scribbling them in a notebook and feeling self-important. You'd think you were getting it out, but really you'd be keeping it inside and quiet. You'd take what upset you and turn it into art, and now it would fester, because you would think other people ought to share your outrage at what happened to you." He looked at me funny. "Do *you* write songs?"

Until that point, telling him about my notebook had been in the back of my mind. I was scared to tell him because he would rope me into the band that way. But I'd been curious to talk to him about it, test him out, see if there was any possible way the band could play a few of my songs. I would have loved to hear them, if only once.

Now that he'd made fun of songwriting, no way. He hadn't even known he was making fun of me, so I shouldn't be offended. It still hurt. I wasn't going to walk straight into his stereotype.

"No, I don't write songs," I said. "But maybe you'll run across a girl who does. You can make out with her and convince her to join your band."

"You know what?" he asked immediately. I'd expected him to pause as my insult sank in, but he jabbed back as though he'd seen it coming. "You called me a tease last night, too, and I didn't say anything because I was trying to draw Charlotte off you." He glared at me, lips pursed, shadowed face gaunt. He was never more handsome than when I was pushing him away.

"Sorry," I said. "I took that too far."

He kept glaring at me, unmoved.

My heart sped up as I realized he was angry, and I deserved it. I was no better than Charlotte, taking potshots at him.

"I'm still mad about Saturday night," I admitted, "and Charlotte, and all the girlfriends. I'd thought that—" Telling him I'd hoped we could be together . . . that assumed too much under the circumstances. "I don't know what I thought," I finished. "But Charlotte opening the door of your truck was a shocker."

He sighed, too, much to my relief, and leaned back on one hand in the grass. His anger was over. "There's more to it than that. These past few days, I keep thinking you and I are going to do something, but you're sending me mixed signals."

"No, *you*—"

He broke in, "No, *you* respond when I flirt with you. But then last night, when I was telling you good-bye, you just stared up at me and gave me a polite good night like I was the president of Vandy."

"No, *you* didn't kiss me last night because you were afraid of what Charlotte would think."

"I've told you about that," he reminded me. "She doesn't have any claim to me. I also don't want to be mean to her or piss her off."

"Because of the band," I grumbled.

"Yes," he exclaimed, exasperated, "and I don't think I'm wrong to try to keep the peace in the band, and I don't think I'm being a tease."

"I don't either," I admitted begrudgingly, watching an ant crawl across my bare foot in my sandal. My voice sank lower as I said, "Jealous. Frustrated."

He nodded. "I can't change the past, Bailey. Believe me, I would if I could." He got that far-off look into the sky again but reined himself in before he got lost. He looked into my eyes as he said, "I can't change that I dated her. I can't change that I dated a lot of people. I've told you I wasn't serious with those girls." He moved his hand onto my bare knee, and the afternoon suddenly heated by twenty degrees. "Whatever's wrong between us, I want to get over it, because I'd like to get serious with *you*." His hand moved to cup my whole knee. "I wanted you last night."

I felt my face flush, and my neck, and my chest where he couldn't see. So many times in the past year I'd made out with Toby or some other guy. There had been fewer of them than there had been of Sam's girlfriends, but I'd been no better than him for going to that place with them when I didn't really care.

In those dark moments at parties, my body had gone electric for them. But not in the middle of the day, in an open field, with a boy's hand on my knee instead of down my panties. There was no reason for Sam and me to share this look right now and feel this way about each other, except that we did.

He glanced down at his watch and said in defeat, "And now we have to go." Brow creased, deep in thought, he reached behind my head and pulled me toward him.

Without thinking, for once, I sat up on my knees and leaned forward, bracing myself on the grass with one hand as my lips met his.

He tasted sweet, and the kiss was sweet and chaste, until his hand slipped under my shirt. His touch on my bare waist made me gasp and break the kiss.

Eyes on mine, he said as if convincing himself, "I want to play this gig tonight."

I nodded. "So do I."

He moved his hand around my waist to the button of my shorts, a preview of what was to come. Then he backed away from me and stood, holding out a hand to help me up. "But it's going to be a long night."

11

Sam was wrong. The entire afternoon and evening seemed to flash by in a second, because we were having fun.

Sam and I met Charlotte and Ace at his dad's car dealership. We parked the truck and crawled into the middle seat of the SUV that Ace had chosen for the day. As Ace pulled into traffic, Sam said, "It's like our Mystery Machine. All we need is a Great Dane."

Charlotte leaned around her front seat to say, "My drum kit is our Great Dane. Only it says 'Crash!' instead of 'Rowr?'"

Something about her Scooby-Doo imitation struck me as funny. I laughed uncontrollably for a few seconds. It felt so good that I kept laughing until Charlotte stared at me like I'd grown another head. I supposed my laughing was about as common as Charlotte doing impressions.

Sam was watching me from across the SUV with a bemused look, like he didn't quite know what to make of my laughter either. Finally he called, "Who gets to be Fred, and who's Shaggy?"

"I call dibs on Fred," Ace said.

"You're totally Fred," Sam agreed. "Stodgy."

"I guess we all know who gets to be Daphne, and who's Velma," Charlotte said bitterly.

"I can't see a thing without my glasses," I piped up, quoting Velma and nudging my cat-eye glasses with one finger.

Charlotte turned around one more time and blinked at me. Clearly she'd meant that she was fashion-challenged Velma. I'd thought at first she was mad at me for taking her self-deprecating punch line away. But her expression wasn't angry, just surprised. She said something to Ace that I didn't catch and reached forward to change the radio station.

"That would make a great album cover, actually." Sam grinned at me. "The four of us, dressed like the characters. You would be the sexiest Velma ever. I wonder if we'd have to pay a licensing fee."

Electricity rushed through me when he said I was sexy. I had to fight down that pesky feeling in order to be annoyed with him. "That would be a great idea," I acknowledged, "if we were a band."

He gave me that dangerous look I didn't see very often. My heart raced. For a second I thought we were going to have it out, once and for all, right there in the back of the SUV.

But the look vanished as fast as it had come. "Aw, honey," he said, "let's not fight." He reached around my shoulders and drew me to him, too hard, a joking hug that I put up with because it meant our argument was over for now. He relaxed his hold, but he kept his arm around me.

Though Ace was talking to Charlotte, I saw a flash of his eyes in the rearview mirror, and I knew he was watching us. Then he rolled down his window, letting in the warm summer breeze and the smell of cut grass.

During the drive, I was surprised that Charlotte didn't engineer some excuse to trade seats with me so she could sit with

Sam—*Oh, I must sit near the back so I can put one hand on my tom to keep it from falling*—but she seemed content to keep her place in the front. She was absorbed in conversation with Ace about a TV show they both watched. Sam interjected a joke now and then, but I was utterly lost. I'd spent most of my nights practicing fiddle.

Along the drive from Nashville to Chattanooga, exits and billboards petered out until nothing was left but trees streaming by our windows. The interstate was a wide expanse of asphalt cut through the forest, tilting to one side and climbing mountains. When I blinked, I opened my eyes again and felt dizzy, disoriented because of the strange angle of the ground, and the SUV climbing the road like nothing was wrong.

As I looked around at the scenery that seemed normal and yet not, I glanced at my reflection in the window. The wind blew my short black curls around my head, the longer pieces in front teasing the tip of my chin. The sun lit my face. But what surprised me was that I was scowling at the landscape. That's not how I felt. With effort, I lifted the corners of my mouth into a smile for my own reflection. Then I glanced at Sam so close beside me.

When he felt me looking at him, he smiled. He squeezed my shoulders, more gently this time, then let me go, because two hours would be a long drive with his heavy arm around me. But he rested his hand on my bare thigh.

I would remember this bright afternoon forever.

♪ ♫ ♪

Arriving at the most luxurious house I'd ever seen, we pulled up to the back lawn, at the end of a pristine pool, and the boys got out to unpack Charlotte's kit. I couldn't help feeling curious about the gig. I imagined the record company execs who'd thrown parties for Julie had even more astonishing homes, but I hadn't been invited.

Between trips back and forth from the pool to the van, while Sam wasn't around, of course, Charlotte kindly explained that one of Sam's exes had arranged for us to play this gig, her aunt's surprise fiftieth birthday party. She went on to inform me that the band's Lao wedding circuit was also a result of an ex with an in. She stated these facts as joylessly as she could manage, but I knew her ulterior motive. If she'd decided to back off me after I claimed Velma and let her be Daphne, she'd forgotten all about that when Sam put his arm around me.

It was hard to be angry with her after the party guests started showing up, bused in by a hired service so the birthday lady wouldn't see their cars and suspect what was up. When she came in the front door and two hundred of her closest friends leaped up from behind her living room furniture, she screamed. Then she cackled with joy and dashed upstairs to change into her bathing suit. I hoped I could enjoy life that much when I was that old. Or . . . ever.

I'd never pictured myself playing a gig so crazy, much less playing it in a bikini top and a denim skirt. The party was a riot, full of great food and fun strangers, even if most of them were middle-aged and probably shouldn't have been wearing bathing suits that small. Between sets, the band went in the pool, too. Mostly Sam and Ace and Charlotte and I talked together about music and Nashville and the CMA Festival starting Thursday—I carefully avoided any mention of Julie—but Sam and I kept finding excuses to flirt and rib each other. Several times when I teased him, he found it necessary to grab me, his hands strong around my wrists in the cool water.

The only negative of the night came when Charlotte quipped that I shouldn't get my hair wet because the ink might run. Ace splashed her, and Sam dismissed the comment by putting his arm around me and changing the subject. However, at midnight when the party finally closed down and we packed the SUV with Charlotte's drum kit, I was still thinking about my hair and other people's perception of it, dyed an unnatural black.

After I'd deposited the last cymbal in the back, Sam opened the front passenger door for me. I was afraid he intended to take the back with Charlotte, just to keep her happy and spread the love around, while I sat up front with Ace. I asked Sam carefully, "Oh, are you driving back?"

"I always drive back at night."

As I climbed into the passenger seat, I held my breath to keep from sighing with relief so loudly that everyone could hear. I had another two hours in proximity to Sam—though I would probably sleep through most of it. Three late nights were catching up with me.

"I'll never know whether I inherited the alcoholic gene from my dad," Sam was saying as he slid behind the steering wheel and slammed his door, "but I definitely inherited the barfly gene. I can't sleep at night, and I can't get up in the morning."

I could see that. Sam was creative and dedicated, but his wasn't the plodding bright-and-early work ethic of the morning person, like mine. It was the crazy creative burst of the night owl, long dark hours of despair before dawn.

"Here." He hadn't pulled his T-shirt back on after our last dip in the pool and our last set of songs. Now he wadded it up, crammed it into the console between our seats, and gently pressed my shoulders until I laid my head down. I took a deep breath, exhaled slowly, and tried to relax. Sam was at the wheel, and I trusted him. As he started the SUV and cruised past the mansion's marble columns, I wondered if Julie would buy a house like this in the next few years, and whether she would throw parties like a record company exec, or if she would never get a chance because she would always be gone.

♪ ♫ ♪

I struggled back from sleep, then started upright, sure something terrible had happened to wake me. The SUV droned along the interstate. The wind whooshed through the open window, and the forest spun by at the edges of the headlight beams.

Sam looked over at me and smiled, shadows long across his face and bare chest. "Sorry. I woke you up on purpose. I didn't mean to startle you. Lie down."

I peeked over the seat. Ace leaned against the side of the SUV. On the opposite side, Charlotte had her back to the door with her knees bent and her bare feet up on the seat, nearly touching Ace's thigh. Ace was most definitely touching Charlotte, with one big hand on her ankle. I studied them for a moment, weighing whether their positions were random or "accidentally on purpose" touching, and on whose part. In any case, they were definitely asleep and unconcerned what they looked like. Both snored softly with their mouths open.

I obeyed Sam by settling back down on his T-shirt between us. "Are you falling asleep?" I asked softly enough that I wouldn't disturb Ace and Charlotte over the white noise of the wind.

"No."

"Why'd you wake me up, then?" I grumbled.

"I don't like to be alone."

I stared out the window, so low in the seat that I could see only the tops of the trees racing by. I murmured, "I like it, mostly."

"What do you do when you're alone?" he asked.

"Practice fiddle." I wrote music, too, but that was none of his business. "What do *you* do?"

"That's the thing," he said. "I start thinking, and I drive myself crazy." He moved one hand into my hair and twisted it gently. "You've said you can't be in this band because you'll get in trouble."

"I will."

"But you don't want to be in it anyway. You don't want to major in music in college. You want to do anything but. Which doesn't make any sense to me when you're practicing fiddle so much." He worked his fingers farther into my hair, down to the nape of my neck. "What happened to you when Julie got discovered?"

"Nothing happened to me. I did it to myself."

"Tell me." His fingers stroked the skin beneath my hair that no one ever touched.

"We'd been at a bluegrass festival all weekend," I said. "Before our last performance, my mom told us there was a scout in the audience, so we'd better do our best. Afterward, she and my dad had a meeting with him. Julie and I waited in the RV and watched one of those singing contests on TV, because we liked to critique the job the singers did and guess whether we could do better under that kind of pressure. We didn't seriously think anything would come of our parents' meeting. They'd had meetings before that didn't pan out."

I wondered if he could feel my muscles knotting up underneath his fingertips.

"My parents came in somber, like they had before. I figured we'd lost out again. But they made us all sit down together around the little dinner table. They said the record company was taking Julie and not me. Julie would be traveling for the next year. I would stay home, and my parents wanted me to stop pursuing my own deal. They said it would be better if I quit music altogether. They couldn't back me anymore, anyway, because they couldn't help two daughters in two different places. It would be no fun for me to live my life in competition with someone I loved."

"And you bought that?" Sam asked skeptically.

"I think you'd agree this situation doesn't sound like fun."

"Only when you're on the losing end."

"Which I am."

Sam's hand stopped on my neck. "I don't understand," he said so loudly that I thought he would wake Ace and Charlotte. At least he realized this. He lowered his voice before he asked, "I don't mean to insult you, but what kind of people *are* your parents?"

"I don't blame them," I said quickly. "They're normal." My mom came off as mean sometimes to people who didn't know her well. In truth, she was only ambitious, and she never let anyone get in the way of her drive—not even Julie and me, when her drive was on our behalf. My dad was the opposite. He hung back and let her make the rules, then supported what she said. But if it weren't for him, my mother would have gone off the deep end a long time ago. He consoled me after she screamed at me, cleaning up the mess she'd made. He kept her stable so the friction generated by her own body didn't tear her into pieces. In public I could always find him a pace behind her. At home or in the RV he would rub the knot in her neck—

I sat up faster than I had when Sam woke me.

"What is it?" he asked sharply.

I slouched against the door and curled my legs on the seat, rubbing my own neck with one hand. "You know what? I'm *not* normal, and you're a nice person, and I don't want to tell you this story."

His mouth quirked sideways in disagreement. "Girls tend to think I'm a nice person because I'm polite and I may make you feel good, but you have no idea what I'm thinking." His tone was so dark that sparks raced across my skin.

I hesitated. When we'd first played together at the mall, I'd thought we had a lot in common. I was thrown for a loop when I told him about Toby's wreck and he acted holier-than-thou. I didn't want to feel rejected like that again.

But I'd never shared with anyone what happened with my family that night. It had eaten away at me in the form of a song I was trying desperately to write, like Sam had said, playing on an endless loop in my head. And if anyone would understand my jealousy, it would be him.

I sighed. "My parents didn't intend to hurt me. I'm sure they just wanted to get all the news out of the way at once. I'd always been responsible before—believe it or not—and they thought I could handle anything they threw at me. It wasn't their fault they were wrong."

"Mm," Sam said as though he doubted my explanation but wasn't quite willing to say it out loud.

"After they told me, I sat there a minute, and then I left the table and climbed to the upper deck of the RV, where Julie and I slept. They let me go. I guess they figured I wanted to be alone to sulk, and I would get over it soon enough. I found my scissors, and I pulled my hair back into a high ponytail and started to chop through it—"

Sam gaped at me. Quickly he put his eyes back on the interstate, but he kept his mouth open, horrified at me.

"—and the smaller bits of hair were falling down around me, glinting golden in the lamplight, and I knew I should not be doing this, that I was angry, that I would regret it. Maybe I didn't quite realize it would be the worst thing I ever did in my life. Regardless, I was halfway through it and I couldn't stop then. I kept hacking until I was holding my ponytail." I made a fist. I could still feel the long, heavy skein of hair in my hand. "Of course, the way I'd cut it off, it had fallen longer around my face, and I was almost bald in the back. That's how I climbed down the ladder."

Sam watched the road. I watched his chest. He was holding his breath.

"And I threw it—" Flexing my wrist, I tossed my hair onto the table. I wasn't aiming really, but I meant for it to land right smack between my parents. Instead, it skidded across the slick tabletop and into Julie's lap.

I winced. "I meant to say something to go along with it. 'You want me to disguise myself, too, so nobody will recognize me and embarrass your precious Julie, is this what you wanted?' But I didn't get any words out, because Julie was crying." Screaming, really, on what should have been the happiest day of her life, and the night she'd always waited for.

"And then I slammed out of the RV, and my parents have hated me ever since."

The roar of the truck filled the silence between us. Sam was breathing again, blinking against the interstate lights, thanking God he didn't have a brother.

"Where did you go?" he asked quietly.

"Oh, there wasn't anywhere to go. I walked over to the bonfire that the festival had built for overnight campers and sat there for a long time and thought about throwing myself into it."

He eyed me uneasily. "Would you have?"

"No. That would have hurt." I laughed. Laughed too loudly and choked a little, trying to quiet myself. Laughed until my sides hurt and I winced with the pain.

He put his hand on my ankle, unintentionally mimicking Ace and Charlotte. "You laugh when you're uncomfortable. You laughed Saturday night when you told me about your wreck with your boyfriend and I got so mad at you." He ran his thumb back and forth across my ankle bone. "I can tell you're not happy."

I snorted at that understatement.

"And you haven't been happy for a long time. You blame yourself. You feel like your whole life hinges on that one night, that one incident you can't take back."

"Yeah."

He licked his lips. "What if you hadn't done that? How would your life be different now?"

"Julie would still be speaking to me, for starters," I said, "because she and my parents wouldn't have gotten so furious with me about Toby's wreck and the party last week. I wouldn't have set that up all year as the way they expected me to act. I wouldn't have spent the year trying to live up to that stupid show of defiance."

"Right, but what *would* you have done?"

Confused, I thought about it, and then I saw his point. If I'd accepted Julie's success and my parents' decree that I remain a failure—if I'd stayed blond—they would have involved me more in Julie's meetings and travels. I would have been a pillar of strength for Julie during her climb to the top. I would have kept that bond with her.

But what was in it for me? I'd loved being Julie's responsible older sister who took care of her. I wanted to be that person again. But that's not *all* I wanted to be. If I'd still had that, but I'd given up the tumultuous but certainly colorful relationship with Toby, and the wreck, and the parties, and the failed experimentation with drugs and alcohol and sexy times, and countless hours of defiant practice on my fiddle, and five notebooks full of wistful songs, my senior year would have been an uneventful blank—except for the adventures of Julie.

"You wouldn't have gotten your job at the mall," Sam pointed out. "You wouldn't have played with this band for the past three nights." He wagged his eyebrows at me. "You wouldn't have met me."

I giggled.

Realized I was giggling.

Felt a huge weight lift off my chest and slip through the roof of the SUV, into the Tennessee night.

"This is self-serving," he said. "You know I want you in the band. I think you've had such a bad experience with your family that you've left them, as best you can, and you refuse to join any other group. The problem is, as long as you won't form any other ties, the only ones you have are the ties to the very family you've tried to leave. Without even knowing, you've become a little kid who acts up to get attention. You can't even live your own life because you're so totally focused on whether and how your parents are going to see every move you make, and what they'll think."

Distasteful as that sounded, it rang true.

"But now you *are* living your own life by playing in this band. You're finally breaking their first commandment."

"Yeah."

"How does it feel?"

The roar of the wind filled the silence again, and I blinked at the brightening interstate ahead as the exits and billboards crowded closer together, leading into Nashville. "It feels lame," I said, "because if they catch me, my mother will run after me screaming, 'How could you do this to yourself? How could you embarrass the family, doing something we trained you to do?' They'll probably stage an intervention."

"Fiddlers Anonymous."

"Exactly. At meetings we'll go around the room sharing how we've disappointed people. When it's my turn, I'll admit I started by playing with Elvis at the mall, and I thought I could handle it, but it led to harder stuff."

Sam wasn't laughing anymore. I was afraid he thought I was making fun of his dad, and I'd offended him. It was weird that he seemed so friendly and open, yet I kept feeling I had to tiptoe around him. I'd never had a friend with real problems, life problems, an addict for a dad. My so-called friends for the past year had problems of their own devising.

But that didn't seem to be what he'd been thinking about after all when he said, "You know what my dream is. To make it big with this band."

"Yes."

"And I think you should try it with us. Then you wouldn't need to go to Vandy. You wouldn't have time. Your parents' opinion wouldn't matter anymore."

Not true. Caring about their opinion was a part of me, like an ID chip implanted in a pet dog.

"But I don't think that's your dream," he said. "What is it?"

The lighthearted feeling had left me. Wishing I could have it back, I rolled my head against the window. "This isn't going to happen. But for the past year, I've had a fantasy that my parents and the record company crawl back to me and tell me Julie can't go on without me. They made a mistake. Julie and I should get the development deal together after all. They need me, desperately. And then they beg."

"That's why you felt so awful when your family got all over you about your wreck," Sam said. "Julie told you she'd lost respect for you, and you were as far away as you've ever been from that fantasy coming true."

I closed my eyes, but through my eyelids I could still see the lights of the interstate passing overhead, closer and closer together. And I felt like Julie was watching me, judging me. In that fantasy I'd had for the past year, I'd wanted my parents and the record company to beg me to come back to them. Julie was always standing to one side, though, because my downfall had never been her fault.

Now I realized Sam was right about my trip to the bottom nearly a week and a half ago. I'd told myself I still didn't blame Julie—but ever since then, in my fantasy, she had begged me, too.

Slowly I opened my eyes, which stung with tears. My vision was blurry but . . . Julie *was* watching me. Looming ahead, placed near the interstate so several hundred thousand cars a day could see it, was an enormous billboard with Julie's picture on it. Ten-foot-tall letters proclaimed "Julie Mayfield" with the date of her Grand Ole Opry debut tomorrow.

I'd known this was coming, more or less, for an entire year. It had seemed a lot more real by last Christmas, when the dates for her first single and her album were set in stone, and more real still when she was scheduled for the Grand Ole Opry tomorrow and a huge single release party on Wednesday and the CMA Festival on Thursday and Friday, four of the biggest gigs she could have gotten short of her own sold-out stadium tour.

But I hadn't actually seen ads for her appearances or her single or her album, either in magazines or online. For the past month I'd purposefully stayed away from the media because I'd known what was coming. Now, for the first time, she was so big I couldn't avoid her. As I looked up at her sweet grin, her blue eyes enhanced by professional makeup, and her blond hair arranged by her own personal version of Ms. Lottie, my first thought was how pretty she was. Her looks wouldn't have substituted for talent, though. In L.A., maybe. Not in Nashville. Luckily she had both.

My second thought was amazement that my first thought was pride in Julie, not jealousy of her, for the first time in a year.

My third thought was that if Sam had seen the sign, too, after I'd just told him what had happened between my family and me, he might have realized how much this huge monster girl would have looked like me if I'd still had long blond hair. In that case, I was in trouble.

Yesterday at my house, I'd half wished Sam would notice one of Julie's star-studded photos, realize what was up, and put me out of my misery. Now that he'd helped me past some kind of barrier in my life, and I was free on the other side, this was the worst thing that could happen.

I didn't dare glance over at him. If he *hadn't* seen the billboard, he would want to know why I was looking at him funny and what was wrong.

I stopped wondering when I heard the blinker switch on. He raced down the exit ramp. After our long conversation and two hours of high winds, the SUV settled into an uncomfortable silence as he stopped at the light, then pulled into the parking lot of the nearest gas station, which glowed weakly, closed for the night. He parked the SUV directly under Julie's sign, killed the engine, and bailed out, slamming the door behind him.

Ace started awake at the same time Charlotte yelled, "Oh!" In the rearview mirror, I watched them glare at each other warily as they backed away to opposite ends of the seat. Judging from their expressions, I wasn't sure who'd been the first to touch the other, and who blamed whom.

"What's happening?" Charlotte asked. At first I thought she was caught up in her tangle with Ace only, but she was looking at me in the rearview mirror. She wanted to know why we'd stopped.

"Well, I'm not sure, but I'm guessing Sam found out my sister is going to play at the Grand Ole Opry tomorrow night, and he's upset that I haven't told him." I pointed through the ceiling of the SUV.

Charlotte and Ace exchanged a quizzical look, then opened their doors and got out.

The noise of the interstate rushed in, like the noise of the wind before, but more distant, just a dim rush in the background. My heart raced so fast that it hurt. My relationship with Sam was probably over. But I didn't feel anything. I was back to that place where I'd spent the past year, with no emotion at all. Just panic.

Sam startled me by jerking open my door. He scowled at me for a moment with his fists on his hips. Behind him, Charlotte and Ace gazed up at the sign and whispered together. The sign was directly above the SUV, so close I couldn't see it myself, but I knew it was there.

"I think this goes without saying, Bailey," Sam barked. "You've got to get us an in with your sister's record company."

I responded without hesitation. I'd known for three days this was bound to happen sooner or later, and how Sam would react when it did. "I think *this* goes without saying, because I've already told you. I'm not allowed to be in a band. Julie's company doesn't want me to. They're afraid it will ruin her PR. They're not going to give a contract to someone defying a direct order. That's not the way to make a good first impression."

"Then, a different company," he said. "Surely your sister and your parents have other connections, after a year preparing for her freaking *album and Grand Ole Opry debut!*" He balled both fists like he wanted to hit the side of the SUV, but that would injure his guitar-playing hands. With a groan he backed away from the SUV and walked across the clearing under the sign, past Charlotte and Ace, with his hands on his head.

I got out and called after him, "I can't ask them to do that. They'll take my college tuition away."

Ace and Charlotte turned to stare at me with resentment and no understanding whatsoever. Over their heads, Sam yelled, "Your parents threatened you with that when they thought you were going to end up in a tabloid magazine for crashing into a lake with your cokehead boyfriend. If you disobey them by playing with a kick-ass band, your punishment won't be the same. That just doesn't make any sense."

"We'll never find out, because I'm not going to ask them."

Charlotte stepped close to me, wearing a sour look. "You'd give up a chance at a recording contract, for *all* of us, just to get your parents to pay for your college? My mom isn't paying for *my* college."

"Maybe if she was, you wouldn't be so desperate to get a re-cording contract." I felt ugly saying that, but I just wanted them all off my back now, because I wasn't going to do what they were asking me to do.

"Wow," Ace said flatly. That's when I knew I was beyond hope. I'd expected Charlotte to get emotional, and Sam. But Ace had more sense than both of them put together. If *he* was disgusted with me, I deserved it.

"Even if my parents weren't threatening me," I spat, "I would never ask them for anything else again."

"*That's* really the problem, isn't it?" Sam yelled. "You're just too stubborn to ask for help, or forgiveness, or *anything*."

"Oh!" I cried. "You were *just asking me* what is *wrong* with my parents. You understood perfectly well *then* where I was coming from. It's only now that *you* want something from them that you suddenly can't fathom why I wouldn't apologize to them."

Face dark with anger, Sam stalked toward me. As he passed Ace and Charlotte, Ace reached out and put one hand on Sam's chest to keep him back. Sam brushed Ace off and kept coming for me, holding two fingers an inch apart. "We're *that close,* Bailey."

"If you can't get any farther without me groveling to my parents, it looks like you're going to stay *that close.*" I measured an inch with my own fingers.

"You—" Sam started, taking another step toward me.

Ace shoved him backward. "Man, come on. We're arguing under a billboard at two o'clock in the morning, and you don't have a shirt on."

Sam turned on Ace. "What the fuck do—"

"Stop," Ace said. He glanced toward the service road, where a cop car cruised slowly by.

Sam looked, too. "Fine," he said, stomping toward the SUV.

"Let me drive," Ace called after him.

We heard a door slam on the far side of the SUV.

"So, Bailey, things *might* have been better if you'd never showed up," Charlotte said smugly.

"Can you stop? I swear to God." Ace encircled the back of her neck with one hand and gave her a gentle shove toward the SUV. He seemed to be steering her toward the backseat with Sam. Her heart must be all aflutter, I thought bitterly.

I waited until everyone was inside the SUV. That way, any individual person would be slightly less likely to take a shot at me. I slipped into the front passenger seat again. As an afterthought— though that's not what it seemed like to me—Sam half stood and jerked his wadded-up T-shirt out of the console beside me and put it on.

Ace drove the rest of the way to his father's car lot. Nobody turned to me to say, "You'd better let Ace drive you home because Sam is done with you," but that was the message, and I got it loud and clear. Sam pulled his guitar case out of the back of the SUV and drove off in his truck without a word.

Ace asked me for my address and plugged it into the GPS. As the robot lady commanded him to drive down the boulevard and turn at Music Row, he commented, "So. Not Bailey Wright. Bailey Mayfield."

I said defensively, "Bailey Wright Mayfield."

"It must really hurt to have your sister playing at the Grand Ole Opry," Charlotte said.

I let that insult lie there, like an egg frying on the hood of a car on a summer day in the desert. She didn't care what I thought of her, but she cared what Ace thought, and he wasn't going to like that stab at me.

He didn't defend me, though, just kept driving past the record company offices.

Charlotte tried again. "It's a shame that your sister got the blond hair, and you got the jet-black hair. After seeing her, I'd almost say your hair color wasn't natural."

If she'd known how close we were to my granddad's house, she might have started insulting me earlier. Now she'd run out of time. Ace pulled up at the bottom of my granddad's cement stairs.

"Thanks, Ace," I said genuinely. "It's been a pleasure knowing you."

"Oh," he exclaimed like *I* was the one who'd insulted *him*. "We're not done with you. You said you were in the band for four more days. This was day one."

"What?" I protested. "No! Sam doesn't want me playing with you now."

"Sam does not cancel a gig," Ace reminded me in a warning tone.

"There *are* no gigs." I opened my hands. "I told him I couldn't play tomorrow."

"I know for a fact he's scheduled us at Boot Ilicious on Wednesday," Ace said.

"Oh, come on!" I cried. Toby had no idea I was playing in a band, I hoped. But he'd discovered a place to snag booze, and he wasn't going to give it up anytime soon. I'd likely see him there, and now I would be doing exactly what he'd always made fun of me for.

"No," I said. "Sam didn't say anything to me about another gig."

"He was probably waiting for the right time," Ace said, "because you *freak out* every time he tries to get you to play with us again."

Charlotte burst into laughter. I let her laugh. I felt stunned. It was the first time Ace had raised his voice at me.

He turned around. I didn't see the look he gave Charlotte, but she stopped laughing.

"And Sam sent in our video to audition for a Broadway gig on Thursday," Ace said. "Since it looks like you and Sam might not be speaking, I'll call you both days to make sure you're coming. If you don't answer, I will come find you."

"O-*kay*!" So much for my sweet parting with my understated friend. I opened the door and jerked my beach bag and fiddle case off the floorboard.

Just before I slammed the door, Charlotte chirped from the backseat, "Good night, Bailey Mayfield!"

I took a step back and opened her door. "Shut up," I said to her face before closing the door again. I jogged up the steps.

Upset as I was, I had the wherewithal to stuff my fiddle case into my beach bag before opening the front door. If I *had* been harboring some inkling of an idea that Sam was right and I could make it big with his band, thereby breaking away from my parents completely, those hopes were dashed now. I needed more than ever to keep my moonlighting a secret from my granddad.

But as I entered the dark house and peeked out the front window to watch Ace drive away, I knew my Wednesday and Thursday nights with the band wouldn't be all I saw of Sam. I had a mall performance to get through tomorrow afternoon, and then I was making a date.

12

After I got off work the next evening and changed from Dolly Parton's helper back into my bad-ass self, I found Sam's dad's address online, then parked in front of his house. It looked a lot like my granddad's house, actually, but in a neighborhood that hadn't been kept up as nicely: a house people bought when they weren't a hundred percent sure what they would get paid from month to month. I called Sam.

"Hey, Bailey," he said sleepily.

"I didn't mean to wake you," I said, then waited for him to deny he'd been asleep. When he didn't, my heart twisted. All day I'd thought how unreasonable and selfish he was, if he would throw away our relationship just because I wouldn't give him a shortcut to success. But he must have gone home last night, then stayed up so late that he was still asleep at six the next evening. That made me want to comfort him, run my fingers through his hair with his head in my lap as he'd done for me last night, even though I was the one who'd caused the trouble.

"My granddad wouldn't let me sleep that late," I said by way of conversation.

Sam yawned. "My folks aren't home. My mom had an early meeting before night shift. My dad's on a bender."

"He's not driving around, is he?" I hoped I didn't sound as alarmed as I felt. Sam's real problems surprised me every time, even now that our whole relationship had turned dark.

He laughed, a pale echo of his musical laughter from the rest of the days I'd known him. "No, he stays put. My mom makes him go to a motel."

I took a deep breath. "I'm parked in front of your house, I think. Or I'm about to get arrested for staking out the wrong guy."

I watched his house—or the house I was sitting in front of, anyway. The blinds opened in a second-story window.

"I see you," he said somberly.

"Well." Maybe I should have given up on the night and driven away. Instead I said, "I was hoping you might come out with me. I have something I want to show you."

"Give me ten." He hung up.

In seven, he was locking the side door and running past his truck, down the driveway. When he was still several paces away, I noticed he was wearing his T-shirt from two nights before, the one I'd cartooned on with Charlotte's marker. I wasn't sure whether the marker was especially permanent or he'd washed the shirt carefully, but his heart was still on his sleeve.

He got into my car with his usual bluster, smelling of toothpaste and soap and shampoo, his hair hanging in damp waves as on the first day I'd met him, when he'd played an old Scottish tune in the sun. But nothing else about him was as usual. He didn't ask where I was taking him. He didn't make small talk. He sank down in the seat like he wasn't quite awake and stared stonily in front of him.

Until I drove down the exit ramp to the Grand Ole Opry. Then he sat up.

I found a spot in the crowded parking lot. "Do you have an umbrella?" was the first thing he said the whole trip. As we slammed the car doors and followed the crowd toward the theater, the sky rumbled overhead, and violently pink clouds raced across the twilit sky.

"No," I said, not that I cared. "Five Feet High and Rising" started playing in my head.

When it was my turn at the box office, I asked for two tickets, half hoping they would be sold out and I wouldn't be able to go through with my plan. I was dying to see Julie on the Grand Ole Opry stage, and then again, I dreaded it. And when Sam saw her, I wasn't sure how he would react.

No such luck. Even during CMA week, the Grand Ole Opry wasn't selling out on a Tuesday, when the headlining acts were mid-dling stars and Julie was unknown.

While I was talking to the cashier, choosing seats, someone slipped my billfold out from under my elbow on the counter. I turned in alarm. When I saw it was just Sam, I continued my conversation until I came away from the window with tickets.

Sam held my billfold open, staring grimly at my driver's license. At my real name.

He looked up at me, and the accusation in his eyes hurt.

He already knew I'd lied about my name. But I suppose see-ing it on my license hit it home to him, like seeing Julie onstage tonight was going to hit it home to me that country music was her life, not mine.

Our seats were high in the large, steep auditorium. To know what was going on, we relied on one of the huge screens that fo-cused on the star onstage. I could tell by the way Sam expressed no surprise at the show that he'd been here as often as I had over the years. The Grand Ole Opry was a theater production but also

a live radio show that had been ongoing and pretty much un-
changed since the twenties: some old-fashioned commercials for
potato chips and ice cream, an elderly man in a sequined cowboy
getup telling jokes about his sex life, a musical act—often bluegrass
rather than country—that had been an Opry staple for decades but
never made it big, and finally a newbie the record companies were
trying to promote, or a genuine star. Repeat four times for a two-
hour show. Julie was the newbie for act three.

I thought the announcer would never stop reciting his commercial for hand salve—and then, before I was ready, Julie was
walking onstage amid polite applause, wearing a fixed grin, her
face turned purposefully toward the audience.

The thing that struck me about her was how beautiful she
looked on the jumbo screen. With her face blown up the size of
a Chevy, every imperfection in her face should have been notice-
able, but she didn't have any. Her skin was flawless, her lipstick
glossy, her brilliant blue eyes outlined in smoky shadow, her blond
curls shining in the spotlights. She might have been nervous, she
might have sounded off, but the camera loved her, and she looked
like a star.

But underneath the gorgeous hair and perfect makeup, I could
tell she was terrified. Her easy smile when we used to play together,
even onstage, had morphed into a tight one. Her hands moved ro-
botically across the guitar strings. Normally she was good at using
the whole stage so the audience didn't get bored watching her. This
time she stayed rooted to the lighter circle in the very center of
the wooden floor, hauled here from the Grand Ole Opry's original home, the Ryman Auditorium, and saved again after this new
theater's flood. She stood on it like it was her life raft in the vast sea
of the empty, brightly lit stage, her backup musicians pushed to the
edges and too far away to save her.

She played two songs, both insipid, the upbeat first one better than the slower follow-up. They were cute and they would get radio airplay, but the tunes weren't catchy. The conceits in the lyrics I'd heard a hundred times. The upbeat one was about going away from home and missing her dog (first verse), her friends (second verse), and her family (third verse). The other was about her true love for her boyfriend (first verse), her parents (second verse), and God (third verse). Nobody would remember them in a year. She would be exactly as successful this week as the record company's marketing efforts made her, coupled with whatever notoriety she could gain from being only sixteen. These songs wouldn't help her.

The second song ended with a big buildup. Though I hadn't heard it before, I could tell she was supposed to hit a money note. She took it down a fifth, like a spooked figure skater at the Olympics attempting a double axel rather than a triple. As the tune wrapped up, my self-absorbed thoughts assaulted me. I'd never wanted Julie to fail. But I did feel a bit self-righteous. If my family hadn't shut me out, I might have prevented this fiasco by pointing out how crappy the songs were, or just by standing in the wings, supporting her, when she went onstage.

And I was bitter. Bitterness and I were old friends by now, but at the moment bitterness was trying to go down my bra in public. I had spent the last year so depressed that Julie got this opportunity when I didn't, yet *this* was the upshot of it? It was an opportunity squandered, a year of bitterness over nothing at all.

Sam and I sat through the entire show without getting up, hardly moving. Neither of us laughed at the jokes. We were movie critics, sports writers, record company scouts, leaching all the joy out of watching a performance. And after the heat between us over the past few days, we each stayed in our own cold personal space, never touching.

Finally the show was over. The lights turned up. The audience en masse edged along the narrow rows and up the stairs to the exits. Only Sam and I stayed in the uncomfortable bench seats built to imitate the church pews in the Ryman, staring at the blank screen where Julie's pretty face had been.

"What'd you think?" I asked.

He sighed. "I'm eaten up inside with jealousy. I don't like myself very much right now."

I felt him looking at me. I met his gaze. In his eyes I saw that he understood what I'd been going through for a year. Not that this helped us now.

"You think you could have done better than her," I guessed.

"She was nervous," he said diplomatically. "We want to think we wouldn't be scared shitless if we ever got this opportunity, but we wouldn't know for sure until we got here."

I nodded. "You think her songs were duds." *I* thought her songs were duds. Any second the music notebook in my purse would begin to glow, and we would see the light escaping around the edges of my purse's leather flap.

"I can't write songs," he said, "so I'm in no position to judge."

I wasn't sure why I'd expected Sam to be honest with me, now that he and I had no plans for the future. But I was annoyed that he would flake out on me for the sake of politeness after days of brutal honesty. I baited him, "You think if you got a contract, you would make damn sure your songs were better than that."

"Her songs are . . ." He paused and eyed me, searching his mind for a truthful adjective that wouldn't offend me. "Cute. They have pop crossover potential."

"But not blockbuster potential," I mused.

He said nothing, letting his silence pass for inoffensive agreement.

"What she lacks in catchy songs, she might make up for in pure bubbly personality," I thought out loud.

"If she works on her stage presence." With a huff of impatience, Sam turned to me. "I'll be honest with you, Bailey. I don't know if I'm supposed to try to make you feel better about her chances, or worse."

"That's fair," I said. "I don't know, either." I squinted at the far-away stage, into the wings where Julie had disappeared half an hour earlier. "Her handlers aren't going to like this."

"Oh, you've met her handlers?" Sam asked in surprise.

"Yeah." I added bitterly, "And before you ask, no, I'm not going to tell her handlers about you, or the band, either."

He chose to ignore that remark. "Are they good, like Carrie Underwood's handlers, or do you get the feeling she's going to be like one of the also-rans on the singing contest TV shows?"

Since he was keeping the conversation mature and unemotional, I tried to do the same. "I think they're okay in terms of the advice they give her, but they don't actually talk to her. They talk to my parents." In turn, I would bet money that my mother was giving Julie the lecture of her life right now. *Don't you want this? Didn't your daddy and I give up our jobs and go on tour with you because you wanted this? You need to start acting like it.* On a normal night, Julie would call me in tears at ten o'clock, wishing for her old life back. I would talk her down, reminding her that this was what we'd both always wanted.

Suddenly I realized I was hanging on to the edge of the bench with a death grip, and my fingertips had gone numb. Taking a deep breath and making a conscious effort to relax, I saw that Sam and I were nearly alone in the auditorium. Only a few ushers laughed in the far corner, wondering how long they should give us before they kicked us out.

I turned to Sam. "So, I wanted to come clean with you and show you everything I know about my sister. Her first single is out today. She has enormous record company backing. She may or may not drop the ball. It's too early to tell, I guess. And I am persona non grata. I bought these tickets myself."

"Regardless, you could still use your connections to get us an audition with the record company if you swallowed your pride and asked."

Oh, so he *wasn't* going to play nice after all. Hurt and shocked and insulted, I told him, "I knew it was going to be like this from the moment I met you. I wanted to show you this, and I was hoping we could save whatever we had. But the bottom line is, you don't want to be with me now, and I don't want to be with you."

"I want desperately to be with you," he said quietly. "I just know that I would be angry with you every second of my life, and it wouldn't work."

I met his dark, worried gaze. "You wear your heart on your sleeve." I reached out and touched the heart I'd drawn on the soft cotton of his T-shirt. My finger slipped under the material and stroked his warm skin, then pressed his hard biceps more firmly. His arm didn't give.

The feeling started small, tingles of awareness around my fingertips where they touched him. The feeling raced up my arm and across my chest. I knew my face was flaming, and I tried to figure out why. We'd kissed, after all. He'd put his hands pretty much everywhere there was to put them. There was no reason for me to blush with my ears burning just because I was touching his arm.

But as the strange warmth continued, I realized what was different this time. Instead of him touching me, propositioning me, coming on to me, *I* had touched *him*. He'd talked about my standoffishness, that gulf between us. Without meaning to, I'd reached across it.

And I couldn't take it back now. He was thinking what I was thinking. Head tilted and eyes down, he watched my hand stroking his skin. His eyes didn't rise to mine. Maybe he suspected, as I did, that if our eyes met, we'd be acknowledging what was going on, and the spell would be broken.

The spell was too good. We both wanted to stay under it.

I continued to move my fingers across his skin exactly as I had before, but I needed to make a decision. I had reached for him, but I could back out of it by trailing my fingers down his arm and settling my hand in his, like I wanted us to be friends.

I didn't want us to be friends.

Ever so slowly, I slid my hand up his sleeve, across his shoulder, and up his neck to cradle his jaw, prickly with stubble.

He bit his lip. "Let's go back to my house," he whispered, "and we can discuss our differences in private."

We'd both forgotten about the storm blowing up. As soon as we climbed the stairs and slipped through the doors into the lobby, we could hear the rain beating on the windows.

Sam turned to me in question. I replied, "I still don't have an umbrella."

"Give me your keys and I'll bring your car around."

"I'll get soaked on the walk to the driveway, no matter what."

He continued to look questioningly at me. He'd been raised a southern gentleman. Whether the ladies were already soaked or not, gentlemen brought the car around in the rain. Their alcoholic fathers taught them this. The fathers might not be much good to the family, but they would bring the car around in the rain. This was another song in the making, one I struggled to push to the back of my mind. Now was not the time. I took Sam's hand and said, "Come on."

We agreed silently that it would do us no good to run. The rain came down so fast that no puddles formed, only swift rivers down the sidewalk. Under an awning near the driveway, several people huddled, laughing that they were wet, waiting for a shuttle to the huge hotel nearby, but those were the only folks we encountered all the way across the shining parking lot, empty except for my car. The temperature had dropped twenty degrees since we first entered the theater. A stiff, cold breeze chased us the last few yards.

I shut my door and yelled, "Yuck!" I started the ignition.

"Yeah." Sam turned up the heat. He adjusted the dials as I drove and the windshield fogged up. He placed his other hand on the inside of my thigh, not high enough to distract me from driving, but in exactly the right place to remind me where we were headed.

Back at his house, I parked as close to the side door as I could get. "Let me unlock it first," he said. "Most families would have umbrellas waiting in the vestibule or whatever, but we don't have a vestibule, much less an umbrella." He trudged to the door, unlocked it, then nonsensically came back for me as if I couldn't walk three steps through a downpour by myself, and ushered me inside.

We kicked off our shoes on the rug just inside the door, and he poured water into an automatic coffeepot. Then he came back to me, placing himself between me and the door like he thought I might escape. "Why don't you take your clothes off," he whispered, "and I'll put them in the dryer."

Suddenly I wasn't freezing anymore, even in the air-conditioned kitchen. Heat raced across my skin. I knew what we were going to do. I had accepted this since the end of Julie's show. But every new hint at it was like an electric shock to my system.

He stood in front of the door with his arms folded across his tight, soaked T-shirt, melting my insides with his dark eyes. He wasn't going anywhere. He wanted to watch.

I might have tried very hard in the past year to give off the vibe that I undressed in front of boys every night of the week, but it just wasn't true. Swallowing, I asked, "Could you turn off the light?"

He reached to the wall and flicked the switch. The kitchen vanished. All that was left was his silhouette in front of me, framed by the streetlight streaming through the window in the top of the door. He could probably still see me pretty well. Now that I couldn't see his face, I felt more at ease.

The soaked cotton of my T-shirt felt like a cold compress on a wound. After I stripped it off, my skin burned hotter. All I had on underneath was my black bra.

I tossed the T-shirt to him.

The jeans were harder. Now that they were wet, they hugged me even more tightly. I struggled to force them down my legs, hoping my black lace panties made this striptease worthwhile to Sam. I had no idea what I was doing.

I half expected him to chuckle in the darkness. He didn't make a sound. I finally tossed the jeans to him, and his silhouette caught them with one hand. He cleared his throat. "Be right back." His voice broke. He turned and disappeared into a room just off the kitchen. I heard his own clothes slide off his body and the dryer shift to life. In nothing but boxers, the muted light smoothing his taut muscles, he crossed the shadowy kitchen and poured us each a cup of tea.

With shaking hands rattling the teacup on its saucer, I followed him through the old house, the small rooms and narrow passageways and squeaky wooden floors. Upstairs he led me down a short hall and opened a door for me. I expected his room to be wallpapered with signed posters of the Eli Young Band or the Zac Brown Band. Instead, I walked into a guest room with blank powder-blue walls and a crazy quilt on the bed. The weight bench in the corner was probably his, but everybody stored their exercise equipment in the guest room.

Wondering why Sam was taking me here instead of his own room, I looked back over my shoulder at him. Maybe there was something in his own room he didn't want me to see—in which case I wanted to see it. When I'd first met him a few days ago, I'd tiptoed around him and let him keep his secrets. That time was over.

"My mom erased me," he explained. "The plant shut down for a week in May. That doesn't happen often when people are buying a lot of cars, so she always tries to get as much done around the house as she can. She'd already planned to make my room into a guest room when I went to college. She just did it a little early while she had the time."

"If she erased you," I said, "where did you go?"

He turned around and nodded to the boxes lined up against the wall. Here were the rolled-up posters of country bands, no doubt. In the shadows of one box glinted his gold football trophies. He paused, gazing down at them as if looking for himself.

I took his cup from him. As I moved, cool air brushed past my bare thighs, and I remembered I was walking around a boy's room in my underwear. But that was what I'd come here for. I turned and placed one cup on either bedside table, then crawled onto the bed.

He left the room, then came back with a lit candle and placed it on the dresser. He turned out the light. The candlelight dashed across the room and rippled on the black ceiling like water. His shadow crossed to the far wall and opened a window. The sound of the rain and wind rushed in. The light on the ceiling transformed from a gentle ebb and flow into a stormy sea.

As I watched him, I sipped my tea. My mouth filled with hot sweetness. Now he crawled onto the foot of the bed and moved forward to meet me. All of his bare skin warmed all of mine in the cool room. My heart raced and my skin sparkled with the knowledge that no one would disturb us now. No one would stop us. There was nothing to prevent us from losing ourselves to each other, except logic, and heartbreak, and every sound reason in the world.

♪ ♫ ♪

We moved very slowly. It was like fooling around in front of a glacier. We couldn't see it advancing, but we knew that it was about to crush us, yet we didn't get out of the way.

What felt like hours later, when we were naked and totally open for each other, he interlaced his fingers with mine so that our hands were clasped. He nudged our hands with his prickly chin, watching me. "I want to," he whispered. "Do you?"

Heart pounding, I nodded. "I do."

"Promise?" he asked.

"Promise." My voice came out hoarse.

He rolled off the bed and crossed the room. With a start I realized he'd disappeared out the door. I'd been stuck on the fact that I'd seen him, all of him, naked. Like an afterimage when I'd stared at the sun, I kept seeing him though he wasn't there.

I'd gotten this close to sex with Liam Keel at a party, and with Aidan Rogers at a party, and with Toby at a party initially and lots more times after that. Though I'd desperately wanted to be a bad girl and I'd thought I wanted to have sex, I couldn't go through with it with someone I didn't love. And the setting had been different—the back porch at the house where the party was going on, a truck, Toby's car. Never a bed. Never a bedroom, wide enough to see the boy crossing it and coming back with a condom. Before I'd only seen the guy close up, too close for perspective. Sam I saw clearly in the candlelight, shoulders strong and biceps unexpectedly big and solid for such a gentle guy, his eyes on me, his pace deliberate. I owed it to myself to keep my eyes open and watch him. I wasn't going to dream through this.

He rolled onto the bed beside me again, kissed my forehead, and tore the package open. I watched him put the condom on. And all the while I was thinking through what this meant. He knew I was on the pill. He was using a condom anyway. My doctor had lectured me that the pill protected against pregnancy but not STDs. She'd said I should use a condom too unless I was in a committed, monogamous relationship.

That wasn't what this was. It never would be. And if Sam wanted to protect himself or me with a condom, either he hadn't believed me when I'd said I was a virgin, or he'd been lying himself.

"Hey," he whispered. "My eyes are up here."

I laughed nervously and met his gaze. At some point I'd clasped my hands in front of my mouth. I must have looked to him like I was terrified.

And maybe that was the reason for the condom. He could tell how scared I was, and he wanted me to have no doubts.

He wrapped one hand around both of mine. "Your hands are cold." He inched forward until our foreheads touched. "Are you okay?"

"Yes."

"Ready?"

Was I?

"Yes," I said.

I tried not to think about him and me. I didn't see how things could possibly work out between us, even though he obviously wanted that now, and I did, too. The best-case scenario was that he was a boy I loved, who would break my heart and leave me. We would stay together for days, weeks, even months. When I looked back on it later, though, I wouldn't remember our slow fall out of love. All I would remember was this one night.

So I tried to commit to memory every feeling of my first time. But there was a point when everything turned a corner and left me shocked by what I saw there. He made me feel too good, and I loved him too much. There was no way we could leave each other after this.

♪ ♫ ♪

Much later, the rain stopped, leaving only the sound of the breeze in the window. The candlelight had dimmed on the ceiling. Sam lay facing me with his arm across my waist, and his chin nestled against my shoulder. My body felt completely flattened, so tired and satisfied that I sank into the mattress. Yet every molecule of me was aware of him, as though I were standing in the makeshift dressing room in the mall, naked and listening for his voice or his guitar.

I murmured sleepily, "I thought it wasn't supposed to be any good the first time."

He propped himself up on his elbows and looked at me like I'd gone loco. "Girls may say that. Guys don't." He grinned at me and stroked a lock of hair away from my face. "I hate to say this, but you'd better go. It's getting so late that even I won't be able to explain it to your granddad. I don't want you to have to drive across town so late, but if I drove you, that would—"

"No, that would just be harder to explain," I agreed.

His mouth turned down, and his dark eyes grew serious. The candlelight played eerily across his face as he said, "I want you to know how much this has meant to me. I'm so glad we were each other's first." His brows knitted. "That didn't come out right. This is why I don't write songs."

I wondered if he was backtracking because of the look on my face. He sounded like he was saying we were each other's first, and that was the end of it.

Suddenly he gushed, "Bailey, you have completely turned me upside down in the last four days. Which makes sense, right? There's a country song about this. Deana Carter sings about it. Lady Antebellum sings about it. Gosh, not just country artists. Katy Perry. Everybody has a song about it because everybody's been through it. You find that person at eighteen and you lose yourself. And the tragedy is, it's the person who's completely opposed to everything you've ever wanted. You bond with that person, and that person breaks your heart. I'm that tragedy for you, and you're mine."

This was definitely the end of it.

"What about Alan Jackson?" I breathed.

Sam gazed sadly at me, stroking my bottom lip tenderly with one callused finger. "Not everybody can be that lucky."

Those words were still sinking in as I murmured, "I started the night thinking that way, Sam, but now . . . don't you want to try to work this out?" I sounded a lot more desperate than I wanted to.

His finger stopped on my lip. "Are you going to ask your family to try to get an in for our band?"

"No," I whispered.

He shook his head. "Then we can't be together. In my head I know that's wrong, Bailey, but I have to follow my heart. I'm messed up right now, and I can't give you what you deserve."

Suddenly his touch burned like a cold knife. I slipped out from under him, found my underwear on the floor, and pulled it on. "That's what you said to Charlotte when you broke up with her, Sam. That's what you said to everyone."

I ran out of the room and down the stairs. I stopped in the tiny laundry room off the kitchen and fished my clothes out of the dryer. In the darkness I mistook Sam's shirt for mine until I pulled it on and, in addition to hanging off me, it smelled like him. Cursing, I tossed it into the dryer and found my own.

"I wasn't lying," came Sam's voice.

He was leaning against the doorjamb to the kitchen in his boxers, with his arms crossed, his face grim, his hair wild, looking like the hunky half of an argument in a country music video. "You were special."

"Oh, *was* I, in the past tense?" I shot back. "I was different from your other girlfriends, right?"

"Yes," Sam said.

"Because we screwed."

His lips parted.

"Tell me the truth," I insisted before he could speak. "Was this another one of those life experiences you try to accumulate because they make you uncomfortable? Are you going to channel this emotion and use it when you sing?"

He unfolded his arms and stood up straight.

"I see," I said. "It's that genre of country song, the one where you break it to your lady that you don't love her, and she drives away in tears. Sorry, but I'm not going to give you that satisfaction."

I slipped my shoes on, picked up my purse, and calmly walked outside to my car. Sam stood in the doorway watching me, the mist after the rain curling around him in my headlight beams as I backed down his driveway.

Dead tired, I just wanted to get home and go to bed. That helped me remain calm—right up until railroad crossing guardrails descended in front of my car. The warning signal clanged its bells. The train moaned its off-key tritone, louder and louder and louder until it filled my head and I couldn't hear myself think.

I slapped my hands over my ears and yelled, "I would like out of this country song now. I want out of this country song *right now!*"

I wasn't sure who I was praying to. The ghost of Johnny Cash, maybe. But nothing changed. The train still moaned. The signal clanged and flashed like a migraine. And when the end of the train finally slipped past me and disappeared into the Nashville night, I knew I wouldn't get to sleep until I wrote this song down.

13

I spent the next afternoon suffering through Hank Williams's yo-deling and wondering about the big party that the record company was throwing for Julie that night. At dinner my granddad told me gently that he'd talked to my mom the night before and tried to convince her to invite me, but she was too afraid the record company wouldn't like it. I suspected she was afraid I would jump on the buffet and start throwing canapés just to spite everyone.

My granddad seemed especially gleeful that I was going out with Sam again, as if that made him feel less guilty that I wasn't included in Julie's celebration. The closer the party time came, the more resentful I felt that Julie and my dad hadn't stood up to my mom and invited me, and the better I felt that I was about to dis-obey my parents again.

I just wished I'd been able to do that without seeing Sam. There was the appearance of love, the trappings of it that I put in songs. There was real love, the kind I was afraid I'd felt for Sam last night. And then there was the ache I was feeling, intense and depthless. I had never heard a song like this, either because nobody had ever been this heartbroken, or because a tune that depressing wouldn't sell.

Sam never called me, but I knew he was in communication with Ace. Ace had said Monday night that he would call to make sure I was coming to the gig at Boot Ilicious if Sam and I weren't speaking. I knew he wouldn't have called me *four* times, though, if a nervous Sam hadn't been goading him into it. I parked in the deck Sam and I had used and abused our first night together, then walked a few doors down to the eighteen-and-up bar. My fiddle got me a pass inside without paying cover, and the bouncers pointed me upstairs.

At the top of two flights, on the roof with a view of nearby skyscrapers on one side and the Cumberland River and Titans stadium on the other, the band stood onstage as if ready to start playing without me.

I could see them only because the stage was two feet above the roof. The place was packed with college-age partiers. Some of the first people I spotted were the girls who'd gotten a manicure on Elvis day at the mall last week. I saw a few other boys I knew from school, who didn't recognize me in the tiny, tight red cocktail dress I'd snagged at the mall that afternoon and paired with my red cowgirl boots and red cat-eye glasses in a statement of ironic overkill. So far, no Toby, but there were three floors to this bar, and it was already almost nine o'clock. He was probably here somewhere. The first guy to recognize me would text him so that he could come up here and laugh at me. I could feel it.

But I had a job to do, a work ethic for the forbidden. I sashayed through the crowd. I was still three people deep away from the stage when I saw Sam's face change under his cowboy hat, from worry to relief. He held out a hand and hauled me up onstage with one strong arm.

"Where have you been?" he demanded.

"Ace told me to be here at nine," I said, glancing at my watch. It was five until.

"You know I'm in danger of a stroke until you get here," Sam growled.

I shrugged. "I had other things to do."

"I hope you're not giving her everything you gave to me on her behalf," Ace said, stepping between us. "You look like shit, Sam. Just back off everybody."

Sam *did* look like he hadn't gotten any more sleep since I'd woken him at six the night before. In fact, he looked like his haggard father imitating Johnny Cash. He gave Ace a sullen glare, then pulled out his cell phone to text us the playlist.

"But *you* look beautiful," Ace told me.

I was glad *someone* had noticed I'd outdone myself tonight, if you liked this sort of thing. I gave him a saucy curtsy in thanks, but I wished he hadn't said it in front of Charlotte, who'd come from behind her drum kit to lurk, listen in, and scowl.

"I don't know what to play for these people," Sam was muttering at his phone. "I guess . . . all of the Ke$ha. Then what?"

Because he needed her so badly, Charlotte stepped close to him, looked over his shoulder at his phone, and made suggestions from our repertoire for the playlist. Without looking up, he reached behind her and rubbed the back of her neck in an overly friendly gesture of camaraderie. It was amazing that she stayed upright, because her shoulders collapsed like a rag doll under his hand.

Ace's eyes locked with mine in a mutual understanding of jealousy and disgust. But knowing Ace was dying inside, too, didn't make me feel any better. I wound my way to the back of the stage, brought out my fiddle and dumped my case, and rushed back to the front before the restless crowd started chanting.

When I first surveyed the audience, I'd been afraid they wouldn't like our music, at least after we ran out of Ke$ha. But they were enthusiastic to the point of frenzy, and a couple of fights broke out at the edges of the rooftop. I thought the difference was that this audience was younger than our usual spectators, and some of them were drinking underage and weren't handling it well. It was also the largest crowd I'd seen at Boot Ilicious. The pushing that resulted made everyone testy. Normally the audience would be spread out over three stories of dance floors, but tonight most of them seemed to be crowding here.

It didn't bother me, as long as they didn't touch me or nudge my bow. It bothered Sam, though. Between songs, he kept casting a worried eye across the sea of screaming faces, and he didn't respond with much enthusiasm to the calls of "Sam!" from the groupie girls from his high school who had finally caught up with him. When we'd almost reached our ten o'clock break and I pointed behind Ace, wordlessly asking him to pass me the tip jar, Sam shook his head at both of us and pointed at Ace. Ace got down from the stage and held the jar instead of me. I didn't mouth a thank-you to Sam, but judging from some of the grinding that had been passing for dancing in the crowd, I was grateful.

At the break, Sam set his guitar in its stand and headed inside. I knew I wouldn't be following him. Better to get through this night as far away from him as possible. Instead, I headed to the back of the stage and set one elbow on the guardrail at the edge of the roof. Preparations were still under way for the CMA Festival that started tomorrow. Julie's first performance of the festival would be tomorrow night, almost directly below me at the Riverwalk stage. On the other side of the Cumberland River, the Titans stadium glowed. Tomorrow it would host some headliners for the CMA Festival, probably six country superstars back-to-back in one long concert. The next night, Friday, Julie would be one of them.

Not one member of my family had contacted me about going. Both concerts were probably sold out by now. I hadn't checked. I wasn't going to spend my life following Julie around and lurking in her shadow. I'd had enough of that last night.

Out of the corner of my eye, I saw someone sidling up next to me at the wall. I turned to glare at whoever it was. Nobody but the band should have been back here. Ace wouldn't go out of his way to talk to me, and Sam had *better* not. Not tonight. And the *last* person I wanted to talk to right now was—

Charlotte. "I see you've decided to let the crowd focus on Sam rather than you tonight," she said. "You wouldn't want to distract anyone with what you're wearing."

"You know what?" I turned on her so suddenly that she stepped back. "This may be the last time I'll ever play in public, and I wanted to go out with a bang. Sam gave me the line last night. 'I'm messed up right now, and I can't give you what you deserve.' Remember? You got what you wanted, so turn that frown upside down."

I turned to gaze at the stages along the river again and waited for her to scamper inside the bar in search of Sam.

"That's not right," she said. "That shouldn't have happened to you."

I didn't know what she meant by that, and I didn't care anymore.

"I know I've given you a lot of grief," she said, "but I just didn't want Sam bringing random people into the band without checking with me, when I've worked so hard with these guys. And then it seemed like Ace . . ."

As her voice trailed off, I looked over at her. Her eyes were searching the restless crowd for Ace, not Sam.

She turned back to me. "You don't understand. Ever since Sam's girlfriend—"

"Which one?" I asked sharply.

"Emily." Her tone made it sound like I should know all about Emily. "Ever since she died, it's like that was so intense for him that he can't really feel anymore. He's had a lot of girlfriends, but I don't think he ever got this serious with anybody. He didn't with me. If he did with you, and then broke up with you, it sounds like he's getting worse."

"His girlfriend died?" I echoed.

"He didn't tell you that?"

I swallowed. "He told me he had a friend who died in a drunk-driving accident."

Charlotte watched me carefully now as she realized I knew way less about this than she'd thought. "The police said it was an accident."

I pulled my hand away from my face right before I rubbed under my eye. "Is that why he went to counseling?"

"Grief counseling, yeah," Charlotte said. "I wish they hadn't kicked him out. All he did was ask a girl in the group on a date, and her dad had a fit and complained about Sam, which was exactly what he didn't need right then. If he'd stayed in the group, I think he'd be a lot better now. Ever since then, I don't think he's meaning to be a playboy or to be cruel. It's just that girls are attracted to him and feel sorry for him and want to save him. He likes them, too. He likes everybody. He wants to feel that emotion. But then, when he starts to feel too much for a girl, he's scared she feels the same way about him. And he doesn't want anybody to feel that strongly about him again, because of Emily. He tells me he doesn't believe she killed herself over him, and he doesn't feel guilty, but I think that's just what he's telling himself so he can survive."

She met my gaze. "I'm really sorry, Bailey. I am honestly shocked that you got the line from him, too. I thought you were different."

"I knew I wasn't." I pushed off from the wall, snagged my purse from the top of my fiddle case, and shoved my way toward the door inside. I probably should have thanked Charlotte for all the information, but I wasn't in a grateful mood.

Inside, I wound around knots of bawdy frat boys and giggling fashionistas to find Sam and Ace in a dark corner. When Sam glanced up at me and stopped talking, I knew they'd been conferring about me. As if that wasn't obvious enough, Ace turned to look at me, too, and his eyes widened.

I stood in front of them. "Can I have a minute with Sam?" I asked Ace.

Ace cut his eyes to Sam, who looked like he wished Ace wouldn't abandon him there with me. Ace didn't dare stay after he saw the look on my face, but he did tap his watch. "We don't have much time," he said as he dove back into the crowd.

I turned to Sam. "Now," I said, "tell me about your girlfriend."

Some small part of me held out hope that Charlotte had been wrong, or lying, and Sam would have no idea what I was talking about. But he knew exactly who I meant. My heart sank into the pit of my stomach as he eyed me and said, heartbreakingly serious, "I told you about Emily."

"No, you didn't," I assured him.

His brow furrowed. "I didn't want to mess things up between us."

"Maybe you shouldn't have screwed me and then broken up with me."

"I did not *screw*—" His eyes flew to the girls in clubbing dresses who turned to look us up and down. Then he whispered to me, "You can't do this to me right now."

"*I* can't do this to *you*?"

"At a gig," he explained. "We're still in this band together."

I could tell from the blaze behind his eyes that he was not backing down. Nothing mattered except this gig, until the gig was over.

I wasn't backing down either. Not this time. "You need to get over that," I said. "What if the next girl you take advantage of confronts you right before you go onstage at the Opry?"

"No," he said firmly, forgetting that he was trying not to attract attention to our fight. "Do not go there. Girls always say guys took advantage of them or talked them into something. Guys say girls seduced them. What you and I did was mutual. Don't you dare say it wasn't."

"You have some kind of problem," I told him, "and you used me to try to get over it, like you've used a hundred other girls in the past year."

"A hundr—" He stopped himself with a grimace, glanced around at the crowd, and started again. "I don't want that kind of excuse. The truth is, Emily and I dated for a year. That's a long time for me, longer than I've ever dated anybody. At first she was really excited about my gigs, and I was excited about her being excited. But we started to get on each other's nerves. She never seemed to have her own . . . not a gig, exactly. She didn't play gigs. But she never had her own metaphorical gig. A thing. An event. A sport she played, something she did so *I* could come watch *her*. Maybe I should have been flattered by that, but it got to be too much. I felt suffocated because all her attention was on me all the time, and I didn't feel the same way about her.

"I'd decided to tell her that and break up with her, but I didn't want to hurt her feelings, because we'd had a lot of fun together and I still liked her. Then she wanted to go to a party and I refused to go. Sometimes I skip parties if there's drinking. I don't mind other people drinking, but at parties the assholes want to get me drunk for the first time because they think it would be hilarious. So I told her I wasn't going, and I planned to tell her the next time I saw her that it was over between us. At the party she got drunk. She didn't have a ride home. She crashed her car into a guardrail and died."

He said all of this matter-of-factly, with no change in the tone of his voice. But his fists tightened, and the muscles moved in his forearm.

"Her family wanted me to sit with them at the funeral, which I did. All her relatives and friends were telling me if only she hadn't died, we would have been together forever."

"They *said* that to you?"

"Yes, which . . . you forgive people for saying weird shit when somebody dies. The thing is, none of it is true. She wasn't the love of my life, and I'm not going to pretend she was just because she's dead."

He peeked out from under his cowboy hat at the crowd, like he was about to get caught with his hand in my dress. I wished now that our problems were that simple. I wished for the fight from our first night together.

He said, "And then sometimes I think I'm being really weird about that because as long as I'm angry about the whole thing, I can't panic."

"What would you panic about?" I asked. "That you weren't there?"

"To drive her home. Yeah. I had told a couple of friends that I was going to break up with her. After the wreck, some people were saying she'd heard about that, and she drove off the road on purpose. In another version, she just got really drunk at the party because she was so upset about me, and that's what caused her to have a wreck later. Either way, it's my fault. Maybe I was put on this earth to do one thing, to get her home safely, and I didn't do it."

I looked around the bar, at the girls sipping beer and laughing. The way they eyed Sam, I knew any one of them would be glad to comfort him in his grief and loss. Maybe valuing myself as much as I valued him made me strangely cold. As his friend, I would have been glad to help him get over his problems. I didn't appreciate being surprised by them as his lover.

"You date a girl until you start to have feelings for her," I told him, "and then you break up with her. But you never got very far with anyone. Which means one of two things for me. Either I'm incredibly easy, and you knew that and took advantage. *Or,* you felt less for me than you've ever felt for anybody, because you were able to get so far with me before you got uncomfortable and ended it."

His nostrils flared in distaste, and he stood up straighter against the wall. "You think I'm a nice guy and you can say anything to me, but there's a limit to how much bullshit I'll listen to from you. Emily doesn't have anything to do with you. I didn't break up with you because of her. I just realized we can't ever be together. You'll always wonder whether I'm just using you for your sister's connections."

"And you really *will* be using me."

He looked down, half an acknowledgment.

"Anyway," I said, "I'm not saying you broke up with me because of Emily. Charlotte also told me that when Emily died, that's when your emotional problems started."

He looked sharply at me.

"At first it seems like you feel more than other people," I said.

"But I've finally figured out Charlotte's right. You feel less. You're numb. And you're trying to get some of that emotion back, even if it hurts. Even if it hurts other people. I really thought you and I had a connection. I know I didn't always show it. I tried not to. But when you broke up with me, you broke my heart. And I swear you made it worse on purpose. You wanted to make it the ultimate breakup by consummating our love first."

"The way you acted, I honestly didn't think you cared," Sam said. "Not like I did."

"I see." I nodded. "You're telling me I'm an emotionless bitch."

"Not a bitch," he said levelly, ever the gentleman.

"Really," I said. "Here's how much I care about you, Sam." I opened my purse and pulled out my illustrated notebook of songs. I flipped through the pages and ripped out four together. "Here's a song about you screwing me and then breaking up with me, thus trapping me forever in a fucking country song. This is how I felt about that last night." I shoved the pages at his chest.

He opened the pages in his hands, but I didn't watch him read them. I was already searching backward through the notebook for another choice song. "Here's how I felt when I first met you, since *that* obviously wasn't clear. Oh, wait." I flipped in the other direction. "Would you rather know how I felt when we couldn't get along, but I knew we'd be onstage together the next night anyway? Or how I felt when you undressed me in your truck?"

"Bailey," he said sternly, like I was a little girl making a scene. "We have a gig."

"I beg your pardon," I exclaimed. "A gig! There's nothing more important." I yanked the torn pages from him, folded them inside the notebook, and shoved the whole thing back into his chest.

"Here are my songs, my emotions about you, that I will never have again. Take them and climb to the top with them. I have no use for them or for you."

I spun on my boot heel and pushed through the crowd and the stuffy air to the rooftop. As I emerged under the stars and the twinkling lights strung along the walls, I saw Charlotte and Ace at the guardrail where Charlotte and I had talked. She was on her tiptoes, about to kiss him. The hair on my arms stood up.

"Oh, don't do it," I said to myself, but I meant it for her. Whatever was standing between them, they hadn't worked it out, and she was about to ruin everything.

He stayed stock-still for a moment. Then he slipped one hand behind her head and kissed her deeply. Just as suddenly, he stepped away from her. He was angry at her, pointing his finger in her face, pointing out at the crowd. I saw him mouth, "Sam," and Charlotte burst into tears.

"That's right," I told her, though she still couldn't hear me and it was none of my business, anyway. "You should never start something when you haven't finished the last thing. People feel used that way."

"What?" Sam demanded. He'd caught up with me.

"Absolutely nothing," I said, grasping the hand that Ace offered me from the stage. Charlotte still stood against the guardrail, sobbing.

"Well, *this* will be a fun set." As I grabbed my fiddle and tuned up, I noticed that the manicure girls stood near the door, talking with Aidan Rogers. He gazed up at me and opened his mouth in utter amazement. Immediately he pulled out his phone and thumbed the keyboard.

I muttered, "And here comes Toby."

I had no doubt Aidan really texted Toby then, but it took Toby three songs to reach the roof, probably because he was three sheets. Despite the fact that he'd changed his hair from dyed black to bleached blond and gotten a second eyebrow piercing in the week and a half since the wreck, I recognized him right away because he was so tall and thin, a head above the crowd. He stood next to Aidan for a moment, talking with Aidan but never taking his eyes off me. Then he started to move in my direction.

I had nothing to worry about. He could stare all he wanted, but I felt safe several feet above the crowd and him. I turned away from him and watched Sam for the signal to start the fourth song.

The next time I looked around, Toby was alarmingly close. Despite the tightly packed crowd, he'd managed to push within three people of the stage. He locked eyes with me. I lifted my chin and looked at the Nashville skyline, concentrating on my solo.

Then when I looked down, he was right next to me. My heart jumped, but I didn't. I didn't even glance over at Sam for help. I didn't need his help. Toby would never intimidate me again.

Even though I'd made an effort not to signal to Sam about what was going on like a helpless female, somehow he knew. "Next we'd like to do an easy Johnny Cash tune for you," he said into the microphone. "'Cocaine Blues.'"

I had no time to check for Toby's reaction. "Cocaine Blues" was a doozy, not the kind of song that the lead singer of a band should drop into the playlist and spring on his fiddle player, especially after he'd lulled her into a false sense of security with Justin Timberlake and Ke$ha. We got through it okay, though, because we were professional musicians. And then when I glanced down at Toby, he was looking straight up at me and licking his lips.

I pulled Sam's handkerchief from the pocket of my dress and wiped both my sweating palms, holding my fiddle and bow in the crook of one elbow and then the other.

"Switch places with me," Sam called. His voice didn't register with me at first because he'd said it outside the range of the microphone. When I understood what was going on and looked over at him, he nodded toward Toby, then moved his finger between himself and me.

I hadn't asked for his help, but I wasn't going to refuse it, either. Obediently I switched places with him. We took a moment to detangle our cords while the crowd whooped impatiently. Sam glanced behind him at Ace and Charlotte, who must have been motioning that they wanted to know what was going on, because Sam put up his hands and shrugged. His one-night stand's leering ex was hard to explain during a set. He signaled to Charlotte to start the next song.

I tried not to look toward Toby. I kept my chin up and my eyes above the crowd. But he was so close to the stage that I couldn't miss his white-blond head and the angry curses from other guys as he pushed his way from Sam's side of the stage to my new side.

When the song ended, Sam took a moment to stare Toby down silently. *Don't do this,* I messaged telepathically to Sam. Challenging Toby would only make things worse. But Sam and I had no psychic connection. The crowd got restless. Someone yelled, "Play 'Freebird'!" Sam glared at Toby for a few seconds more and finally signaled to Charlotte, who started the song.

And Toby grabbed my ankle.

I never stopped playing. The crowd didn't notice mistakes. They noticed hesitation. I could play right through this number and then deal with Toby.

His hand slid up my calf to pause at the back of my knee.

Now I was shivering, afraid he would yank me offstage and forward into the crowd. My fiddle might get scratched, and my mother would never forgive me.

His hand moved up the back of my thigh, under my skirt.

Sam's voice and guitar riff disappeared. *He'd* stopped playing and was staring at Toby. Slowly I lowered my fiddle like Toby was a snake I didn't want to startle with any sudden moves.

It took Ace and Charlotte another few seconds to stop playing. Even the crowd noise slowed to a halt. Into the dead silence on the rooftop, Sam growled into the microphone so that his words echoed against the brick walls, "Get your hands off my fiddle player."

Holding my fiddle and bow, I didn't have a hand free to defend myself. I could only shudder as Toby's hand crept higher.

Sam dropped his guitar. I felt a spike of adrenaline and the urge to leap forward and catch it. But before the electrified strings' earsplitting complaint sounded over the speakers, Sam was off the stage, shoving Toby.

Guys shouted. Girls screamed. I reached blindly into the crowd to grab Sam and only succeeded in dropping my bow. Ace leaped past me. The entire crowd shifted to the left, then parted, drawing Toby and Sam away from each other, despite some idiot hollering, "Fight!"

The door to the interior of the bar burst open. "Break it up!" a burly bouncer yelled. Two even bigger men followed him. The crowd stopped moving toward Toby and Sam then and began to drain sheepishly out the door. One of the bouncers grabbed Toby by the collar of his T-shirt and made a show of muscling him out, even though Toby had gone limp. In two minutes, nobody was left but a couple of older men who probably owned the bar, and the band.

I jumped down from the stage to retrieve my bow, which didn't seem any worse for wear after I'd retightened the screw. Then I sat down on the edge of the stage, crossed my legs primly, and listened to the owners cuss Sam out because they'd had to clear everyone into the first and second stories until the next rooftop band set up, and a lot of those people would probably leave.

"Your patron had his hand on my girlfriend's ass!" Sam shouted right back at them. "I won't start a brawl if your security people do their jobs!"

That's when Ace walked over. "Please excuse us for a moment," he told the owners. He put his hand on Sam's chest and pushed him backward across the floor, all the way to me on the stage. Then he hissed, "Shut up. Let me handle this."

"Ace," Sam cried, "they—"

"Shut. Up!" Ace insisted. He gave Sam one last glare, then sauntered back to the group of men with his hand out for introductions like he was selling them a car. Sam scowled after them for a moment, then took out his phone and scowled at that.

Charlotte sat down beside me—not between me and Sam, for once, but on my other side. With her eyes on Ace, she whispered to me, "Do you think you could possibly take me and my drums home?"

"Sure," I said with lots of fake enthusiasm, "if they'll fit in my car."

"Ace isn't talking to me," she said. "I think I fucked up."

"I think you did, too," I said.

"Thank you," Ace called to the men, who were retreating through the door into the bar. "See you soon." When they'd disappeared, he turned to us with rage in his normally placid face. "Well, we're not blackballed," he said, "but we have five minutes to clear out before the next band. I swear to God, I'm not sure I even want to be in this band anymore. I am sick to death of you." He pointed at Sam. "And you!" He had a special scowl for Charlotte. Then he turned to me. "And . . . I don't know *what* the fuck you're doing half the time. The way things are going, I'd just as soon quit."

"That's too bad," Sam said quietly, handing Ace his phone with an e-mail message open, "because tomorrow night, we're playing on Broadway."

♪ ♫ ♪

The next afternoon, at the end of a long four hours touring the mall with Mr. Crabtree and Elvis, I slipped into Ms. Lottie's chair.

"Well, hon," she said by way of greeting, "I didn't think your face could get any longer than it already was."

Suddenly angry and tired of her teasing, I burst out, "Remember when you told me Sam Hardiman was a heartbreaker?"

She stared at me in the mirror with two hairpins in her mouth and two hands on my ponytail wig.

"I am done with all the sage advice Nashville has to offer. If you're going to hurt, not help, what are you dispensing advice for?"

Frowning, she spat out the pins, which made the smallest *clink*s as they hit the floor, and spun me around in the chair to face her. She towered over me with her hands on her hips. "Sam Hardiman is a good man," she declared angrily.

"O-kay," I said, hoping my ironic tone would kick her out of my business and shut her up.

No such luck. "He is not a drinker," she said, tapping her pointer finger with a long, French-manicured nail. "He is at work every time he's supposed to be." She tapped her middle finger, then paused on her thumb. "He didn't cheat on you, did he?"

A lump formed in my throat. I couldn't even answer her. He had *better* not cheat on me. But now that we weren't together, he could do what he wanted. The thought of him hooking up with someone else stopped me from breathing.

"Then you need to get your ass off your shoulders," she told me, "and figure out how to make it work."

"There's more to it than that!" I exclaimed. "You make it sound stupidly simple, like a country song."

She looked over her bifocals and down her nose at me. "Country songs are so simple because they're about what really matters."

"Would you *stop* it with the *aphorisms*?"

Abruptly she spun me back around in the chair. We faced each other in the mirror. Muttering to herself, she took the rest of the pins out of my ponytail wig and lifted it off my head. I scowled down at my hands in my lap. I should have been relieved our confrontation was over, but the lump in my throat hadn't gone away. I swallowed.

"Bailey."

I looked up at Ms. Lottie in the mirror.

She put her hands on my shoulders and asked my reflection, "Do you have a gig with Sam tonight?"

I nodded sadly.

She fingered my black hair. "I see the look you've been going for. Do you want me to help you do it better? Like a real country star?"

I pictured Goth-country, rebel-hearted me, but better. Just as Julie had looked like herself at the Grand Ole Opry, but better. That's what a professional like Ms. Lottie could do for me.

And whether Sam only thought it would help the band's reception, or his heart raced because his latest ex looked so beautiful, he would take notice.

I told her, "Yes, ma'am." And then, as she got to work with her comb, I whispered, "Thank you."

♪ ♫ ♪

When I got back to my granddad's house, with my makeup dramatically perfect and my hair in a glamorous version of itself like I was headed to the Grammys, my granddad had already left to fight the CMA Festival traffic and take his VIP seat for Julie's performance on the Riverwalk stage. It was easy for me to dress in an outrageous country getup to go with my starlet hair and slip out of the house for one last gig. Picking up Charlotte at her run-down apartment complex made saying good-bye to my life as a performer a little easier, because I didn't have to ride with Sam and talk to him, or drive alone and obsess about him. I'd had a couple of song ideas since last night, but I hadn't written them down.

Because we'd made it up the musician pecking order to a Broadway bar, the city had reserved a parking space for me in back. We pulled into the place in plenty of time before the gig so Sam didn't have a stroke. The summer solstice was approaching, and the sun hadn't quite gone down. Sam leaned against the wall outside, pretending to focus before he sang, but actually making sure we showed up. Ace stood on the other side of the door, with his back to Sam, talking to a group of college-age girls.

I cut the engine, but neither Charlotte nor I made a move to get out of the car.

"Maybe we could find a way to make the band work with none of us dating," she mused, eyes on Ace.

"I don't think so," I said.

"Maybe we'll have such a great time tonight that we'll forget what we were fighting about before."

"Maybe," I agreed, because she wanted to believe there was still hope for her and Ace, and she wasn't listening to me anyway.

"I guess we'd better get out," she said, and I was about to agree when my phone rang. The ringtone signaled the call was from Julie.

I pawed through my purse so violently that even clueless Charlotte knew to ask, "What's wrong?"

Ignoring her, I said breathlessly into the phone, "Julie?"

"You have to get down here to the Riverwalk stage," my mother said. "Julie has her first CMA Festival performance in just a few minutes, and she's refusing to go onstage."

I stared through the windshield at Sam. He was still pretending I wasn't here, but I knew he was hyperaware of me and was *dying* to go onstage. What my mother was saying did not compute. "Let me talk to Julie."

"She's not allowed to talk to you," my mother said. "Not while she's refusing to go onstage. She's grounded from her phone. You come down here and talk to her right now."

"Mom," I said. "Tell me what's going on and how serious it is. I'm in the middle of something."

"You're in the *middle* of something?" my mother shrieked. "You're spending the summer sanding guitars for your grandfather, and he's here. What could you possibly be in the middle of? What could be more important than your sister?"

With a pointed look at me, Sam slowly pushed off from the wall, crossed in front of the door to the bar, and laughingly joined the conversation with Ace and the college girls.

"I'll be right there." I clicked my phone off and turned to Charlotte. "I have to go. I'll try to be back before the gig, but no guarantees." I jumped out of the car.

"Then you can't go!" Charlotte exclaimed, jumping out, too.

"Go where?" Suddenly I had Sam's full attention. He and Ace forgot all about the other girls, meeting Charlotte and me at the back of the car.

"Julie's playing at the Riverwalk stage in a few minutes," I told Sam, "and she's refusing to go on. She needs me."

"You can't go." He repeated Charlotte's words as though they were obvious, spray-painted on the back of this row of nineteenth-century buildings.

"I promise you I can," I said, taking a step in the direction of the river. I could have assured him, as I'd assured Charlotte, that I would try to be back in time for our gig. But I didn't even care when he was ordering me around.

He stepped in front of me. "No, you can't!" he shouted. "We have a gig, Bailey! There is nothing more important than this gig right now."

I put my hands on my hips. "There are a lot of things more important than this gig. My sister is more important. *I* am more important. *You* are more important. But you'll never understand that, and that is your whole problem." I walked around him.

"This is not your fantasy that the record company and your parents and Julie decide she can't do this without you, Bailey," he called after me. "She's been doing it without you for a year. There is *no way* they're scrapping a year of work and deciding at the eleventh hour that they need you."

I turned around backward and called, "That's not what I think."

"That *is* what you think, or hope. Otherwise, you wouldn't be going."

Oh. We'd known each other less than a week, but he sure knew how to keep me around—at least as long as it took me to tell him off. I stomped all the way back to him on the uneven pavement of the alley. "Yes, I *would* be going, because I'm not you. Just because *you* don't care about anything but performing doesn't mean you should judge everybody else by your own low standards."

He blinked, but his jaw was set. "If you walk away from this gig, that's it for us. Don't come back to the gig, and don't come back to me. Ever."

I looked at him. Really looked him up and down—the cowboy hat mashing his dark hair, his handsome face half-hidden by now with dark stubble, his chocolate eyes—because I knew I might not see him again. I made sure I took in what I was leaving, and then I turned.

He caught me by the arm. "We have to rely on you to make gigs, Bailey. Nobody will book us anymore if they can't rely on us to be there. All four of us."

"It doesn't matter why," I said. "You told me don't leave or we're over. And I'm leaving." I turned one more time, but, aware of what I was putting behind me, I circled back around and stopped directly in front of Ace.

"It's not that Charlotte doesn't love you," I told him in a rush. "She's just so insecure that she can't imagine *you* would love *her*. The only reason she's hung up on Sam is, she didn't have to guess how he felt about her. Once upon a time, Sam told her that he loved her and she was beautiful. You're going to have to do the same." I turned and flounced down the alley. When nobody called their thanks to me, I turned around, gave them a little curtsy, and called, "You're welcome." They were all staring at me, motionless, and I was a little afraid that I'd ruined whatever chance Ace and Charlotte had with each other.

But before the back door of the bar disappeared beyond the curve of the steep hill, I spun around one more time. Ace stood in front of Charlotte, hands on her shoulders, head bent, lips close to hers. She gazed way up at him, then inched closer. He kissed her mouth.

As I watched them, heat spread across my face, and my lips tingled. At least one good thing had come out of the past wonderful, horrible week.

Sam stood only a few feet from what must have been a shocking sight for him, his two best friends finally making out. But he wasn't looking at them. He stood with his feet planted stubbornly far apart, like he was ready for someone to try to push him over, with his strong arms crossed on his chest, watching me go.

I put my eyes on the alley ahead of me and tried to think of the best way to cut through the crowded streets to the Riverwalk stage.

That's when I started to cry.

14

I sobbed all the way down the alley, worried about what could have happened to change Julie's mind about wanting to be a star. Wondering what was wrong with Sam that he wanted to be a star more than anything. Sad for myself.

In that short walk, I cried for everything I'd stopped myself from crying for over the past year: how unreasonable and unkind Toby had been. How cold everyone had been at school. How unfeeling my parents had been. How far I had fallen for Sam so quickly, with no rope or handhold to climb back out of that hole.

But by the time I reached the bottom of the alley and needed to cross the street and wind my way through the throngs of tourists to the Riverwalk, I was pulling Sam's handkerchief from my pocket and dabbing the tears from under my eyes. I might not be the front chick in a rockabilly band anymore, but I still had a style to uphold. I wasn't going to ruin Ms. Lottie's hard work.

And I wanted to look like a million bucks when I saw my parents and Julie.

Near the stage, I shouted over the music for a guard to tell me where to find my family. They must have called ahead to him that

I was coming, or I looked enough like hot new country sensation Julie Mayfield that he recognized I was related. He pointed me toward a line of country stars' trailers lined up at one end of the parking lot. I walked along them until I found my parents' RV. I stood at the door for a few seconds, wondering whether to just go on in, and then I knocked.

My granddad let me in. I passed right through the living area. My parents sat around the kitchen table where they'd told me Julie was going to be a star and my career was dead. My mother started yelling at me that Julie had come this far, and now she was going to throw it all away out of immaturity and stubbornness. Ignoring my mother, I climbed the ladder into the upper sleeping area.

Julie was watching for me. When she saw my head appear, she spread her arms wide.

"Bay!" she squealed.

I smiled. "Hey, Julie."

We hugged for a long minute, sitting on the mattress, and then we lay down, staring at the ceiling only a few feet above our heads, and talked just like we used to when we dreamed of making it big. All the photos of stars that I'd taped to the ceiling on my side of the mattress were still there. I hadn't crawled into this space in a year, but Julie hadn't taken any of my stuff down.

"Even though the single's only been out a day," she said, "they can tell it's selling well, and the album is racking up presales. They want to go back to contract with me right now for another album. I told Mom and Dad that I want something in exchange this time. I want some of your songs on the second album. They say that's ridiculous and they won't even approach the record company about something so childish. Therefore, I am not going onstage. My God, you look beautiful."

I was flattered for about half a second, first about my songs, then about the hair and makeup Ms. Lottie had done for me so I looked as put together as Julie, but that quickly turned to annoyance. "You can't just not go onstage, Julie." I had walked away from a gig myself, for Julie. And that made me angry. "You don't get it. My songs are something I wrote as a child. You have an adult job. You signed an adult contract to get on that stage and entertain the thousands of people who bought tickets."

"No, *you* don't get it," she insisted. "You wrote those songs only a year or two ago. You were my age when you wrote them. If you were a child then, I'm a child now. And you know what that means? I can't sign a contract. My parents can sign it for me, but nobody can make me perform. Not unless I get what I want."

I was astounded that she seemed so sure of herself, so defiant. She scared me. All of a sudden, she was reminding me of me. "Why are you doing this?"

"It's the only way I could think of to get what I want. I could go on a hunger strike, but I would get so *hungry*. Mom would make her chocolate chip cookies and I'd be toast."

"No," I said, shaking my head. "Why do you want any of my songs on your album? You don't have to do this to bolster my ego and keep me from riding with coked-up drivers."

"That's ridiculous. If I wanted to keep you from riding with coked-up drivers, I'd just ignore your calls for another week and a half. I can tell that's been working, because your voice mails have sounded increasingly desperate." She grinned at me, her blue eyes looking angelic and self-satisfied.

I said slowly, "You little devil."

"Fact," she said. "I want to sing your songs because they're good. They're different. They're real. They're about being a teenager. Mom and Dad didn't care I was signing away all my rights to choose what songs I perform. Now the company is picking shit for me, and I have to put my name on it. I need you to help me get my career back on track. I wouldn't want you if you weren't good."

I rolled over on the mattress—carefully, so my hair didn't get crazy—and looked at her, as we'd gazed at each other up here a million times as children. Julie had understood me better than anybody. I thought I'd lost that in my life, and maybe I would never completely regain it. But as she grinned at me, I felt like I was getting a little piece of it back.

"Are you sure that's the only reason you don't want to go onstage?"

Her pretty face fell. "I screwed up at the Opry, Bay."

I poked her. "Of course you didn't. You looked a little nervous, but it was your first time at the Opry, for God's sake! You'll do better tonight, and even better when the Opry asks you back."

She shook her head, and now her eyes were welling up with tears. "You don't know how bad I sucked. You weren't there."

"I *was* there."

She stared at me and sobbed once. "You *were*?"

"Yes."

"Even after we didn't invite you?" she wailed. "Even after I wouldn't talk to you on the *phone*?"

"Yes," I said firmly. I felt around on the mattress and took her hand. "Listen to me. Whatever happens between us, I will always come to your Opry."

She squeezed my hand and kissed my cheek. "Thank you."

I slid off the mattress and climbed down the ladder. I hadn't even reached the bottom when my mother asked, "Did you tell her to get onstage?"

As I set my feet on the floor of the RV, my mother patted the seat beside her at the table. I kept standing and folded my arms. "I told Julie that she's worked hard and she's done everything you asked her to do for a year. If she wants you to fight for one item in her contract, she's within her rights to withhold something you want until you promise her what she wants."

"I knew you would pull something like that," my mother sneered. She turned to my dad and asked, "Why didn't you stop me from calling her?"

My dad opened his mouth, and my granddad moved toward the table, but I didn't need their help this time. I said, "You can't ask for my opinion, then say my opinion isn't worth anything when you don't like it. I am part of this family, too. You are one of the many reasons Julie is a success, but so am I. *I* worked hard and did everything you asked me to do, too, for seventeen years. The way you raised Julie made her want a career in music. You raised me that way, too, and you can't penalize me now for doing what you raised me to do." My mother took a breath. Before she could speak, I went on, "Granddad got me a job playing fiddle with those tribute bands that walk around the mall."

"You did *what?*" my mother shouted at my granddad.

I continued in a louder voice, just as she'd yelled over my protests my whole life. I quoted her line that she'd used on me so many times: "Excuse me, but I have the floor."

She stopped talking and stared at me with wide blue eyes. I'd been shocked in the past at some of the similarities between us. She was having that reaction now.

I said, "I'm in another band, too, that has a gig on Broadway tonight. Or, I *was* in a band. And it's not right for you to take away my college tuition because of that. Parents pay for their children's college if they can, and you certainly can. It's not right for you to take that away because I pursue the career you taught me to pursue. But if that's what you're going to do, so be it. I will join another band. I will try not to embarrass you or Julie, but I'm not going to live my life denying this huge part of myself just because you want to keep me a secret."

For once in her life, my mom seemed shocked into silence. It was my dad who said quietly, "We don't have time to talk about this right now, sugar bear. We've got to get Julie onstage. We're back in Nashville for the next few months. You can move back home, and we'll have plenty of time to work it out."

"You just made me move to Granddad's," I said. "I'm comfortable where I am, if he'll let me stay."

I felt my granddad's hand on my shoulder.

"Well, come by tomorrow afternoon," my mother said weakly, "and we'll talk."

"I can't. I have a gig from two to six." I looked at my parents' forlorn faces. Standing firm had felt good, but I did want to work this out with them. I said, "I can come by your house in the morning."

As I stepped from the RV onto the pavement, the hot sunset hit me full in the face. It was a moment before I glimpsed Sam, Ace, and Charlotte talking behind the orange tape with the security guard watching them from a few yards away. When they saw me, they waved me over.

Part of me didn't want to go. But I couldn't spend the rest of the night going around being firm with people. That felt good only while I was doing it, and I knew better now than to take rash action that I would regret for a year. I walked toward them. When Sam held out his arms, I ran the rest of the way in my cowgirl boots and didn't bother crossing under the tape before I lost myself in his hug. The tape stretched between us, and we hugged around it.

"I'm sorry," he said in my ear. "I was wrong. I didn't mean it. What you said about cutting your hair, that you knew as you were doing it that you would be sorry for the rest of your life, but you were so angry that you couldn't stop . . . that's how it was when I was saying that to you. And I don't want to be sorry for the rest of my life. Please come back to us." He held me at arm's length. "Please come back to *me*."

I looked into his dark, intense eyes, then over at Ace and Charlotte. They both gazed at me somberly, with Ace's arms wrapped around Charlotte's chest like they couldn't believe they'd finally gotten together and now they had no intention of letting each other go.

Finally Julie's voice came from behind me. "You'd better say yes, Bailey. You haven't had a boy that cute come on to you since that blond guitar player at the bluegrass festival. The one you looked for for years? The one you had such a crush on?"

Sam stared dumbfounded over my shoulder at Julie. His eyes slid to mine.

I felt myself blushing hard. There was nothing left to do but duck under the tape and walk forward into his arms again.

"Thank God," Ace said.

"Hi, I'm Charlotte," I heard Charlotte say to Julie, "and this is Ace, and that's Sam. We're Bailey's band."

"You're in a *band*?" Julie shrieked at me. "Bailey, you didn't tell me you're in a *band*!"

"You haven't been speaking to me," I murmured against Sam's chest. I never opened my eyes, just listened to his racing heart.

Suddenly I backed away and looked up at him. "Are you missing your gig right now? For me?"

He looked stricken. He said carefully, "I am *willing* to miss my gig for you." Gesturing to the parking lot and the distant crowd around the Riverwalk stage, he said, "I am here, potentially missing my gig, for you." He glanced at his watch. "If we hurry, we can still make the gig. But if you want me to miss it to prove how much I love you—"

"Bailey doesn't need that proof, do you, Bailey?" Charlotte prompted me.

"No, I don't," I said. "I didn't mean what I said before, either. Missing a gig would be completely out of character for you. I wouldn't love you if you weren't you."

He eyed me a moment more. "My God, you look gorgeous. You always do, but tonight you wanted me to eat my heart out." Suddenly he shouted, "Okay, let's go!" and dragged me by the hand down the sidewalk, toward Broadway.

As we ran, I turned around and called to Julie, "Good luck with your gig!"

"Good luck with *your* gig!" she hollered back.

The four of us hustled around the crowds and up the hill. I didn't think about Julie again that night. I had a show to put on.

♪ ♫ ♪

But late the next morning, I sat on the bed in my old room at my parents' house as Julie asked, "Are you sure you're not going to move back home?"

She and my parents and I had spent an hour talking our problems out. Now that Julie and I had retreated upstairs, she lay in my very old beanbag chair—she'd gotten a pink one and I'd gotten a yellow one for Christmas one year—with her blond curls spilling across the carpet, looking at me upside down. When she was in that position, I couldn't read her expression, but her voice sounded pleading.

"I've hardly seen you for a whole year," she said. "My tour kicks off in a few weeks, and I know you'll still want to move to the dorm at Vanderbilt. But in the meantime, you and I can hang out here, like always."

"I don't think so."

"Come on. Don't tell me you'd honestly rather live with Granddad!" She sat up and spun around to face me, her mouth in a cute pout. "It sounds to me like you *said* in the family meeting that you'd forgiven Mom and Dad for the way they've treated you, but you haven't *really* forgiven them."

I pushed my glasses up on my nose—the glasses Mom had had the nerve to tell me didn't become me yet again. "It's not that I haven't forgiven them," I explained. "It's just that I can't live with them anymore. They didn't think they were pitching me out on my own just by making me stay with Granddad for the summer. That's what it felt like to me, though, and now I can't come back. Just like you couldn't go back after you put your foot down and told them you will have a say in your next album or else."

There was one big difference between her assertion of independence and mine. Hers was likely to make millions of extra dollars for her and the record company—or lose that much—whereas mine mattered to nobody but me. A year ago I would have pointed out this difference, bitterly. Today I was able to put it in my pocket. I had learned to play in a group.

"Besides," I said, "if I moved back here, we wouldn't see each other that often anyway. You may be in town, theoretically, but I know you've got meetings and concerts and interviews lined up. I have a lot of gigs." There was my mall job, which I planned to continue until conflicts popped up. And for the first time, I was hopeful they might.

I lowered my voice. "I didn't want to tell Mom and Dad this unless something comes of it"—more residual bitterness, maybe, but my secrets were mine to share or not—"but the gig on Broadway last night went great. After our set, the owner asked us not to pack up just yet. She introduced us to a record company exec who'd been watching in the audience."

Julie's eyes widened with excitement. I'd intended to tell her this whole story soberly, because it was only a nibble, and maybe it wouldn't pan out. But when I saw her expression, I couldn't help grinning as I told her the rest.

"When the place closed, he went to get his guitar from his car. He played with us for another hour. Then he asked for Sam's number and said he'd try to set something up for us."

"What does that meeeeean?" she squealed under her breath.

"I don't know. Maybe nothing. But I'm glad I went."

I cocked an ear toward the window. Two stories below, gravel popped in the driveway. Someone was coming. Much as I loved being in love, I wished my heart didn't race into overdrive at the very thought that I might catch a glimpse of Sam. There was no reason for him to be driving up to my house this morning. It was probably the mailman.

But sure enough, moving to the window, I saw Sam's truck parked in the driveway, dust settling around it. He got out of the cab and glanced toward the window where I stood, like he knew I was there.

"Who is it?" Julie asked. "Sam?"

"Yes," I said. "Lucky me."

As I bounded down the stairs, though, I remembered that he hadn't met my parents. I'd put my foot down with them that morning, but that didn't mean they wouldn't harbor some residual ill will about me joining a forbidden band. They might blame him. I sped up, hoping to catch him before my parents did, and nearly tripped on the last step.

I shouldn't have worried. Yes, he was already in the kitchen, but he was doing the Sam thing he did so well, looking my dad straight in the eye as he shook his hand, and complimenting my mom on the scents of the big family lunch she was about to serve us.

"Won't you join us?" my mom asked him.

"I would love to," Sam said, "but I came over—I'm so sorry to interrupt—because I was hoping to steal Bailey away for a gig."

My dad just raised his eyebrows, but my mom looked at me accusingly, like I'd known about this beforehand and hadn't told her.

"What kind of gig?" I asked Sam.

He opened his mouth, about to tell me. Then his eyes darted sideways to my dad and back to me. "I need to talk to you about it."

I couldn't imagine what this gig could be. An impromptu Lao wedding? "Let's go outside," I said, taking him by the hand.

As I opened the door to the porch, my mom called after us, "Can I make you both a plate to take with you?"

"Ma'am," Sam said, "I wouldn't put you out, but it smells *really* good."

My mother smiled to herself and turned back to the stove, murmuring, "You got it."

"Sir, nice to meet you." Sam reached over to shake my father's hand again before he followed me.

I closed the door behind us. When Sam and I had come here a couple of days before, I'd thought the place seemed dead without the familiar braying of farm animals, but I supposed it was all in my perspective. Today it seemed quiet but peaceful and welcoming, warm with the memories of all the years Julie and I had spent playing in the creek and rolling in the grass.

I slid onto the porch swing, patting the seat beside me. "Look at you!" I told Sam. "You really know how to lay it on the folks."

"You ain't seen nothing yet." He weighed down his end of the porch swing, but instead of nudging us into motion, he turned to me and put both hands on my knees. "I came out here to tell you I got a call from Mr. McAdory this morning."

The record company exec. "What'd he say?" I breathed.

"He can't schedule us this weekend because he's waiting for all the CMA folks to clear out. But on Monday he wants to meet with the band in the studio at his office. He's asking his boss to listen to us."

"And . . . what if they like us?"

"He's being cagey. You know how they are. He's not going to make us any promises unless his boss likes what he hears."

I nodded. "I want you to be prepared that they might not pick us up."

"Of course I know that. I'll bet they do, though."

"I know they'll pick *you* up," I said.

"What?" He seemed honestly surprised.

"And if they do, I want you to go."

"No. I don't think that's going to happen. I'm the one Mr. McAdory has been communicating with. If he wanted just me, he's had plenty of opportunity to tell me that by now. Anyway, I've said before that I don't want to be this talking head that the record company controls—this singing head—this solo act who might or might not get the good songs. I want the band. I want your songs. I want *you*. I love you. Not that your parents and Julie don't, but with you and me it's different because we're coming from the same place. You know?"

I smiled at him. "Yes, I know."

He paused. "After we had that fight at Boot Ilicious, I went home and played through all your songs."

"*All* of them?" I asked. "You must have stayed up until noon the next day." He *did* have that hard, Johnny Cash look about him again, like he'd been missing sleep.

He acknowledged this with a small shrug. "And Bailey. If Julie really gets your songs on her next album, that's going to be great for her. Our band sounds terrific, in my humble opinion, but your songs are going to put us over the top in the meeting with the record company. Your songs . . ." He swallowed, then smiled wanly. "Some of them are painful."

"Yeah." I wished now I hadn't shoved some of the choicer ones into Sam's chest.

"Though it *was* a relief to find out that you feel as strongly about me as I do about you." He laughed. "You've channeled your pain into something constructive, a lot better than I have. And if the band makes it big, you're going to be why."

I didn't agree. If the band made it big, we would all be why. But I was glad to be a part of it. I was proud my songs were part of it. After a year living in a fantasy of being called in to save Julie, I had saved myself instead, by doing what I loved.

"So!" he said. "We've got today, Saturday, and Sunday to practice some of your songs until they're perfect."

"Oh." No wonder he'd said we couldn't stay for lunch. He knew I had to work this afternoon. We had another gig on Broadway tomorrow night, and on Sunday night, one at the first bar where we'd played in the District. We were all booked up, and now we had to find time to practice, too. Something told me I wasn't going to get a lot of shut-eye between now and Monday.

I had never been so excited about losing sleep.

"We can practice at my house," he said. "My mom doesn't have to work this weekend, which is bizarre. And my dad . . ." His voice trailed off. He looked down at his hands on my knees. "It took me a while to figure out how to tell him I'm not going to make it to the mall this afternoon. For years I looked forward to the day I could tell him to his face that I didn't need him anymore, but when

I finally did, it was a lot harder than I thought. And he didn't react the way I thought he would. At *all*." Sam squeezed his eyes shut.

I held my breath for the horrible thing Mr. Hardiman had said to Sam. It wouldn't be true, but I was afraid Sam would believe it.

His voice broke as he said, "He took his bags, which were already packed because he'd just gotten home from his bender, and my mom drove him to rehab."

I slapped my hand over my heart and sighed with relief. "Sam, that's a good thing, not a bad thing. Isn't it?"

Nodding, he said, "My dad thought now would be a good time. He said he'll be gone for a while, but I'm about to go to college, and I don't need him anymore. My mom, on the other hand, said I'll always need him, and he'll always need me. She said he should go to rehab now anyway because it's never a bad time to stop being a jackass."

I laughed. "I love your mom."

"Me too." His eyelashes were wet, but he grinned at me. "And when I told my dad we're auditioning for a contract, he said he knew it all along, and it was about time."

I slid my hand on top of Sam's. "It was."

He nodded slowly. I knew he was worried about his dad. But I could tell by the way his eyes moved to the ceiling of the porch, and the sky beyond, that he was already thinking through what else we needed to do before Monday.

I helped him. "I'll make a hair and makeup appointment for Monday morning before our meeting, for me and for Charlotte. I'll try to enlist Ms. Lottie."

"For Charlotte?" he asked me dubiously. "Good luck with that."

"They want a whole look for the band," I reminded him. "If the execs are on the fence about us, Charlotte's makeover could make all the difference. We'll ask Ace to explain this to her."

"Ah! Deploying Ace." Sam beamed at me. "I like how you think."

"And we have to choose another name for the band," I warned him, "pronto."

"Now, wait a minute," he protested. "Redneck Death Wish is very catchy."

"Tell you what. Julie's learned a lot about marketing music over the past year. Let's go back inside and run it by her. If she laughs us out of the house, we'll think of something else by Monday. Deal?"

"Deal. I know she'll love it."

"Redneck Death Wish," I grumbled. Then, as I thought through the coming weekend, I realized that what he'd been telling me hadn't quite sunk in. I stared at him with my mouth open for a few seconds. But as a grin slowly spread across his face, I realized what this meant.

"Oh, Sam." My hands found his and clasped them. "You're about to get what you wanted."

He nodded. "I already did." He leaned down and touched his lips to mine.

As he kissed me, I was aware of the morning sun slanting onto the porch and across my legs, and the sound of birds, and the smell of freshly cut grass. The wind swayed us in the porch swing. After all the work to become a star, the dashed hopes, the heartache, and trying to heal myself in all the wrong ways, I was still living my life inside a country song.

Only this one had a happy ending.

♪ ♫ ♪

Julie snagged us VIP tickets to her show in the Titans stadium at the CMA Festival that night. I looked around for my granddad but didn't see him. He must have been backstage with my parents. This time around, I didn't resent that they were with Julie and I wasn't. They had their hands full. They couldn't worry about me, and I didn't need them to. My place was here with my band, because our gig on Broadway started at nine.

"How are y'all doing?" Julie called over the mike. In response, the crowd emitted a nondescript moan—not an excited scream, but Julie hadn't made a name for herself yet, and there was just so much she could expect.

The crowd's unenthusiastic reply didn't faze her, though. She was a professional musician. She murmured into the microphone, maybe more to herself this time than to the crowd, "It's good to be home." The audience roared. She cut them off as she started her first song.

I jumped a little at the noise as the drums kicked in. I hadn't expected the music to be so *loud,* like a real concert. Then Julie's clear, strong voice sang the tune she'd started with at the Grand Ole Opry. My doubts fell away. Maybe the song didn't make a lot of sense, but the tune was catchy, the beat was infectious, and she sounded like a pro.

In the instrumental break between verses, Charlotte leaned around Ace and Sam to shout, "She's so good!" Ace nodded. I nodded, too, smiling. She *was* so good.

"She's the real deal," Sam said in my ear. "She's going to make it."

Several songs later, as she waited for her rhythm guitarist to switch from electric to acoustic, she asked the crowd, "Is everybody excited about all the great singers you came to hear tonight?"

The crowd gave her an enthusiastic answer this time. Maybe they were responding to the idea of the bigger acts who would follow her, but I thought they were more into Julie herself now that she'd shown them what she could do.

"Me too," she said. "And after that, if you're on Broadway, be sure to stop by between nine and eleven to see my big sister's band, Redneck Death Wish."

This time the roar of the crowd was unmistakable. The hair on my arms stood up and my heart raced as if Sam were kissing me. There must be a lot of locals in the audience, and they must have stumbled into our sets in the last week. Either that or they were responding to our awesome name.

"I told her I'm not sure about this band name," Julie said, laughing, "but my sister has been my rock for sixteen years. She's an incredibly talented musician and songwriter. Do yourself a favor and go hear her play." Reading what she'd inked in her palm, she named the bar and its address.

Nobody sitting in the first four rows had turned around to look at us. Nobody had recognized us. With all the spotlights in her eyes, even Julie couldn't seem to see me close to the stage. But I felt my face flush anyway, like I was the one in the spotlight instead. I turned to my band.

Ace was gaping at me. Charlotte was grinning—*Charlotte was grinning!*—and giving me a thumbs-up. Sam looked slyly over at me as he rubbed his hands together like he finally had Nashville exactly where he wanted it. Dipping his head, he whispered in my ear, "You asked her to mention us. I'm glad you did, but I promise you didn't have to."

"I didn't ask her to," I admitted, looking at Julie again, who was talking about why she loved the next song so much. And then she announced it: "A Lady Antebellum tune called 'Dancin' Away with My Heart.'"

"Hey!" Sam exclaimed over Julie's guitar intro. "That's one of our songs about finding and losing each other."

"That I *did* ask her to do," I told him. "I asked her to play it for you and me."

Here in the comparative dusk away from the bright lights onstage, no one else could see the look he gave me. His lashes cast long shadows across his dark eyes as he looked over his shoulder at me. He was wearing the red T-shirt I'd decorated with a heart on the sleeve.

He surprised me by standing, moving in slow motion as though Julie's music were water around us. I took the hand he offered me. He led me past Charlotte and Ace, into the aisle. I didn't ask what he wanted. He didn't ask me to dance. That's just what we did. I laid my head against his shoulder. He slid his hands down around my waist tentatively, as if he wasn't sure how to hold me, or whether I wanted to be held. One of his hands found one of mine. I pulled his hand close and tucked it under my chin.

He bent to whisper, "Maybe we should dance only the first part of the song. The finding each other, and not the losing each other."

I kissed his knuckles and looked up at him. "Maybe we should enjoy it and feel lucky we're together. I feel very, very lucky."

And for the first time, I did.

Dirty Little Secret
Jennifer Echols

Introduction

Bailey Mayfield is in trouble. After a high school graduation party, she got in a car accident that's put her on probation with her parents. They sentence her to spend the summer before college working with her grandfather with one rule: No playing in bands.

At first, Bailey is going to stick to her word. But when her grandfather gets her a gig playing at the local mall and he vows to stick up for her if her parents find out, she convinces herself this one infraction of her parents' no-bands rule is okay. Then she falls head over fiddle for the sexy Sam Hardiman, a singer with a band of his own. Soon they're playing on the Nashville circuit, where, Bailey says, "a country legend might drop in and change our lives with one phone call" (pages 151–152). Ultimately, Bailey is presented with a choice: her love, her music, or her family.

Topics & Questions for Discussion

1. Early on, Bailey says that the costumer for the mall band "was way too polite to be baited into admitting my look was the stuff of her nightmares" (page 2). Given Bailey's attitude, what was your first impression of her? How does that impression change?

2. Bailey is raised in a musical family. Why do you think music—which is so close to the hearts of her mother, father, grandfather, and sister—is the way she chooses to act out against them?

3. When Sam comes over and speaks to Bailey's grandfather, what sets her grandfather at ease? Why is Sam better at getting him to trust them than Bailey is?

4. Why does Bailey wear a shrug when she's leaving her grandfather's house for her first gig and take it off in Sam's truck?

5. Why is Bailey's grandfather more accepting of her than her own parents are?

6. The first time Bailey and Sam kiss, Bailey thinks, "I didn't want him to know how he was affecting me, in case he didn't feel the same way" (page 96). Given where their relationship is going at this point, why is Bailey so afraid of showing her feelings?

7. When Bailey's nearly mugged, she says she'd rather give up her wallet and ID card than her fiddle. Is there a special object like that that defines who you are, that you wouldn't give up for money or safety?

8. Over and over, Bailey vows to leave Sam's band and never return. What keeps her coming back for more?

9. "Sam was creative and dedicated, but his wasn't the plodding bright-and-early work ethic of the morning person, like mine" (page 198). Are you more of a Bailey—early-rising writer type— or more of a Sam—late-night brooding type?

10. If Charlotte is interested in Ace, why do you think she can't move on from Sam and leave him for Bailey?

11. Why does Bailey, upon seeing the billboard for her sister Julie's show, decide she wants to go to the Grand Ole Opry with Sam in tow, even though she knows it will be painful?

12. What compels Bailey to keep coming through for her sister— going into hiding, then coming to cheer her on for her show— despite all that her mother, sister, and father have done to her?

Enhance Your Book Club

1. "[N]o country costume could have prepared me for dressing up like Dolly Parton's right-hand girl," Bailey remarks during her first gig at the mall (page 20). Have you ever had to wear a uniform—or a silly costume—for work?

2. Bailey and Sam spend a lot of time seeing other bands performing in Nashville. If you can, take your reading group to a restaurant, bar, or other venue that has live music. Perhaps you should even go in costume!

3. To get in the Southern mood for your reading group, serve BBQ ribs, mac and cheese, grits, and cornbread! See more at: http://books.simonandschuster.com/Dirty-Little-Secret/Jennifer-Echols/9781451658040/reading_group_guide#rgg.